Witch Is Where Clowns Go To Die

Published by Implode Publishing Ltd

Chapter 1

"I have two-hundred and thirty-seven now, Jill," Mrs V gushed as soon as I walked into the outer office.

"Good morning, Mrs V. Two-hundred and thirty-seven what? Pairs of socks? Scarves?"

"No, silly. Followers on YarnAgram."

"I thought you said that you were going to give that up?"

"I was seriously thinking about it after I got whacked, but then all those horrible posts disappeared overnight, and I haven't had any problems since. I've posted lots more pictures over the weekend: scarves, socks, and a few jumpers. They've had lots of likes and shares already. And some really nice comments from people I don't even know. And like I said, I've now got, oh, it's two-hundred and thirty-*eight* now. They just keep popping up."

"That's great. I'm really pleased for you. Have you told your friend Mrs Mizus?"

"I phoned her yesterday. She said she was thrilled for me."

I bet she did.

When I walked through to my office, Winky was sitting on my desk, glaring at me. Something told me he was not in a good mood.

"I'm not in a good mood!" He snapped.

See? What did I tell you? It's like I have a sixth sense.

"Good morning, Winky."

"I don't know how you've got the nerve."

"I have no idea what you're talking about."

"Don't come the innocent with me. I know."

"Do you have to be so cryptic? *What* do you know?"

"That you have a dog!"

Oh bum!

"Err, Barry? I've had him for ages. You knew that."

"I don't mean the one in the paranormal world. I'm talking about rat-dog."

"Oh, right. You mean Buddy."

"He's no *buddy* of mine. How long have you had him?"

"Not very long."

"If he can live with you, why can't I?"

"I'd love for you to do that, but there's a problem."

"I thought there might be. Let's hear it."

"My little girl, Florence, is allergic to cats."

"How very convenient."

"Honestly, it's true. When she asked if she could have a pet, I was going to suggest that you move in with us, but then we found out about the allergy. We took her to the doctor to be tested, and they confirmed it."

"And let me guess, she's not allergic to dog hair."

"Apparently not. That's why we got Buddy."

"How do I know you're not lying to me again?"

"What do you mean, *again*? I would never lie to you, Winky. I'd love for you to live with us, but I have to put Florence's wellbeing first, don't I?"

Luckily, I was saved from further interrogation when the landline rang. It was Mrs V.

"Jill, I've got Betty Longbottom on the line. She wondered if you had time for a quick chat?"

Betty Longbottom? That name was a blast from the past. Some years ago, Betty had opened a shop called She Sells, which had sold all manner of marine knick-knacks. Shortly afterwards, she'd opened a marine centre called

The Sea's The Limit. After a dodgy start, that too had proved to be a real money spinner. Over the next three years, she'd opened several more marine centres around the country. Then, from what I heard, there had been a dramatic downturn in trade, and she'd been unable to keep up the massive loan repayments. Eventually, the business had folded. I hadn't seen hide nor hair of her since then.

"Put her through, Mrs V, would you?"

"Will do."

"Jill, is that you?"

"Betty. Long time, no speak. How are you?"

"Very well, thank you. What about you? I hear you have a little girl now."

"That's right. Florence. She's five and she's just started school."

"How lovely for you."

"I haven't seen you in ages, Betty, where are you living these days?"

"I've moved around a lot, but I recently moved back to Washbridge."

"For good?"

"I think so. I wondered if I might pop into your office to see you, when you can spare the time."

"I'd like that. When did you have in mind?"

"Is tomorrow morning okay?"

"That'll be fine. How about nine-thirty?"

"That works for me. I'm looking forward to seeing you again."

"You too, Betty."

Fortunately, that short distraction had given Winky the chance to calm down. He'd jumped off my desk and disappeared under the sofa, where he was no doubt still sulking.

Provided he never found out the truth, that Florence didn't have an allergy to cats, I should be okay.

A little later, Mrs V came through to my office.

"Jill, your ten-thirty is here."

I opened my desk drawer, took out my diary, and flicked to today's page.

"Mr Black. Yes, I'm expecting him." I pointed to the entry. "Aren't you impressed, Mrs V?"

"At what?"

"That I remembered to put him in my diary?"

She rolled her eyes. "Shall I send him through?"

Sheesh! If that was all the appreciation I got, I wouldn't bother in future.

When Mr Black had made his appointment, he'd told Mrs V very little about himself, so I wasn't sure what to expect. The man who walked into my office had an air of sadness about the way he carried himself. He was wearing trainers, which had probably once been white, blue jeans and a black V-neck jumper over a black t-shirt.

"Mr Black, I'm Jill Maxwell. Pleased to meet you." He shook my hand but barely made eye contact.

"The name's Phil." He spoke so quietly I could barely hear him.

"Why don't you take a seat, Phil? Would you like a drink?"

"No, thanks."

It was clear the guy wasn't in the mood for small talk, so I cut straight to the chase.

"Why don't you tell me why you came to see me today? Take your time. There's no hurry."

"Okay." He took a deep breath. "When I was nineteen, I was convicted of murder."

"Oh?" I hadn't seen that coming.

"I didn't do it. I was released from prison five weeks ago."

"Who were you convicted of murdering?"

"Liam Roberts. My half-brother."

"Right."

"He was four years old."

Oh boy. I was beginning to think that I might be out of my depth, but I owed it to him to at least hear him out.

"And the reason you came to see me today?"

"I want you to prove I had nothing to do with Liam's murder. I can't live the rest of my life as a convicted murderer."

"Cases like this can be very difficult. I could end up spending a lot of time on this and still not be able to prove your innocence. Are you sure you wouldn't rather just move on with your life now that you're a free man again?"

"No. Unless I can prove to the world that I had nothing to do with Liam's death, there's no point in my being alive anyway."

"There's one thing I feel I must mention before we go any further. If I agreed to take on your case, there would be substantial costs involved, and you just told me that you've spent some time in prison. Are you in a position to pay my fees?"

"I wouldn't be here if I couldn't. I live with my grandmother now. She's the only person who has always believed in my innocence. She was the only one who came to visit me in prison. She's agreed to cover your fees. Will you do this? Will you help me?"

"I'm not sure. I'll need to know much more about what happened before I can make that decision."

"What do you want to know?"

"Everything. You said that Liam was your half-brother?"

"That's right. I don't know who my biological father is. He walked out on us before I was born."

"What about your birth mother?"

"She married Andy. Liam was their child."

"So that makes Andy your stepfather."

"Unfortunately, yes."

"Why do you say that?"

"Because Andy Roberts is a complete loser. I can't stand the man. My mother actually wanted me to take his name, but no way was I going to do that."

"Do he and your mother still live in the same house?"

"No, they split up not long after Liam died. Mum still lives in Washbridge, but I don't know where Andy is now. And I certainly don't care."

"Are you still in touch with your mother?"

"No, she hasn't spoken to me since I was convicted of Liam's murder."

"Can you tell me what happened to Liam? How did he die?"

"No one knows. His body was never found."

This was getting worse and worse.

"You'd better tell me exactly what happened."

"On the day he went missing, I'd gone fishing."

"By yourself?"

"Yeah. There's a river not far from the house we lived in. I often used to go there. When I got back home, my mother asked where Liam was. I had no idea. I hadn't seen him at all that day. Apparently, he'd told my stepfather that he was going fishing with me."

"But didn't you say he was only four? Surely they would have checked that he was with you before they allowed him to leave the house?"

"They were having a lie-in that morning. My stepfather had got up to go to the loo when he saw Liam who told him I was taking him with me. I did that occasionally, so I guess my stepfather took him at his word and assumed I was waiting for him downstairs."

"Why would Liam tell his father that if it wasn't true?"

"He knew they wouldn't have let him go alone. Anyway, when I told them I'd not seen him, they called the police who launched a search, but they drew a blank."

"How come you were charged with his murder?"

"They found traces of his blood on the rocks where I'd been fishing and on my fishing rod, which was back at the house. I have no idea how the blood got on it, I swear. After that, everything started to go crazy. The police were convinced I'd done it, and nothing I said could persuade them otherwise. They interrogated me for hours. In the end, I didn't know what I was doing. Or saying. I would've said just about anything as long as it meant they'd allow me to go home."

"Are you telling me that you confessed to his murder?"

"I must have, but I don't remember doing it. Like I said, I just wanted to get out of there. Can you help me? Will you take the case? Please."

"Before I make a decision, I'd like to speak to your

grandmother. Could that be arranged?"

"She's not in the best of health, but I'm sure she'll talk to you. She believes in me, and she wants to help to clear my name."

"Okay. Talk to her and if she agrees, give me a call to set up a meeting."

***

Normally, at lunchtime, I would just grab a sandwich, but Aunt Lucy had invited me over to her house for something to eat.

When I got there, she was busy in the kitchen.

"Something smells nice, Aunt Lucy."

"I thought we'd have shepherds' pie. I hope that's okay for you."

"That'll be lovely. I see you have your trophy on display."

The small silver trophy, which she'd won in the Candlefield in Bloom competition, was standing in the kitchen window.

"I thought I'd put it there, so that I see it every time I look out at the garden."

"How did you feel when you found out that it was Charlie who'd vandalised your flower beds?"

"Shocked. I didn't believe it at first. Until then, he'd been so kind to me. I never would have dreamed he was capable of doing something so horrible, but that doesn't mean I approve of what your grandmother did to him."

"Putting him in the snow globe, you mean?" I grinned.

"Yes, that was just too much."

"I hate to say it, Aunt Lucy, but for once I'm on

Grandma's side. I think he deserved everything he got. What he did to you was despicable. Is he back home yet?"

"Yes. I saw him come back yesterday. I'm fairly sure he saw me too, but he pretended that he hadn't."

"Isn't it going to be a little awkward living next-door to him now that you know what he did?"

"Very."

A few minutes later, we were seated at the kitchen table, tucking into the shepherds' pie.

"Mmm, this is delicious. My shepherd's pie never tastes like this, but then mine usually comes out of a box."

"I could give you my recipe if you like."

"That would be great, thanks. I'll pass it on to Jack."

"How's my favourite grand-niece?"

"Florence is great. She went to school with a spring in her step this morning. She's made a new friend in the village; a little girl called Wendy."

"That's nice."

"She's actually a werewolf."

"Does Florence know?"

"Not yet. I'm still trying to figure out the best way to tell her. Wendy and her parents are the only other sups in the village."

"Not for much longer." Aunt Lucy grinned.

"Oh, yes. I'd forgotten about Grandma's hotel. Did you know she'd bought it?"

"No, I would have told you if I did. It came as a total surprise to me. I can't think why she's done it. I thought the whole point of selling her Ever empire was so that she'd be able to put her feet up and take it easy. Has it actually opened yet?"

"Not yet. She did hold an open day for the locals, but I don't think it opens for guests until this weekend."

"I'm not sure I'd want to stay at a hotel run by your grandmother."

"Me neither. How's Lester doing?"

"He's as happy as a lark, but I do wish I didn't have to wash his smelly clothes. They reek of fish. It's got to the point where I can't bear the thought of eating fish anymore, which is a real shame because it would cost me next to nothing. Have you been to Cuppy C today?"

"No, I came straight over here. Why? There's nothing wrong, is there?"

"No, but every time I see the twins these days, all they do is complain about one another. Before their girls started school, only one of the twins was working in the shop at a time, and everything was okay. Now they're working together again, they argue all the time. It's beginning to drive me crazy."

Just then, I heard the thump of paws on the stairs and Barry came charging into the kitchen.

"Jill, I didn't know you were here. I was asleep."

"You look a mess."

"Aw, don't say that."

"Sorry, but it's true. What happened to him, Aunt Lucy?"

"It's my fault, really. When I took him for his walk yesterday afternoon, I had the bright idea of going somewhere different, so I took him by the river. I hadn't realised the recent heavy rain had caused it to break its banks in a number of spots."

"Oh dear."

"*Oh dear*, indeed. There were huge puddles and the

ground was really muddy. Needless to say, Barry thought it was great and he went rolling in it. By the time I got him home, he was absolutely caked in mud. If you think he looks bad now, you should have seen him yesterday before I brushed the worst of it out. I called the groomers first thing this morning, but it appears they've closed down, so I'm going to have to try to find another one."

"If you get stuck, I might be able to help. A dog groomer, called Bubbles, has opened just down the corridor from my office. The lady who owns it seems really nice. She's given me a fifty percent off voucher for shampoos. I don't really want to take Barry to the human world, but if you can't find anywhere in Candlefield, give me a call and I'll see what I can organise."

"Thanks, I'll do that."

"Where's my dinner?" Barry whined. "I'm hungry."

"You'll have to wait a few minutes until we've finished ours," Aunt Lucy said. "Go out in the garden and play. And don't trample all over the flowerbeds."

Chapter 2

Winky was tearing open a brown paper package.

"What have you got there, Winky?"

No response. I wasn't sure he'd even heard me because he was so intent on getting the package open.

"Ta-da!" He held up four eye patches: those awful ones with the eye on the front. A red one, a blue one, a green one and a yellow one.

"Those are absolutely horrible," I said.

"Rubbish. They look great. I think I'll wear the yellow one today."

It was so weird seeing a two-eyed Winky, but before I had the time to dwell further on that, my phone rang.

"Is that Jill?" The voice was familiar, but I couldn't put a name to it.

"Err, yes. Jill speaking."

"It's Don Keigh. I don't know if you remember me."

How could I ever forget him? Don Keigh (best name ever) was a committee member of NOCA, which stood for the National Organisation of Clown Acts. Some years ago, the then chairman of that organisation, a Mr Andrew Clowne, had hired me to investigate a case of extortion. It turned out that the extortion demand had in fact been fake. Andrew Clowne had been trying to cover up the fact that he'd been stealing money from NOCA for years. And to make matters much worse, he'd murdered a clown called Mr Bobo, in an attempt to give credence to the extortion demand.

"Of course I remember you, Don. How are you?"

"Very well. I'm the chairman of NOCA now."

"Congratulations."

"Thanks. I find myself with a tricky situation on my hands, which I think would benefit from your help. I was hoping to come and talk to you about it."

I hesitated because I hated clowns. I always had. They're evil—every last one of them. I didn't particularly want to take on another clown-related case but earnings for the year were down, so I wasn't in a position to turn cases away.

"I guess so, Don. When did you have in mind?"

"Would tomorrow be okay?"

"Sure, but I'm busy in the morning. How about the afternoon? Say two-thirty?"

"Okay, I'll see you then."

A few minutes later, Mrs V came through to my office. "I have your two-thirty out there, Jill."

"My *two-thirty*?"

"You sound surprised. Surely, you have a note of it in your diary."

I knew without checking that I didn't because Phil Black's appointment was the only one I'd entered for that day.

"Of course I do, Mrs V."

"And you'll have a note of the lady's name?"

That PA of mine could be such a smarty-pants sometimes.

"Naturally, but you might as well tell me anyway. That way, I don't have to waste time getting the diary out."

Mrs V gave me that unimpressed look of hers. "It's a Ms Georgina Walpole."

"*Ms Walpole*. I remember. Send her through, would you?"

Georgina Walpole reminded me a little of Rosemond Starr, with her sharp suit and no-nonsense hairstyle. I hoped she wasn't about to quiz me on blue sky boxes.

"Jill Maxwell, thank you for seeing me." She marched over to my desk and gave me a firm handshake.

"My pleasure. Would you care for a drink?"

"Not for me, thanks. I'd like to get through this as quickly as possible." She opened her briefcase, took out a couple of sheets of paper, put them on my desk, and then handed me a pen. "Sign this, would you?"

"What is it?"

"It's nothing to be concerned about. Just a standard NDA."

"NDA?"

"Non-disclosure agreement."

"Of course. And why do you need me to sign it?"

"What I'm about to tell you, Jill, is commercially sensitive, so I need to be sure you won't repeat anything you hear today to anyone."

"That's the way I normally operate. PI/Client confidentiality, and all that."

"Still, just to put my mind at ease. If you wouldn't mind signing it."

I didn't see I had anything to lose, so I signed the form and handed it back to her.

"So, Georgina—is it okay if I call you Georgina?"

"Actually, everyone calls me Georgie."

"Right. How can I help you today, Georgie?"

"I'm here on behalf of my client, Margaret Plant. You've probably heard of her."

"Is she that celebrity chef?"

"No, she's one of the world's bestselling authors in the

mystery genre."

"Right. I actually don't read very much." She looked appalled to hear that. "In the mystery genre, I mean."

"The reason I'm here is that Margaret's latest manuscript has been stolen. I don't need to tell you that this is an unmitigated disaster."

"Doesn't she have a backup on her computer? Or on the cloud?"

Did you notice the way I said *cloud* as though I actually knew what it was?

"Unfortunately not. Margaret is rather old-fashioned. She still uses an electric typewriter, so it was the only copy she had."

"Oh dear. How was it stolen, exactly?"

"There appears to have been a break-in. One of the windows was smashed. The strange thing is that nothing else was taken. It's as though the thief was targeting the manuscript."

"Have you been to the police?"

"Certainly not. We can't afford the bad publicity. This book is already one year late. Margaret has a lot of very loyal readers, but this is beginning to test even their patience. If we were to announce that they were going to have to wait another year—maybe longer—I dread to think what the reaction would be. When the book is published, it's expected to sell a hundred thousand copies straight out of the gate, so there's a lot of money at stake."

"Can I ask why you chose to come to me?"

"We need to avoid publicity at all costs, and I figured that no one would have heard of your little outfit." A backhanded compliment if ever I'd heard one. "So, Jill, do you think you can help?"

"I'm sure I can."

"Excellent. What else do you need from me?"

"First, I'll need to speak to the author herself."

"No problem. I've already primed Margaret. How about Wednesday? Would that work for you?"

"Sure. What time?"

"Why don't I email you with Margaret's address after I've had a chance to speak with her? We can arrange a time then."

"Okay, great. Thanks."

Not long after she'd left, Winky jumped onto my desk. "What's it worth to keep quiet?"

"About what?"

"The missing manuscript of course. What's it worth not to go to the press?"

"You wouldn't do that."

"What's to stop me? I'm not the one who signed the NDA."

"What do you want?"

"How about an extra bowl of salmon?"

"Red?"

"Obviously."

***

I was just about to call it a day when my phone rang; it was Aunt Lucy.

"Jill, I've asked around and it seems that there's now only one dog groomer in the whole of Candlefield. I've just got off the phone with them, and they don't have a free appointment for over a week. Is there any chance you could check if that dog groomer down the corridor from you is able to fit Barry in any sooner?"

"Sure. I was just on my way out, so I'll pop into Bubbles and see what they say. I'll call you back either way."

"Okay, Jill. Thanks."

"Did I hear you say you're going to Bubbles?" Winky said.

"You, sir, shouldn't be eavesdropping on my phone calls."

"Why not? You eavesdrop on all of mine. Why are you going there?"

"Barry managed to get rather dirty yesterday and could do with a shampoo, so I'm going to see if Bubbles can fit him in."

"I hope you're not thinking of bringing him into this office."

"I might have no choice."

"If he tears me apart, I hope you'll be able to live with yourself."

"Barry? Tear you apart? He's more likely to lick you to death. Anyway, I have to get going."

"I'm going to call it a day, Mrs V."

"Okay, Jill. I've got two-hundred and fifty-two likes now."

"That's brilliant." Yawn. "I'm going to call in at Bubbles, then I'll shoot off home."

"Why are you going to Bubbles?"

"I need to book an appointment to get my dog shampooed."

"I can't wait to see that little Chihuahua of yours. You

will bring him in to see me, won't you?"

"Err, yeah. Of course. Anyway, I must get going."

Delilah was behind the desk in Bubbles.

"Hello again." She beamed. "Thanks ever so much for not snitching on me the other day about the poodle."

"That's okay."

"I've double and triple checked all the locks on the cages since then."

"That's good. Is there any chance you have a free slot tomorrow for my Labradoodle? Just for a shampoo."

"Let me take a look." She tapped away on the computer. "We could squeeze him in at eleven, would that be okay?"

"That would be great. Thanks."

"What's his name?"

"Barry."

"That's a great name. I love Labradoodles."

As soon as I was out of Bubbles, I made a call to Aunt Lucy.

"It's me. Bubbles can do a shampoo tomorrow. I'll pop over late morning to pick Barry up. She said it should only take an hour or so."

"That's fantastic. Thanks very much, Jill. You'll have to let me know how much I owe you."

"Don't be silly. Barry is still my dog, remember."

"Okay, I'll see you tomorrow."

***

I'd just pulled up outside the old watermill, and I was about to head in when I heard someone shouting my name. Running towards me, very unsteadily, was my neighbour, Olga. The woman clearly had a penchant for high heels, but she didn't have the first idea how to walk in them.

"Jill, I'm so glad I've caught you. We're having a barbecue on Saturday and we'd love for you all to join us."

"Saturday? I'm not sure if we can. I seem to think we might be doing something on that day."

"Do say you'll try, at least. The weather looks like it's going to be gorgeous."

"Okay. I'll have to check with Jack. If we can make it, I'll let you know."

As soon as I walked through the door, Florence threw herself at me.

"Mummy, you'll never guess what."

"Has Buddy stopped chasing the ball again?"

"No, silly. Something much more exciting than that."

"Go on, then, you'll have to tell me."

"Wendy said that she can turn herself into a wolf."

Oh bum!

"Did she?"

"Yes. I don't think it's true, though. People can't turn themselves into wolves, can they, Mummy?"

"I—err—I think I heard Buddy barking. Why don't you go and see what he's doing?"

"Okay."

She ran through the house and out into the garden. I went in search of Jack who I found in the lounge.

"What's all this about Wendy, Jack?"

"Apparently, Wendy told Florence she turns herself into a wolf whenever there's a full moon. I don't think

Florence quite knows what to make of it. When I picked her up from school, she asked me if it was true. I didn't know what to say, so I just stalled. What do you think we should do?"

"I probably should tell her about werewolves because she's going to find out sooner or later."

"Do you think I should be there when you talk to her about it?"

"I think it might be best if I did this one alone. If that's okay with you?"

"Sure. I'd prefer you did. It's not like I'd have much to contribute. Who was that woman I saw you talking to just now?"

"That's the next-door neighbour that I told you about. Olga. She's invited us to a barbecue on Saturday."

"A barbecue? Great."

"No, Jack, it isn't great. It's the exact opposite of great."

"Why? I love a barbecue."

"We could have our own. We don't need to spend time with the weird neighbours."

"What makes you think they're weird?"

"There's her high heels for a start."

"*High heels*?"

"She can't walk in them."

"Right. I'm not sure that makes her weird. I find it always pays to be on friendly terms with your neighbours."

"You were certainly friendly with Megan, I seem to remember."

"Now you're just being ridiculous. The barbecue could be fun."

"Like a visit to the dentist."

"Don't mention the dentist." Jack shuddered. "I have to get a filling next week."

"I don't know why you're making such a fuss. Getting a filling is nothing."

"That's not what you said the last time you had to have one."

"Rubbish. Anyway, I'm starving. Is it steak and kidney pie like you promised?"

"I'm afraid not."

"Aw, I've been looking forward to that all day."

"Sorry, I hadn't realised we were out of them. I did pop over to the village store, but of course they didn't have any. Did you know that they have everything on the shelves in alphabetical order now?"

Chapter 3

Overnight, Jack and I had discussed the situation regarding Wendy, and we'd reached the conclusion that I needed to have a talk with Florence before she went to school. If I didn't, there was the possibility that Wendy might raise the subject again and that would have left Florence even more confused.

We had decided that it would be best for me to speak to her alone because, as Jack rightly pointed out, there wasn't a great deal he could contribute on the subject. He went for a walk around the village and I called her in from the garden.

"Florence, can you come in please?"

"Is it time for school already?"

"Not yet, but Mummy would like to talk to you for a minute."

"I found a spider. Do you want to see him?"

"Err—maybe later, after we've had our little chat."

"But he might have gone by then."

"There'll be plenty of others to see. Come on in, darling."

"Okay." She skipped into the house.

Why is it only young children skip? It always looks so much fun and yet for some unfathomable reason, you never see anyone over the age of six doing it. What happens? Does the 'skip gene' disappear as soon as you reach your sixth birthday? I should start skipping. Later, after I'd parked the car in Washbridge, maybe I'd skip all the way to the office.

"Take a seat at the kitchen table, Florence, so I can talk to you."

"Is it about the pillow, Mummy?"

"Err, no. What about the pillow?"

"I spilled some juice on it last night." She lowered her gaze. "Sorry."

"Don't worry about that. It'll wash out. I want to talk to you about Wendy."

"Is she coming to my house to play? You said she could."

"And she can, but I don't know when. We'll need to talk to her mummy first. I want to chat about what she said to you yesterday."

"About being a wolf?"

"That's right."

"I think she was telling a big fib, wasn't she?"

"No, I don't think she was."

Florence looked very puzzled by my response. "But little girls can't turn into wolves, Mummy."

"Do you remember when we talked about sups?"

"Yes. You're a sup. And me. But not Daddy."

"That's right. Daddy's a human. And do you remember what sups are?"

"They're witches and wizards who can do magic like we can."

"That's right, but there are other types of sups too."

"What are they?"

"There are lots of different types, but I just want to talk to you about one particular type today. They're called werewolves."

"Are they like wolves?"

"Kind of, yes. Werewolves are half human and half wolf."

"Which half is the human? Is it their head or their

bottom?"

"I don't mean half and half like that. I mean that sometimes they're a human and sometimes they're a wolf."

"Is Wendy a werewolf?"

"Yes, she is. So are her mummy and daddy. And her sister."

"I don't think I'd like to be a werewolf. I don't want to turn into a wolf. Do you think Wendy likes it?"

"I'm sure she does."

"Will she turn into a wolf for me?"

"No, and you mustn't ask her to. Werewolves who live here in the human world have to be very careful not to turn into wolves because they mustn't let anyone see them."

"Why not?"

"Because they have to keep it secret."

"Like we have to keep it a secret that we can do magic?"

"That's right. Do you understand everything I've said?"

"Yes. I'm glad Wendy wasn't telling lies because that's not a nice thing to do to your friend, is it?"

"No, she wasn't telling lies, but you have to keep her secret."

"I will. I promise."

After we'd finished our little chat, Florence went back out into the garden to look for her spider. Jack arrived home a few minutes later.

"How did it go, Jill?"

"Okay, I think."

"It didn't scare her, did it?"

"Far from it. Florence wanted to know if Wendy could

turn herself into a wolf for her to see. I told her that she wasn't allowed to do that in the human world."

"Right, I'm glad that's all sorted."

"Jack, when you take Florence to school today, if you see Donna, why don't you ask her if Wendy can come over to play? Maybe this Sunday?"

"I'll do that. Oh, by the way, while I was walking around the village, I bumped into Olga."

"Was she in her high heels?"

"Yeah." He grinned. "I see what you mean about those. She asked if we'd be able to go to their barbecue."

"And you told her no."

"Actually, I said we'd love to go."

"You did *what*? I thought we'd agreed that we didn't want to go."

"That's not true. I said that I did want to go."

"But I said I didn't."

"That's why I spoke to Florence earlier and gave her the casting vote. She voted yes."

"Great." Outvoted in my own house.

***

I tried skipping from the car park, but I simply couldn't do it. Every time I tried, I ended up doing a lopsided run, which drew a lot of strange looks. One man even asked if I'd hurt my ankle and needed any assistance.

"Three-hundred and two," Mrs V said, as soon as I walked through the door.

"Sorry?"

"Three-hundred and two followers on YarnAgram."

"That's—err—great."

"I know. And the cuckoo clock jumper I put up last night has already got one-hundred and sixteen likes."

"That's really impressive."

Yawn and double yawn. I was so *very* pleased that Mrs V had decided to give me a blow by blow commentary on her YarnAgram account. It was definitely the highlight of my day.

Winky was wearing the blue eye patch, and appeared to be messing around with a watch strapped to one of his front legs.

"Is that a new watch, Winky?"

"It's not a watch." He held it up for me to see. "This is a FitCat."

"A what?"

"You must have heard of them. It tracks how much exercise you do."

"In your case, that would be none. You just sit around this office all day. The most you ever do is jump from the sofa to this desk, and onto the windowsill."

"Rubbish!" he scoffed. "You have no idea what I get up to because you're out of the office for long periods of time. I get plenty of exercise both in here and outside. I often go for long runs."

"Don't make me laugh."

Just before nine-thirty, Mrs V came through to my office.

"Jill, I've got Betty Longbottom out here to see you."

"Right. Send her through, would you?"

Since I'd last seen her, Betty had gone blonde, and it quite suited her. Just like Rosemond Starr and Georgina Walpole, Betty was power dressing. What was it with all these women? I was beginning to feel left out. Perhaps it was time to refresh my wardrobe. Some chance given the state of our finances. The money Jack's father had left him in his will had helped us to buy the new house, but we still had hefty bills to pay each month.

"Hi, Betty. Nice to see you again."

"You too."

"Mrs V, could you get us some tea, please? Unless you'd prefer coffee, Betty?"

"Tea's fine for me, thanks."

While we waited for Mrs V to make the drinks, Betty told me about the terrible ordeal she'd gone through with the marine life centres. How she'd fought to try to keep them in business, but in the end had been forced to admit defeat.

"It was the worst day of my life, Jill. The day I had to close the doors."

"It must have been terrible for you. What happened to all the fish?"

"Fortunately, I managed to find good homes for all of them. But when the centres closed, my dreams went with them."

"I really am sorry, Betty. What are you doing now?"

"Luckily, I was able to return to my previous career."

"In the tax office?"

"That's right. They're on a recruitment drive at the moment, so they snapped me up. I'm now a senior tax inspector."

"That's great. I really couldn't be happier for you. Where are you based?"

"Here in Washbridge. In fact, that's the main reason for my visit today."

"Oh? I thought you'd popped in to catch up on old times."

"Obviously that was nice, but I mainly wanted to warn you that you're due an inspection."

"Really? It can't be that long since the last one."

"It's actually overdue."

"Still, it'll just be a formality, I assume?"

"Let's hope so, but one can never be sure."

Talk about outstaying your welcome! Betty was with me for over an hour, and most of that time she spent updating me on the many changes to the tax regime. Not a subject I was particularly interested in. What a nerve! Coming here on the pretence of catching up on old times when all she really wanted to do was to tell me I was due an inspection.

I should have known better. I first met Betty when we lived in the same apartment block. She'd been a little shady even then. There was her kleptomania stage for a start—not exactly the ideal qualification for a tax inspector. The only reason she hadn't been caught was because I'd saved her bacon.

And this was all the thanks I got for it.

Not long after Betty had left, while I was still busy thinking of different ways I could dispose of her body, Winky jumped onto my desk.

"It looks like you're in big trouble." He grinned.

"What do you mean?"

"You'll never survive a tax inspection."

"Of course I will. Everything I do is above board."

"Not if some of Luther Stone's comments are anything

to go by. He was always telling you that you were charging things against profits that had nothing to do with the business."

"Most of that was stuff you'd ordered."

"I'm not sure blaming the cat will wash with the tax inspectors."

"It'll be fine. I have a new accountant now. He can deal with Betty."

"He'll need to be good to outsmart that Betty woman. Is he a bit of a dynamo, this new accountant of yours?"

"Err—" I glanced at my watch and realised that I only had a few minutes before Barry's appointment at Bubbles. "Sorry, I have to go."

I magicked myself over to Aunt Lucy's.

"Where's Barry, Aunt Lucy?"

"Upstairs, I think. Sorry, Jill, I got carried away with my baking. I should have had him ready for you."

"That's okay. I'll go and get him."

I hurried upstairs and into the spare bedroom, but there was no sign of Barry. Rhymes was sitting in a corner reading a book.

"Do you know where Barry is, Rhymes?"

"Under there." He pointed at the bed.

I got down on all fours and peered underneath. "Barry, come on out."

"No! Don't want a shampoo."

"Come on, Barry. Your coat is a mess. You need a good wash."

"Not going. Don't like it."

Moments later, Aunt Lucy came into the room.

"Have you found him?"

"He's under here. Did you tell him about the

grooming?"

"Sorry, yes I did."

"He won't come out."

"Let me try."

She knelt down beside me.

"Come on, Barry. Jill doesn't have all day."

"I'm not dirty. Don't need a shampoo."

"You're filthy. Come on."

I was beginning to lose my patience.

"If you don't come out, there'll be no more Barkies for you ever again."

"You don't mean that," he said.

"Yes, I do. If you're not out by the time I've counted to three, there'll be no more Barkies for you. One, two—"

He poked his head out from under the bed. "They won't get soap in my eyes, will they?"

"No, I'll tell them to be extra careful."

"Okay, then." He crawled out. "Can we go for a walk first?"

"No, because I have to take you to the human world." I clipped the lead to his collar and magicked us to Washbridge.

If I'd had my wits about me, I wouldn't have landed in my office. But I didn't have my wits about me.

"Barry! No! Come here!"

Luckily, I had a tight hold of his lead because when Barry saw Winky, he tried to rush over to him. Winky took one look at Barry and bolted for the window.

"I want to play with the pussycat."

"You can't. We're already late. Come on."

As I stepped into the outer office, Mrs V looked thoroughly confused.

"Where did that dog come from, Jill?"

Oh bum! What was I thinking?

"Err, this dog?"

"Yes, the one you're holding onto."

"This is Barry."

"But where did he come from, and who does he belong to?"

I'd got myself into a hopeless predicament, and I wasn't going to be able to talk my way out of it anytime soon. I had no option but to cast the 'forget' spell, and while Mrs V was still a little hazy, I dragged Barry out of the office and down the corridor.

"I didn't think you were going to make it," Delilah said.

"I'm sorry I'm a few minutes late. I had a bit of trouble getting Barry here."

Barry jumped up and put his front paws onto the counter.

"Isn't he a lovely boy?" She gave him a fuss.

"Delilah, would you ask Farah to be careful not to get any soap in his eyes, please?"

Chapter 4

Just before two-thirty, Mrs V came through to my office.

"Jill, I have a clown out here to see you. He says he has an appointment."

A. Clown? Andrew Clowne?

"I think you must have got that wrong, Mrs V, Andrew Clowne is in prison. I was expecting Don Keigh."

"I know I'm getting on in years, Jill, but I still know the difference between a clown and a donkey, and I can assure you that I have a clown out here."

"No, you misunderstood me. I said Don Keigh. Not donkey."

"It doesn't matter how many times you say it, it still isn't a donkey out there. Would you like to see the clown or not?"

"Err, yeah, send him through, would you?"

The clown who walked through the door could have been anyone underneath that stupid wig and makeup. It was only when he spoke that I was sure it was Don Keigh.

"Thanks for seeing me at such short notice, Jill." He offered his hand.

"Ouch!" As I shook it, I received a small electric shock.

"I'm so sorry. I thought I'd switched that off."

"That's okay. I wasn't expecting you to turn up in your clown's outfit."

"I didn't really have a choice. When I've done here, I have to go straight to a kid's birthday party, which was booked a while ago. There won't be time to get changed."

"So, what brings you here today, Don?"

"Something awful has happened, I'm afraid. We hold a

meeting of the NOCA committee every month. During the last two meetings, one of the committee members has died."

"Died how?"

"Heart attacks. If this continues, there'll be no one left on the committee."

"That's terrible, but if they died of a heart attack, I'm not really sure why you came to see me."

"I don't believe that it was a heart attack. I think there was foul play of some kind."

"What makes you say that?"

"The day after the second death, I received an envelope in the post. The only thing inside it was these Scrabble tiles." He took an envelope out of his pocket and tipped the tiles onto my desk. Most of them had a white background, but some had been coloured red.

"Did the envelope come in the regular post?"

"No, someone had pushed it through my letterbox."

"Do you have any idea what the Scrabble tiles are supposed to mean?"

"Only that if you use only the red ones, they spell the word: R-E-V-E-N-G-E."

"*Revenge*? What do the police have to say about the tiles?"

"Nothing much. The coroner's verdict in both cases was a heart attack, so the police pretty much dismissed the tiles as someone's idea of a sick joke. I don't buy that. It's obvious to me that someone is targeting NOCA members. Someone with a grudge."

"I'd have suggested Andrew Clowne if he wasn't in prison."

"He isn't."

"Has he been released already?"

"No, he's dead. He died of natural causes during the second year of his sentence."

"I guess that rules him out. Is there anyone else you can think of who might have an axe to grind with NOCA?"

"No one. That's why I came to see you. This has got me really shaken, Jill. Will you take the case?"

"Of course."

"Excellent." He checked the clown watch on his wrist. "Sorry, but I have to get going or I'll be late for the birthday party. Could you come and see me at Chuckle House tomorrow? I can introduce you to my second-in-command and answer any questions you may have."

"Okay, but I'm busy tomorrow morning. How about tomorrow afternoon?"

"That will be fine."

"Do you think I could hold onto the Scrabble tiles, Don?"

"Sure. I'll be glad to see the back of them."

***

No sooner had Don Keigh left than Winky came scrambling back through the window.

"Have you got rid of that stupid dog?" He glanced around.

"Don't call Barry stupid." Only I'm allowed to do that. "He's being shampooed at Bubbles."

"Why did you bring him in here? If I hadn't scarpered when I did, he would have torn me limb from limb."

"Don't be so melodramatic. He just wanted to play with you."

"I could report you for animal cruelty."

"Give it a rest, Winky. You weren't really scared of Barry. You're just putting it on."

"If I need therapy after this, I'm going to send you the bill."

Mrs V popped her head around the door.

"Jill, while you were with that clown, the young lady from Bubbles came to see you. She said that your dog was ready for collection."

"Oh, right. Thanks."

"You haven't forgotten that you promised you'd let me meet your little Chihuahua, have you?"

"Of course not, and I will, but there isn't time today because I have an appointment with Phil Black's grandmother. I'll bring him in to show you next week."

"Oh, okay then." She was clearly disappointed. "You won't forget, will you?"

"Of course I won't."

I hurried down the corridor to Bubbles where Delilah was behind the desk.

"Hi, Jill. I'll just go and get Barry for you." She returned a few minutes later with a spotlessly clean Barry.

"They didn't get any soap in my eyes, Jill," he said.

"I told you they wouldn't."

"I want to come here every time."

"We'll see."

It was only then that I noticed Delilah's puzzled look. She was clearly wondering why I was having what appeared to be a one-sided conversation with a dog.

"Err, tell Farah she did a great job, would you, Delilah? I'll definitely bring him back the next time he needs a shampoo."

"Would you like me to make the appointment now?"

"Err, no, that's okay. I'll pop in nearer the time."

Delilah led him around the counter and handed me his lead. "See you soon, Barry."

Out in the corridor, I was just about to magic Barry and myself to Candlefield when Mrs V stepped out of the office.

Oh bum!

"Jill?" She looked at me, then at Barry. "I thought you said you had a Chihuahua?"

"Err, yes I do."

"Who's this big guy? Who does he belong to?"

In the absence of any credible explanation, I was forced to cast the 'forget' spell on Mrs V for the second time that day. While she was still out of it, I magicked myself and Barry to Aunt Lucy's house.

"He looks much better." Aunt Lucy made a big fuss of him.

"I like Bubbles," Barry said. "They didn't get any soap in my eyes."

"That's good."

"I'm hungry." He licked his lips. "Is it time for dinner?"

"It is. In fact, we're running a little late."

"I'm going to leave you to it, Aunt Lucy," I said. "There's somewhere I need to be."

"Okay, Jill. Thanks very much for taking him."

***

After magicking myself back to the car park in

Washbridge, I drove to Phil Black's grandmother's house. He'd told me that his grandmother, Edie, was the only one who had stood by him after his conviction. He'd also warned me that she wasn't in the best of health. When she answered the door, she was walking with the aid of a metal frame, and she looked very frail.

"You must be Jill," she said in a weak voice.

"That's right. Edie, isn't it?"

"Yes. Come through to the kitchen." She led the way very slowly through the house to the small kitchen, which overlooked the back garden. The room, which looked like it probably hadn't changed since the seventies, was spotlessly clean. "Have a seat, Jill. I was just about to make myself a cup of tea. Would you like one?"

"Yes, please, but why don't you let me make it?"

"I wouldn't hear of it. I may not be as sprightly as I used to be, but I can still make a cup of tea."

She handed me the drink, then hobbled over to the cupboard, and brought out a biscuit barrel. "I'm afraid I only have one type of biscuit. Custard creams."

Clearly a woman of taste.

"Thanks very much. I'll just have the one."

"One's no good to anyone. Take at least two."

"Okay, if you insist."

She parked her frame and joined me at the table. "I really appreciate you trying to help Phil. The way he's been treated by the justice system and even by his family is appalling. I'm ashamed of the way my daughter has abandoned her own son like this. I assume Phil told you that I'll be paying your bill?"

"He did. Are you sure you'll be able to afford it?"

"Yes, that's not a problem. Ever since he was sent to prison, I've put a little money aside every month. I thought he could use it towards a house when he got out, but he insists that he wants to use it to clear his name so he can get on with his life."

"What can you tell me about your daughter's relationship with Phil's stepfather?"

"I never really liked Andy. I couldn't see what Felicity saw in him, but they seemed happy enough, particularly after Liam came along."

"How did Phil get on with his stepfather?"

"Not very well at all. They were always at each other's throats."

"Did it ever get physical?"

"No."

"Would Phil have told you if it had?"

"Yes, he's always confided in me."

"What about Phil's relationship with his stepbrother, Liam?"

"Phil was very good with him, and Liam seemed to look up to Phil."

"I understand your daughter and Andy have split up."

"That's right. About six months after Liam's disappearance, Andy walked out. The stress was too much for both of them. Felicity has remarried since then. I broke off all contact with her after Phil was sent to prison. I couldn't accept the way she'd abandoned her son. We haven't spoken in years."

"Do you know where Andy is now?"

"No. I heard he moved abroad, but I couldn't tell you where."

"Phil told me that he'd occasionally take Liam with him

when he went fishing."

"Yes, but not very often. As you can imagine, a young boy of that age soon becomes bored and starts to mess around. It was no fun for Phil having Liam there because he took his fishing very seriously."

"Phil insists that he never saw Liam on the day he disappeared."

"And I believe him. Phil may have his faults, but he's not a liar."

"Edie, have you ever asked Phil about the blood that was found on the rocks and on his fishing rod?"

"Of course. And he's always said the same thing, that he has no idea how it got there."

"Do you have any theories as to what might've happened to Liam?"

"The only thing I can come up with is that a stranger must've snatched him. After all this time, I suppose we have to assume he's dead, don't we?"

"Unfortunately, yes, I think so."

"Do you really think you'll be able to help Phil, Jill?"

"I'll tell you the same as I told Phil. Cases like this one are notoriously difficult, but I'll do my best."

"Thank you. I can't ask any more than that."

"Do you think Felicity will talk to me?"

"I really couldn't say, but I'll give you her address."

***

I'd just parked in front of the old watermill when someone hammered on the driver's side window. Miss Drinkwater was standing next to the car, beckoning to me to get out. She was red in the face and clearly angry about something.

"Is there a problem, Miss Drinkwater?"

"A *problem*? Yes, I would say so," she snapped. "Is it correct what I hear that your grandmother has taken over the hotel?"

"That's right. Who did you hear that from?"

"Never mind that. I understand she's going to be offering afternoon tea."

"I don't know, but it wouldn't surprise me. The hotel does have a restaurant."

"Tweaking Tea Rooms has been offering afternoon tea in this village since before you were born, and I've never had to put up with competition before. I'd like you to have a word with your grandmother, young lady. Tell her that it's not on."

"I'm sorry, Miss Drinkwater, but it's not for me to tell Grandma how to run her business. Not that she'd take any notice of me anyway. Why don't you have a word with her yourself?"

"Don't you think I've tried? Every time I go up there, there's no sign of her. If you ask me, she's got wind that I'm on her case and she's probably hiding."

"I think that's very unlikely. You'll find that Grandma isn't the kind of person to scare easily."

"I simply won't stand for this. You can tell her that." And with that she huffed, puffed and walked away.

"What did Miss Drinkwater want?" Jack asked when I walked through the door.

"She's not very happy because, apparently, Grandma is going to be offering afternoon tea in the hotel."

"What does she expect *you* to do about it?"

"I've no idea. I'd like to know who told her that the new owner was my grandmother."

"It sounds like there could be a showdown."

"If there is, my money is on Grandma."

"Mine too. I managed to grab a word with Wendy's mum, and she said Wendy can come over on Sunday afternoon about two."

"Great. Where is Florence, anyway?"

"Upstairs, playing with her dolls' house the last time I checked. By the way, Jill, have you remembered what date it is next week?"

"It's not your birthday, is it?"

"No, it's our wedding anniversary."

"Oh yeah, of course. I knew that."

"I've come up with a really great idea for how we can celebrate it."

"A slap-up meal at my favourite restaurant?"

"Much better than that. I've organised a dinner with both of our parents. Won't that be brilliant?"

Chapter 5

Jack sat down at the kitchen table and began to spread marmalade on his toast.

"Are you still not talking to me, Jill?"

I ignored him.

"I'll take that as a no, shall I? I really don't know why you're so upset. I thought you'd be pleased that I'd arranged a dinner party for our anniversary."

"We went through all this last night."

"Oh, so you *are* talking to me."

"As I said last night, a quiet romantic dinner for two would have been lovely, but what on earth possessed you to organise a dinner party with our parents? Have you forgotten about the bust-up our mothers had?"

"But that was years ago. Surely, they'll both be able to let bygones be bygones, won't they?"

"What planet do you live on, Jack? Of course they won't."

For a short period, Jack's mother, Yvonne, had worked at Cakey C, the tea room owned by my parents, and their new partners, Alberto and Blodwyn. Things had been okay for a while, but then there had been an almighty bust-up. I never did get to the bottom of what caused it, but it definitely had roots in Yvonne's previous occupation. When she'd been alive, she'd worked as a witchfinder.

Just then, Florence came running down the stairs. "Mummy, Daddy, Great-Grandma's here."

This morning was going from bad to badder.

And before you lot start, we've already had the conversation about the word badder. Of course it's a word.

"Come on, Mummy." She grabbed my hand and dragged me through to the hallway.

"Florence, why don't we play a trick on Grandma and pretend we aren't in? We could hide and not answer the door."

"No, Mummy, that wouldn't be very nice." Before I could stop her, Florence had already opened the door.

"If it isn't my favourite great-granddaughter." Grandma took Florence into her arms and gave her a big hug.

"I've learnt a new spell, Great-Grandma."

"Have you, now?" She smirked at me. "And which spell has your mummy taught you?"

"The 'grow' spell. It makes plants bigger. Can I show you?"

"Of course you can, but I need to have a quick word with your mummy first. Why don't you go through to the garden and I'll be with you in just a minute?"

"Okay, Great-Grandma." Florence went skipping through the house. And, she made it look so easy.

"So, Jill?" The smirk was still plastered on Grandma's face. "You decided to take my advice after all. I assume you're going to ramp up the lessons now?"

"Yes, but we don't intend to overdo it. We decided I'd teach Florence one new spell a week."

"*One*? Is that all? At that rate, it'll take forever to teach her all the spells she needs to know. Why don't I help? That would move things along much quicker."

"Absolutely not. Jack only agreed to this on the condition that you weren't involved, and that I would be the one to teach her."

"Why does that human have a say in it?"

"That *human* is Florence's father. Keep your voice down or he'll hear you. Anyway, why are you here? What do you want?"

"I don't need a reason to visit my granddaughter and my great-granddaughter, do I?"

"No, but if you try to teach Florence any more spells, you'll be barred."

"Good luck with that. Now, let me go and see how Florence is doing with that spell."

"Before you do, I should warn you that Miss Drinkwater is on the warpath. She's not very pleased with you."

"Who's Miss Drinkwater when she's at home? I've never heard of the woman."

"She owns Tweaking Tea Rooms, and she's heard that you're going to be offering afternoon tea in the hotel."

"What does that have to do with her?"

"Apparently, Tweaking Tea Rooms have offered afternoon tea for over thirty years, and they've never had to put up with any competition in the village before."

"That's about to change. Why did she come to you? Why not come and tell me herself?"

"She tried to, apparently, but you were never in."

"That's because I'm a very busy woman. If you see her again, tell her I'd be happy to *discuss* the matter with her."

"Don't you dare go and do anything stupid."

"Like what?"

"I don't know. Turning her into a frog maybe."

"Don't go giving me ideas."

***

Ahead of my visit to see the author, Margaret Plant, I'd carried out a little research. Although I'd never heard of her, it seemed that she was something of a phenomenon, having published two books a year for the last twenty years—the majority of which were bestsellers. Curiously, she hadn't published anything for the last two years. During my research, I'd come across numerous posts from her readers who were becoming impatient over a series of delays to her latest book. I now understood why her agent, Georgina Walpole, didn't want news of the missing manuscript to break.

Margaret Plant lived in Lower Tweaking, in a beautiful house called the Quill. From my research, I knew she was in her late sixties, had never married and had no children. Georgina Walpole had informed me that Margaret had a live-in housekeeper called Mrs Flattery, and it was she who answered the door.

"Mrs Flattery? I'm Jill Maxwell, here to see Margaret Plant. I believe she's expecting me."

"She is indeed. Come in."

Mrs Flattery's long black hair was tied neatly back, and she was wearing a smart blue uniform. I considered complimenting her on her appearance, but I figured that wouldn't get me anywhere.

"Before I take you through to Mrs Plant, would you like to see where the thief got in?"

"Yes, please. That would be very helpful."

She led the way to the kitchen, which was at the back of the house.

"They broke the pane on the right. When I came downstairs that morning there was glass all over the windowsill and on the floor."

"I understand from Georgina Walpole that the only thing taken was the manuscript."

"That's correct, which is weird because Mrs Plant has some very valuable ornaments and jewellery."

"Have you worked for Mrs Plant for long?"

"Almost twenty years now. I feel so very sorry for her. She'd worked so hard on this latest book, which has taken much longer than usual to write. She works such long hours too; she locks herself away in the study and only comes out to eat or sleep. She's in there now. I'll take you through to her."

For a woman who rarely left her study, Margaret Plant was dressed to the nines.

"Jill Maxwell, I assume. I'm Margaret."

"That's right. Georgina Walpole told me this would be a good time, but if you're just on your way out, we can always reschedule."

"There's no need. I'm not planning to go out today. Do have a seat. I'm very grateful that you were able to come at such short notice. I assume that Georgie has filled you in on what happened?"

"She has, yes. It must have been a terrible shock when you discovered the manuscript was missing."

"I was devastated. I still am. The thought of having to write that book again from scratch is simply too much to bear."

"Do you still have your notes on the book?"

"I didn't make an outline—I never do. I'm what's known in the trade as a *pantser*. In other words, I write by the seat of my pants. I just dive in and see where the book takes me."

"I see. Have you ever considered using a computer?"

"I've tried it a couple of times, but I found the creative juices wouldn't flow, not like they do when I'm using Daisy."

"*Daisy*?"

She patted the typewriter. "I call her that because she has a daisy wheel. I don't imagine that means much to you. You're far too young. It's that disc-like thing with the letter keys on it."

"I see. Where was the manuscript taken from?"

"This desk. It was just behind the typewriter. That's where I leave it every evening."

"And nothing else was taken?"

"Nothing. If it wasn't for the broken window and the missing manuscript, you wouldn't know anyone had been in here. Have you read any of my books, Jill?"

"I'm afraid not. I don't really get the chance to read much, what with work and looking after my little girl."

"How old is she?"

"Florence is five."

"I never had children, but I look on all of my books as my babies."

"Mrs Flattery tells me you spend most of the day in here."

"That's right. Nose to the grindstone. I chose this room for my study because it looks out onto the back garden, and if I need some fresh air, I just go through there." She pointed to the door next to the window. "When the words won't come, I take a walk around the garden, weather-permitting, and wait until inspiration strikes."

"It's hard to imagine why a random thief would take nothing but the manuscript. Can you think of anyone who might have taken it?"

"No. My first thought was that someone was going to try and extort money from me. I half expected to receive a note demanding payment, but I've received nothing. It's a total mystery."

"What about visitors, Margaret? Do you have many?"

"Very few. The only family I have is my sister, Ruth, but she seldom visits. It's months since she was last here."

"What about your neighbours?"

"That's a bit of a sore point, I'm afraid. I've fallen out with the neighbours on either side. My fault entirely. When I'm in the garden, trying to get the creative juices flowing, I don't want any interruptions. On several occasions, I've been rather short with the neighbours, and now they don't talk to me at all."

"Would it be possible to take a quick look outside?"

I figured that in order to gain access to the kitchen, the thief must have come through the garden.

"Of course." She stood up from the desk and led the way out of the door. "I'm afraid it's a bit of a mess out here, as you can see. I keep intending to find myself a gardener, but I never seem to get around to it."

I considered mentioning Peter, but I thought that wouldn't be very professional. Maybe later, depending on how things turned out.

There were tall hedges to the left and right, with a wire fence behind them. It would have been difficult, although not impossible, for someone to gain access from the neighbouring gardens. At the far end of the small garden was a high wall in which was set a wooden door.

"Where does that door lead to, Margaret?"

"Into the garden of the property on the other side of the wall."

"How come there's a door between the two properties?"

"Apparently, when these houses were built, they were owned by the same family. The door provided easy access. It's locked now of course. There's a padlock on the other side so no one can get through."

"Do you know who owns that house?"

"Err, yes, it's a widower by the name of Mr Stanley Trotter."

"Do you know him well?"

"Not particularly."

***

I had hoped that Margaret Plant might offer me a drink, but it didn't seem to occur to her. By the time I came away, I was rather peckish and ready for a cup of coffee, so I magicked myself over to Cuppy C. Although the shop itself was quiet, the twins were going at it hammer and tongs behind the counter.

"Hey, girls, keep it down. You'll upset the customers."

"It's her fault," Amber said. "Tell her."

"Rubbish," Pearl countered. "She's the one who started it."

"No, I didn't."

"What are you arguing about anyway?"

"Business has been a little slow of late," Amber said. "We're trying to come up with a way to get more customers through the door. I suggested that we do a two-for-one offer."

"I think we should do buy-one-get-one free," Pearl said. "That's a much better idea."

"No, it isn't!" Amber insisted. "Everyone does that.

Two-for-one is far better."

"Girls, I don't know how to break this to you, but this argument is nonsense. Your suggestions are one and the same thing."

"No, they're not," Pearl said. "I said we should do buy-one-get-one free. Amber wants to do two-for-one."

"I know that, but two-for-one is exactly the same as buy-one-get-one free. Just think about it."

The twins looked at one another, thought about it for a moment, and then burst out laughing.

"You're right, Jill. It is, isn't it?" Pearl said.

"Silly us." Amber at least had the good grace to blush.

"Right, now that's settled, can I have—"

"I think we should knock up a sign straight away," Amber said. "It can say, *two cupcakes for the price of one*."

"No," Pearl objected. "It should say, *buy one cupcake, get one free*."

Give me strength!

Eventually, the twins managed to reach a compromise by agreeing to include both of the terms on their sign: Two-for-one *and* buy-one-get-one-free.

At long last, I had my coffee and muffin. Nectar!

"Hey, girls, how do you go about teaching the Lilys magic?"

"What do you mean?" Amber said.

Both of them seemed confused by the question.

"I mean, do you teach them a certain number of spells each week?"

"I don't teach Lily any magic," Pearl said.

"Me neither." Amber shrugged.

"How do they learn magic, then?"

"Mainly at school. They have one magic lesson a day."

"How are they coming along?"

"My Lily hates it," Pearl said.

"My Lily does too. She says it's boring."

"But they're witches. They should love magic."

"I never did." Amber shrugged.

"Me neither," Pearl said. "Mum was always giving us a hard time about it, but we couldn't be bothered."

"What about Grandma? Didn't she get on your case?"

"At first, but after a while she gave up on us, thank goodness."

"Florence loves it. She'd learn a new spell every day if I let her."

"Sounds like she's a swot," Amber said.

"Just like her mum." Pearl laughed.

Chapter 6

As soon as I walked into the outer office, Mrs V got up from her desk and held up her phone triumphantly like some kind of trophy.

"Would you like to know how many followers I have now, Jill?"

Definitely not.

"Of course I would. How many?"

"Three-hundred and forty-eight. I can't believe it."

"Me neither. That's—err—fantastic, but I really must crack on."

"Look, there's another one. That makes it three-hundred and forty-nine."

"Great."

Winky was fast asleep on the sofa. Meanwhile, Bobby and Bertie, the two overweight pigeons who had made their home on the ledge outside my office, were perched near the open window.

"Good morning, Bobby. Morning, Bertie."

They both seemed somewhat subdued, and they could barely find the energy to raise their wings in acknowledgment. That wasn't like them at all; something was clearly amiss, so I walked over to the window.

"Are you two okay?"

"We're just feeling a little blue today, Jill," Bertie said.

"I can see that, but why? Has something happened?"

"Nothing in particular. We're just lonely."

"But you have each other for company, don't you?"

"Yes, but neither of us has a girlfriend. We haven't had one for ages."

"Two handsome birds like you? I'm sure that'll change

soon."

"I very much doubt it," Bobby said. "We've both been trying to find a girlfriend for ages, but with no luck at all. It can be very lonely without someone to snuggle up to."

"I'm sure it can."

"It's alright for you two-leggeds. You have dating agencies and even dating apps to help you find a partner. There's nothing like that for pigeons."

"I guess not, but then it's not like you have phones anyway, is it?"

"Of course we do," Bobby said, and they both produced a phone from under a wing. "How else do you think we communicate with one another?"

"Sorry, I had no idea. Maybe someone will come up with a dating app for pigeons soon."

"I certainly hope so." Bertie sighed. "Anyway, we'd better get going. The lunchtime sandwich crowd will be headed back to their offices now, so there should be rich peckings down there. We'll see you later, Jill."

"Okay. Keep your chins up."

All ten of them.

What do you mean that's unkind? Have you ever seen a pigeon that didn't have at least a double chin?

While I'd been talking to Bobby and Bertie, Winky had woken up, no doubt in time for his bowl of salmon. Curiously, though, he'd disappeared under the sofa. I went over to the cupboard, opened a tin of salmon, and filled his bowl. Normally by then, he would have been weaving around my legs, but he was still under the sofa, so I got down on all fours and looked underneath, to find him tapping away frantically on his tablet.

"Winky, I've just put your salmon out."

"I'll be there in a minute."

"I thought you'd be hungry by now."

"I am, but it'll just have to wait. I'll get to it as soon as I can."

Charming! I would never understand that cat. Most days, he pestered me non-stop for his food. Whatever he was working on must have been very important because it certainly had all of his attention.

***

I really wasn't looking forward to this meeting.

Even though there had been a clown school just down the corridor from my office for a couple of years, I was no fonder of clowns now than I had been when I was a kid. That's why the thought of returning to Chuckle House filled me with dread. Last night, I'd had a horrible nightmare in which I was being chased all around Washbridge by a gang of killer clowns.

The exterior of Chuckle House had been given a complete facelift. So had the interior, which was nothing short of spectacular—in a *freak-you-out-of-your-mind* kind of way. I'd never seen so many statues, paintings and photographs of clowns in one place. Behind the reception desk was a woman who, unsurprisingly, was wearing a clown costume.

"Good afternoon," I said, all cool, calm and collected, like clowns were my favourite thing. "My name is Jill Maxwell. Don Keigh is expecting me."

"Ah yes, of course." Her bow tie spun around and lit up as she spoke. "He's in the conference room on the next floor. You can take the Chucklevator."

"Sorry? The what?"

"The Chucklevator." When she pointed, I realised she meant the elevator.

"Oh, right. Thanks."

I stepped out of the elevator (I refuse to call it a Chucklevator) onto a red carpet so thick that I could barely see the top of my shoes. On the walls on either side of the corridor were numerous framed photographs of clowns. Beneath each one was a small plaque, which commemorated the life of these apparently famous performers. One in particular that caught my eye was Mr Cheese who had been Washbridge's Clown of the Year for three consecutive years during the nineties. Mr Cheese's main claim to fame was that instead of the customary red nose, he had what appeared to be a lump of cheese on his face where his nose should have been. You had to hope that his act was funnier than his appearance.

While still trying to put creepy Mr Cheese out of my mind, I knocked on the door marked conference room. From inside, I heard Don Keigh shout for me to come in. Dressed in a regular suit, he was seated at the head of a large conference table. Unfortunately, the man sitting next to him was in full clown costume.

"Jill, do come and join us." Don gestured to the seat next to him. "This is my second-in-command, Trevor Hee. He has a performance booked for later this afternoon, hence the outfit."

"I'm very pleased to meet you, Jill." Trevor stood up and offered his hand. He must have sensed my hesitation because he said, "No shocks, I promise." He held out his open palms to prove the point.

"Nice to meet you too, Trevor."

I'd no sooner got the words out than I was hit in the face by a gush of water, which came out of the flower on his lapel.

"Sorry, Jill. Force of habit. Funny, eh?"

"Hilarious." I took a tissue from my pocket and wiped my eyes.

"I've told Trevor about our brief meeting yesterday," Don said. "I thought it might be helpful if you spoke to him too."

"I agree. Trevor, I assume you're aware of the Scrabble tiles."

"Yes, but to be perfectly honest, I've already told Don that I share the police's view on this. I don't think they're of any significance. The cause of death in both cases was confirmed as a heart attack and tragic as that is, I don't see anything sinister in it."

"What do you make of Don's theory that this might be the work of someone with a grudge against NOCA?"

"Like who, though? I have to say that I think we're wasting our money pursuing this, but Don's the chairman, so it's his call."

"What can you tell me about the two clowns who died?"

Don fielded that question. "The first was a great guy called Mickey Vallance. His clown name was Webby, and he'd been runner up for Clown of the Year on three separate occasions. Most of us were hoping that he might win this year. He specialised in wearing oversized clown boots which were twice as long as the normal ones. They were really something to behold."

I bet.

"How old was Mr Vallance?"

"In his early sixties."

"Had he been ill at all?"

"He'd had a little trouble with his ticker. Nothing too serious though."

"What about the other clown?"

"That was Randy Seaburn who was about the same age as Mickey. As far as I'm aware, he'd been in good health. Randy's clown name was Jolly Jelly, and as his name suggests, his act was predominantly built around jelly. He specialised in taking jelly pies to the face. He had it down to a fine art."

"Were both gentlemen married?"

"Yes, their widows are distraught, as you would imagine."

"I think it might be helpful to my investigation if I could speak to those two ladies. Do you think that would be possible?"

"I don't see why not. I'll give you their names and addresses before you leave, and I'll give them a call to warn them that you'll be contacting them."

"Thanks."

"What do you think we should do about the next committee meeting, Jill?" Don said. "Should we press ahead with it?"

"We have to," Trevor interjected. "I can see no reason to do otherwise."

Don clearly wasn't so sure. "What do you think, Jill?"

"For now, at least, there's no evidence of foul play, so I think you should proceed as normal. If I uncover anything untoward, I'll let you know and then maybe you'll need to have a rethink."

"I'm still convinced this is the work of someone with a

grudge against NOCA. Or maybe just against me," Don insisted.

"You really have to let go of that idea," Trevor said. "It's time for us to move on."

"This is your call, Don," I said. "Do you want me to investigate the deaths or not?"

"Definitely, and I don't want you to leave any stone unturned."

"Okay, you're the boss."

"And you'll keep us posted?" Don stood up.

"Naturally."

***

Kathy had called earlier to ask if I'd like to pop over to her house for a coffee after work. Her place wasn't exactly on my way home these days, but I'd had a long day, so I decided to finish early and have a drive over there.

"Jill, I almost didn't recognise you without the candyfloss in your hair."

"You're so funny, Kathy. You should do stand-up."

"Freaking Tweaking was a blast, wasn't it? It was a pity about the strong winds. We'll have to go again next year."

"Yeah, I can hardly wait."

"I thought we could go through to the orangery for our drinks."

"La-di-da. Listen to you with your *orangery*. Don't you mean the conservatory? You, Kathy, are turning into a proper snob."

"Says the woman who lives in the old watermill."

"The watermill is lovely, but it isn't nearly as big as this place. There's just enough room for the three of us."

"What will you do when the next little one comes along?"

"There isn't going to be *another* little one. I've already told you that. Florence is more than enough for me."

"How about Jack? Does he feel the same?"

"Yes, he does. I've told him that he does."

Kathy went to make the coffee and I went through to the 'orangery'. I'd no sooner sat down than I spotted *them* and burst out laughing.

"I take it you've seen the gnomes." Kathy handed me my drink.

"I assume they're some kind of ironic statement."

"I wish they were. When Pete told me he was getting them, I thought he was joking, but he insists that they give the garden character. He wanted to get six of them, but I put my foot down and insisted that two was enough."

"More than enough, I'd say."

"Between you and me, Jill, they're freaking me out."

"I'm not surprised. They're freaking me out too."

"I don't mean the look of them, although that's bad enough. They're freaking me out because I reckon they're possessed."

"*Possessed*? What are you talking about?"

"I swear they keep moving around."

"Have you been at the wine again?"

"No. Do you see the one with the fishing rod? Last night when we went to bed, it was underneath that tree. And the one with the bucket was over there by that bush. This morning when I got up, they'd swapped places."

"Now you're just being ridiculous. The kids must have done it before you came downstairs this morning."

"That's what I thought, but when I asked them over breakfast, they said they'd had nothing to do with it."

"If it was a practical joke, they're hardly likely to admit it, are they? They're just trying to get you at it, and it looks like they've succeeded."

"I suppose you're right. Anyway, I've been meaning to ask you for some time. How are you settling into village life?"

"I'm getting used to it slowly but surely. I could do without the long journey to and from work every day, but otherwise it's all good. Except for Grandma of course."

"What's she done now?"

"Bought the hotel in the village."

"Oh dear." Kathy laughed. "Rather you than me. I wouldn't like to think she was my neighbour."

"There are quite a few strange characters in Middle Tweaking."

"Such as who?"

"There's the woman who owns the tea room for a start. She's so scary it's a wonder anybody ever goes in there. And then there are the Stock sisters who run the village store. They never have anything you need in stock, and even the stuff they do have, you struggle to find. Their latest brainwave is to put everything on the shelves in alphabetical order. Oh yes, and we've been invited to a barbecue by our next-door neighbours."

"I didn't think you had next-door neighbours."

"They live in the house nearest to ours. It's about fifty yards up the road. I'd thought we could make an excuse to get out of it, but Jack went and told them we'd go. Anyway, how come you aren't at work today?"

"The managers and staff are more than capable of

running the shops without me looking over their shoulders. I just pop into each one from time to time to make sure everything's running smoothly."

"Nice work if you can get it."

"What about you? Are you busy?"

"I'm run off my feet at the moment. I have three cases on the go."

"Have you ever thought of taking on any help?"

"Like who?"

"Another investigator who could share the load. You'd be able to take on more cases that way."

"I've never really thought about it."

"You should. Delegation, that's the name of the game."

Chapter 7

The next morning, as soon as Florence had finished her cornflakes, she jumped up from the table and rushed upstairs to her bedroom.

"What's going on with Florence?" I said. "She's spending an awful lot of time up there."

"She seems to have rediscovered her dolls' house." Jack had forsaken his beloved muesli in favour of Shredded Wheat. That guy was a glutton for punishment.

"I didn't think she was very bothered about the dolls' house."

"She wasn't until a couple of days ago. Now, every time I check on her, she seems to be playing with it. I guess we should be pleased if it gives us a little peace and quiet." Buddy yawned and gave a huge stretch (for such a tiny dog). "I bet Buddy's pleased too. He gets a break from chasing the ball around the garden."

"Talking of Buddy, I'm going to take him into the office one day next week."

"How come?"

"I made the mistake of telling Mrs V that we have a dog, and she made me promise to take him to show her. According to her, Chihuahuas are sweet."

"She might change her mind after she's met Buddy." Jack grinned.

"I told you that I was taking Barry for a shampoo at Bubbles yesterday, didn't I?"

"Yeah, how did it go?"

"Okay. Barry was happy because they didn't get any soap in his eyes. The only problem was Mrs V saw me with him, which confused her because I'd told her we had a Chihuahua."

"How did you talk your way out of that one?"

"There was no way I could, so I had to use the 'forget' spell on her."

"Poor old Mrs V. By the way, I didn't get the chance to ask if Kathy had anything interesting to say when you went around there for coffee."

"Can you believe it?" I laughed. "They have garden gnomes."

"I like gnomes."

"Don't be ridiculous."

"I mean it. We should get some too."

"Over my dead body. Kathy was mainly talking about her shops, and how they practically run themselves these days. She just pops into each one now and then to make sure things are ticking over okay."

"It sounds like she's becoming quite the lady of leisure."

"And here's me, always run off my feet. She suggested that I should take on another investigator to share the workload. What do you think?"

"I think it would be an unmitigated disaster."

"Why?"

"You've taken on people before, and it always ends badly because you're too much of a control freak."

"I am not a control freak. I resent that accusation. Hey, don't put your bowl there. It goes on the other side."

He turned to me and smirked. "See, you've just proven my point."

"Because I want you to put your dirty bowl in the right place? That doesn't make me a control freak."

"If you say so."

"Stop smirking. Kathy says it's all about delegation, and

I'm beginning to think she could be right."

***

I was upstairs getting changed for work when Jack shouted from the lounge.

"Jill, you have to come and see this. Hurry up!"

"What is it?" I rushed downstairs.

"Look at that crazy guy." He pointed through the window. "Have you ever seen anything quite like it?"

The man in question was the vicar who, for reasons known only to himself, was walking down the middle of the road, wearing a dressing gown and a pair of flip-flops. As if that wasn't weird enough, he had a pug under his arm. And, to make matters even worse, it was pouring with rain.

"That's the vicar," I said.

"Are you sure?"

"Yeah, he gave me the—err—I mean, I bumped into him in the village shop. What on earth is he doing? And why does he have a pug under his arm?"

"I think he's trying to catch that other dog." Jack pointed down the street where a black Labrador was sauntering in the opposite direction.

The vicar was clearly shouting to the Labrador, but it was paying him no heed. There was precious little chance of the vicar ever catching up with the dog because the flip-flops were slowing him down. And having a pug under his arm definitely wasn't helping.

"One of us should go out there and help him," I said.

"Are you volunteering?"

"I would, but I don't have my shoes on. You'll have to

go. It's the neighbourly thing to do."

"Oh, alright then." Jack grabbed his coat, hurried out of the door, and shot off down the street in pursuit of the Labrador. After a bit of cajoling, he eventually managed to grab the dog's collar, and held onto it until the vicar caught up with the two of them. After the vicar had put the lead on the Labrador, he and Jack exchanged a few words, and then Jack came hurrying back into the house.

"I'm soaked." He ran his fingers through his wet hair.

"Did you ask him why he was carrying a pug under his arm?"

"I did, yes. He asked how else was he supposed to carry it."

***

Thankfully, by the time I left the house for work, it had stopped raining. I was just about to get into the car when someone called to me. I'd seen the woman around the village, but I'd never actually spoken to her before.

"Hello there. I've been hoping to catch you for a while. I'm Barbara. Barbara Babble. I live in one of the bungalows just behind the church."

"Near Mr Bacus?"

"Two doors away, actually. How do you know Arthur?"

"He's my accountant."

"I see, err—sorry, I don't know your name."

"Jill Maxwell."

"I've lived in Middle Tweaking for almost twenty-five years now, Jill. I've seen a lot of changes to the village in that time, I can tell you. Lots of comings and goings too."

"You must have."

"How did you come to buy the old watermill?"

"I knew the lady who lived here some years ago: Myrtle Turtle. And I happened to hear it had come onto the market again."

"Oh yes, Myrtle. I'm afraid she and I never really saw eye to eye. And I certainly had no time for those two friends of hers—their names escape me."

"You mean Hodd and Jobbs."

"That's them. They never should have been allowed to live in Middle Tweaking. They simply weren't village people at all."

"Maybe they'd have been better off at the YMCA?"

"Sorry?"

"I was just saying this is our first time living in a village too."

"Yes, but I can tell you're village people."

"Thank you." I think.

"I assume your husband doesn't have a job at the moment."

"Sorry?"

"I've noticed he takes your little girl to school, but he doesn't go out again after that. I assume he's out of work, is he?"

"No, he works from home, actually."

"Hmm. I see."

"I'm sorry, Barbara, but I'm running a little late for work."

"I'm not a gossip, Jill, as you'll soon find out, but have you heard about the Stock sisters?"

"The ladies who run the village store?"

"Cynthia and Marjorie, yes." Barbara glanced around to

check that no one was within earshot. "I assume you know they're spinsters."

I couldn't remember the last time I'd heard anyone use that term. "I'd never really given it any thought."

"Yes, spinsters, both of them. But I happen to know that they are both seeing a gentleman."

"That's very nice for them."

"But the thing is, it's the same gentleman."

"I see. Still, it's none of our business what the three of them get up to, is it?"

"I don't think you quite follow me, Jill. Neither of them knows that the other one is seeing the same gentleman."

"Oh?"

"And can you guess who that gentleman is?"

"I have no idea."

She double checked that no one was within earshot. "Between you and me, and you mustn't repeat this to anyone, it's the vicar."

"The vicar?"

"Yes, but you mustn't say a word."

"I won't."

"Promise?"

"I promise. Anyway, as I said, I really must get going."

"It's been nice talking to you, Jill. Give my regards to your husband and tell him I hope he finds a job soon."

"Err, right, bye."

Wow! What a very strange woman. I would have to make sure that I gave her a wide berth in future.

***

I'd parked the car in Washbridge and was walking to

the office building. I'd given up on the whole skipping thing because I simply couldn't get my head (or legs) around it. As I approached the office, I noticed two window cleaners working on the building. As I walked by their ladders, I heard someone shout, "Look out below."

Foolishly, I looked up, and a torrent of water hit me on the head.

"Jill, is that you? I'm so sorry." I looked up to see Blaze hurrying down the ladder.

At the top of the other ladder, Daze was laughing her head off. "Sorry for laughing, Jill, but that was priceless."

"I really am sorry, Jill." Blaze was standing beside me now. "I was just reaching for my squeegee and I must have nudged the bucket."

"That's okay. What are you two doing up there anyway?"

"Working undercover. We're trying to track down a gang of roof sprites who we believe are operating in this area. You haven't seen them, have you?"

"I wouldn't know a roof sprite if it poured a bucketful of water on my head."

"I really am sorry, Jill. Is there anything I can do?"

"No, it's alright. You'd better get back to work."

"Is it raining again, Jill?" Mrs V said. "I thought it had stopped."

"No, Mrs V, it isn't raining. A window cleaner emptied his bucket of water on my head."

"Why would he do that? Had you said something to upset him?"

"No, I hadn't. It wasn't deliberate. He accidentally knocked over the bucket and it spilled all over me."

"You should sue him."
"I'm not sure that would do any good. Anyway, what's all this equipment for?"
Mrs V had a digital video recorder, mounted on a mini tripod, on her desk.
"I'm doing so well with YarnAgram that I've decided it's time to extend my social media reach."
"Your social media—?"
"Reach. Yes, so the next logical step is to open a YarnTube account."
"Let me guess. Is that videos?"
"Exactly. It's one thing showcasing photographs of my work, but with a video, people will be able to see me in action, so to speak."
"Right, I see. Does that mean you'll be recording them in the office?"
"Yes, so I'm going to need you to knock on the door whenever you come into the outer office, just in case I'm in the middle of recording."
"Hang on. Let me make sure I've got this right. You want me to knock on the door every time I want to come in here?"
"That's right, so I can pause the recording. Otherwise, I'll have to do a retake because I'm not very good with the editing thing. Is that alright?"
"Just perfect."
"Thanks. I thought I'd start with something simple, so my first video will be a pair of socks."
"Great. I'd better let you get on, then."
Sheesh! My office wasn't my own anymore.
Winky was busy at work on *my* computer.
"Hey, get off there."

"I'm nearly done."

"You're done now. You know you're not supposed to use that."

"I'll only be a minute. Right, that's it. You can have it now."

"What are you up to, Winky?"

"Sorry, no time to talk." He jumped down from the desk, scurried under the sofa, and began to tap away on his tablet.

What on earth was he up to? I'd never seen him so engrossed.

I was still considering Kathy's suggestion that I should employ another private investigator. Jack had been very negative when I'd brought up the idea, and he'd even accused me of being a control freak, which was clearly nonsense.

I went onto one of the large recruitment websites who, fortuitously, were offering a special deal where you could post your job for two weeks at half the normal rate. That was obviously fate telling me this was the right thing to do. I quickly created an account and then clicked on the 'Post New Vacancy' button.

Description: Private investigator.

Duties: Investigation - various types of cases.

Qualifications required: No academic qualifications needed.

Experience required: Experience of private investigation work is essential.

Other information: Private investigator wanted to join a dynamic, forward-thinking company. Must be a self-starter, good communicator and a team player.

Starting salary: I suppose I would have to pay them. But how much, though? I typed 'To be negotiated'.

That was everything, so I submitted the job. Now all I had to do was sit back and wait for the applications to flood in.

I caught up on a little paperwork until it was time for my meeting with Phil Black. We'd arranged to meet at the house where he'd lived at the time of Liam's disappearance.

"Right, Winky, I'm off."

No response. He was still too busy on his tablet.

As I walked into the outer office, Mrs V yelled at me. "Jill, what did I tell you about knocking? I was halfway through this video. Now, I'll have to start all over again."

"Sorry."

Why was I apologising?

Chapter 8

Phil Black was so busy staring at the house that he didn't notice me pull up in the car. It was only when I got out and called to him that he turned around.

"Are you okay, Phil?"

"Sorry, I was miles away."

"Have you been back here recently?"

"No. Not since I was arrested. Believe it or not, I have some really happy memories of this place. When I first got here today, I saw a young boy in the upstairs window and just for a moment, I thought—" His words drifted away.

"Where did you used to go fishing?"

"Do you see the treeline over there?" He pointed across the road. "The river's just beyond the wood."

"Do you feel up to taking me there?"

"Sure."

The road was very quiet; I'd only seen one car go past since I'd arrived. Phil led the way across the road, and along the pavement for about fifty yards until we came to a small wooden gate in the drystone wall. Once through that, we followed a well-worn path that led across the field to the wood.

"Did you used to go fishing often, Phil?"

"Yeah, most weeks during the season."

Once we reached the treeline, the path continued through the wood. The going there was a little slower, but within a matter of minutes, we emerged next to the river, which was quite narrow and slow running at that point.

"Did you fish from a particular spot?"

"Yeah. Over there. I always used to sit on those rocks."

"Can I take a closer look?"

He hesitated for a moment, but then led the way. "I used to love it here. It's so quiet and the fishing was the best on this stretch of the river by far. I tried lots of different spots, but none of them compared to this one."

"You said that Liam had been here with you before?"

"He came with me a few times. He always wanted to have a go, but the rod was too long and heavy for him to hold. All he could really do was watch me. After half an hour or so, he'd get fed up and start messing around, throwing stones in the river. Once he did that, I had no chance of catching anything, so I had to pack up and go home."

"That must have made you angry."

"It was annoying, yeah. I much preferred being here by myself."

"That's understandable."

"I was never angry enough to do anything to him if that's what you're getting at. I would never have hurt him."

"I'm not suggesting that for one minute. I'm just trying to understand the dynamic between the two of you."

"Liam was a good kid and could be a lot of fun, but I still didn't want him with me every time I went fishing."

"You said that Liam told your stepfather he was going fishing with you."

"That's right, but I would already have been long gone by then."

"He must have tried to make his own way to you. Would he have been capable of finding you by himself?"

"Yeah, he'd done it before, even though he knew he shouldn't cross the road alone."

"The police found blood on the rocks, didn't they?"

"So they reckon."

"You sound doubtful."

"I've seen the photographs of it, but there was definitely no blood there when I left that day. I would have seen it."

I was convinced of Phil Black's innocence. Why else would he spend the money his grandmother had saved for him on hiring me? He'd done his time in prison. He could have used that money on a fresh start and put the past behind him. It wasn't just that. It was the way he spoke about Liam; he had clearly been close to his young stepbrother. Proving Phil was innocent was not going to be easy, though, unless I could find out who had actually murdered Liam, and at the moment I had precious little to go on.

After leaving Phil, I drove a few miles and then pulled into the side of the road. I hadn't wanted him to overhear the phone call I was about to make to his mother in case it went badly. I wasn't even sure if the number that his grandmother had given me was still current, but it was the only one I had.

"Hello?" The voice was female. So far, so good.

"Is that Felicity?"

"Speaking. Who is this?"

"My name is Jill Maxwell. I'm a private investigator. I've been hired by your son, Phil."

"Why are you calling me?"

"I wondered if it would be possible to come and talk to you?"

"No."

"Maybe I could ask you a few quick questions now, then."

"I have nothing to say to you."

"I'm trying to find evidence that will prove your son's innocence. I think you may have information that can help me."

"I don't want anything to do with it. I've washed my hands of him. Leave me alone."

"Can you at least tell me where I can find Phil's stepfather?"

"I have no idea. The last I heard, Andy was living in France somewhere."

"Are you sure I can't change your—" It was too late; she'd already hung up.

***

I drove to Washbridge, parked the car, and took a walk down to Coffee Animal. Dot was once again behind the counter, and today she had a yellow bow in her hair. Curiously, her beauty spot was now on her right cheek.

"Hi, Jill. Your usual?"

"Yes, please. What's today's animal? Nothing too vicious I hope."

"Hardly." She reached under the counter and brought out a small glass cage in which there appeared to be just a few twigs.

"This one is empty, Dot."

"No, it isn't." She pointed. "See, it moved."

"A stick insect? Are they even animals?"

"I don't know, but they're kind of cute, don't you think?"

"Not really."

The shop was very quiet, so I was able to get a table

next to the window. I'd just taken a bite of muffin when a tiny voice from inside the cage said, "Hello there. What's your name?"

"Hi. I'm Jill. What's yours?"

"Everybody calls me Sticky."

"It suits you."

"Can you let me out?"

"I'm not sure that's allowed, is it?"

"Don't worry. It'll be fine."

"Do you promise not to run away?"

"I'm a stick insect. How would I do that?"

"Point taken." I was about to open the lid, but then hesitated. "Do you bite?"

"Of course not."

"Promise?"

"I promise."

"Okay then." I opened the lid. "Out you come."

"You'll have to put your hand in here."

"Why?"

"So I can crawl up it."

Gross. I'd never been particularly fond of creepy crawlies, but I was committed now, so I put my hand inside the cage, and gave an involuntary shudder when Sticky began to crawl up my arm.

"Keep still or I'll fall off."

"Sorry."

When he reached my elbow, he stopped.

"Thanks. It's good to get out of there."

"Are you sure you don't bite?"

"I promise, but I do like muffins."

"Stick insects don't eat muffins."

"Only because no one ever gives us one."

"I'm not sure about this."

"Go on. Just a little bit."

"Okay then." I broke off a small piece and put it on my arm next to him. In no time at all, he'd gulped it down.

"Is that all I get?"

What was it with the animals in this place, eating my muffins? Last time it was Jimbob the gerbil, now it was Sticky the stick insect. At this rate, I'd have to start ordering two of them.

Sticky turned out to be good company. For a stick insect, he had a lot of interesting tales to tell. Given a choice of spending half an hour with him or with Mr Ivers, I would have chosen Sticky every day of the week.

When I got back to the office, I hurried up the stairs, and I was just about to walk through the door when I remembered Mrs V's video shoot, so I knocked first.

"Come in."

I poked my head around the door.

"All clear, Mrs V?"

"Yes, come in, Jill. I've finished recording for the day. Would you like to see what I've done?"

"I'd love to, obviously, but I don't have time at the moment. I've only popped in for a few minutes, then I have to go to Little Tweaking."

"Maybe tomorrow."

"Maybe, yeah." Not a chance.

Winky was lying on the sofa. "Where's my salmon?" he demanded. "I'm starving."

"So, you *do* want it today. You weren't interested yesterday."

"That's because I was busy."

“What were you up to, anyway?”

“Nothing to concern yourself about. By the way, have you posted a job vacancy?”

“You’ve been on my computer again, haven’t you?”

“Only for a couple of minutes. So, did you?”

“Yes, for a private investigator.”

“That’s a joke, right? Who’d want to work here? For you?”

“Plenty of people. I’m expecting a ton of applications.”

“You’re clearly delusional.”

Before I could respond, my phone rang. It was Margaret Plant’s agent, Georgina Walpole.

“Jill, it’s Georgie. I just wondered how your meeting with Margaret went.”

“Okay, I think. She’s clearly very upset at having lost the manuscript.”

“I realise it’s early days, but any thoughts so far? Any leads?”

“Not really, other than it’s obvious that whoever took the manuscript must have come through one of the neighbouring gardens. As soon as I’ve finished on this call, I’m going to go and speak to her neighbours.”

“The main reason I called you is that I’m getting a lot of flak from Alistair Furlong, the head honcho at the company that publishes Margaret’s books. He’s demanding to know when he can expect to receive the final manuscript.”

“I take it you haven’t told him that it’s been stolen?”

“No, I just fobbed him off. He wanted to talk to Margaret, but she hates the man and refuses point-blank to have anything to do with him. There’s a limit to how long I can put him off, so time is of the essence.”

"Understood. Don't worry, Georgie, I'm on it."

"Good, because to make matters worse, Richard Watkins, who is one of Margaret's main competitors in the mystery genre, is doing a tour to promote his new book at the moment. He's scheduled to do a signing here in Washbridge on Saturday. He's even gone as far as to suggest that Margaret has retired, making him the King of Mystery, which is a complete joke because the guy's a hack who has no talent whatsoever. Anyway, Jill, I must get going. You'll keep me posted?"

"Of course."

By the time I'd finished on the call, Winky had disappeared out of the window, so I put his salmon out, ready for when he came back.

"Mrs V, I'm going to talk to Margaret Plant's neighbours, and then I'll probably head home."

"Okay, dear. Tomorrow, I'm going to record a video of me making a jumper."

"Fantastic. When you've done that, there is something I'd like you to do, please."

"Of course. The video shouldn't take too long."

"Can you see if you can track down Andy Roberts, Phil Black's stepfather? I believe he's living somewhere in France, but that's about as much as I know."

"I'm on it."

***

I'd planned to start with Mr Stanley Trotter who lived in the house that backed onto Margaret Plant's property, but after knocking on the door and ringing the bell several times, there was no answer. I'd even peered through the front windows but there was no sign of life.

The couple who lived in the house to the left of Margaret's property were Mr and Mrs Comfy who looked like a couple of bookends, dressed in their matching jumpers. They both came across as a little fussy and had an annoying habit of finishing one another's sentences.

"We rarely see Margaret these days," Mr Comfy said. "She keeps herself—"

"To herself," Mrs Comfy chimed in. "We used to invite her over—"

"For a cup of tea, but she always declined."

"She did come over, but only the once. That must have been five years ago."

"It was four, Mildred. Definitely four."

"I do believe you're right, Marmy."

Marmy?

"So, neither of you have spoken to her recently?"

"No. We have tried, but Margaret can be very blunt."

"Rude even. Whenever we've tried to talk to her, she has more or less made it clear that—"

"She was too busy, so after a while, we didn't bother anymore."

"Have either of you spotted anything unusual in the last few days?"

"What kind of thing?"

"Any strangers on the street for example."

"Now you mention it, we did see someone—"

"Hanging around in the road a few days ago."

"What were they doing?"

"*He* was standing on the other side of the road. He kept looking at his phone."

"Can you describe him?"
"He was tall."
"Very tall."
"Middle-aged."
"And he had one of those weird sheepy beard things."
"*Sheepy*?"
"You know. Like a beard, but not quite a beard."
"Do you mean a goatee?"
"That's it. And glasses."
"Did you see him go into any of the houses?"
"No, he just walked up and down."
"And kept checking his phone."
"Then he left."
"Was he in a car?"
"No. He was on foot."

By the time I left the Comfys, my neck ached from glancing back and forth between the two of them.

A Mr Montgomery lived in the house on the other side. Unlike the Comfys, he was a man of very few words.

"I didn't see anything."

"Are you sure? It's quite likely the burglar gained access to Mrs Plant's garden through one of the neighbouring properties."

"Still didn't see nothing."

Resisting the urge to correct his double negative, I persevered. "Do you know Margaret well?"

"No. I've no time for the woman."

"Any particular reason?"

"Yes. That hedge of hers. I've been asking her to cut it back for at least four years, but does she take any notice? No. It's like talking to a brick wall. It's stolen half of the light from my conservatory."

And that was pretty much all he had to say for himself. Was it possible that Mr Montgomery had stolen Margaret's manuscript as payback for the ongoing hedge dispute? Maybe, but it seemed unlikely because he was in his seventies, and probably not capable of getting through the hedge and climbing through the kitchen window.

Chapter 9

The next morning when I came downstairs for breakfast, Jack was standing in the middle of the kitchen, acting very strangely. He was looking to his left, and then to his right, and then back again. He hadn't even noticed me.

"Jack, are you okay?"

"I think this room is haunted."

"By your parents, you mean? Have you been talking to them?"

"No, it wasn't Mum and Dad."

"It wasn't *my* parents, was it?"

"No. I couldn't actually see anyone, but while I was pouring out the muesli, a spoon floated out of the drawer, across the room, and landed on the table over there."

"It was probably my mother, trying to mess with your head. It sounds like the sort of thing she'd do."

"What if there are other ghosts in this house that we don't know about?"

"Did you feel a chill when it happened?"

"Now you mention it, no I didn't."

"You were late coming to bed last night, and you did a lot of tossing and turning, so you're probably still half asleep."

"I know what I saw, Jill."

"O—kay. Why don't we see if it happens again? Where's Florence?"

"Outside playing with Buddy."

"Was she in here with you when the spoon thing happened?"

"No, she didn't come downstairs until just afterwards."

"So, she didn't see it?"
"No, she didn't but that doesn't mean I imagined it."
"I believe you." Not.

Jack was clearly still feeling uneasy as we ate our breakfast. After each spoonful of muesli, he kept looking around, obviously expecting something to come floating past him. In an attempt to take his mind off it, I decided to tell him about Mrs Babble.

"She stopped me yesterday on my way out of the house. She seems to know you."

"Her name doesn't ring a bell. What do you mean, she knows me?"

"She knew you don't go out to work and asked if you were looking for a job. She spent half the conversation telling me how she wasn't one to gossip, and the other half gossiping. Mind you, she did have one juicy piece of gossip. Not that I'm the sort of person to repeat it."

"Fair enough."

"Okay, you've twisted my arm, but you mustn't tell anyone else. According to Barbara Babble, both of the Stock sisters are seeing the vicar."

"*Seeing*?"

"She didn't elaborate, but I got the feeling they were both romantically involved with him."

"Both of them?"

"That's what she said. The thing is, neither of them knows that the other one is also seeing the vicar."

"That is rather scandalous." Jack laughed. "When I spoke to him yesterday, he seemed like butter wouldn't melt in his mouth."

"It's always the quiet ones, but then anyone who walks

down the street in the pouring rain, in a dressing gown and flip-flops, with a pug under one arm, is probably capable of anything."

I'd just finished my scrambled eggs on toast when my phone rang.

"Come up to the hotel."

"Grandma?"

"Quickly. I need a word with you."

"I was just about to go to work."

"This will only take a minute."

Before I could object, she'd ended the call.

"I take it that was your grandmother?" Jack grinned.

"She wants a word with me up at the hotel. I'll get changed first, and then I can go straight to work after I've found out what she wants."

When I came back downstairs, I went in search of Florence and found her in the garden.

"Mummy has to go to work now. Come and give me a kiss."

She ran across the lawn, threw her arms around my neck, and gave me a big, sloppy kiss. "We're going to draw rainbows at school today, Mummy."

"Are you, darling? That'll be fun."

"I told Miss Soap that I'm going to do mine red, yellow and blue."

"Don't rainbows have more colours than that?"

"Mine doesn't. I like red, yellow and blue."

"Fair enough. I'll look forward to seeing it tonight. Love you lots."

"Love you more."

I took a leisurely walk across the village to the hotel where Grandma was waiting for me by the entrance.

"It took you long enough." She tapped her watch.

"Good morning to you, too. I had to get changed for work. Are you still planning to open for guests this weekend?"

"Yes, in fact the first ones arrive tomorrow. We're booked solid for the next three weeks already."

"How did you manage that?"

"Surely you know by now that I'm a marketing genius."

There was no arguing with that.

"Why did you want to see me?"

"We're going to be run off our feet for the next few days, and I haven't managed to recruit my full quota of staff, so I can offer you part-time work in the evening in the restaurant."

"I don't have time to work for you. I have my own business to run in case you've forgotten. I'm really busy at the moment; I have three cases on the go this week. In fact, I've just advertised for another investigator."

"Surely you could spare a little time in the evenings?"

"No, Grandma, I can't. The evenings are for me, Florence and Jack. You'll just have to find someone else."

"This is most inconvenient. Are you sure you can't drop one of your cases?"

"No, I can't. Although one of them is already beginning to look pretty hopeless. A young boy went missing some years ago, and his brother, my client, was convicted of his murder."

"Did he do it?"

"I'm convinced he didn't. I had him take me to the spot

on the river where his brother is supposed to have died, in the hope it might yield some clues."

"And did it?"

"No. Nothing."

"You need to speak to Gwen Ravensbeak."

"Gwen who?"

"Ravensbeak. I don't particularly like the woman, but she does have an incredible power. She can stand in any location and see everything that has happened there in the past."

"Is she a witch?"

"Yes, but she doesn't use magic to do it. No such spell exists, you should know that."

"So how does she do it, then?"

"I don't know. I'm not sure even she does."

"Do you think she'd help me?"

"If the location was in Candlefield, I'd say yes for sure. The problem is that Gwen hates the human world. I suppose you could have a word, to see if you can persuade her to make an exception."

"Where would I find her?"

"She spends most of her time at Candlefield Bowling Club."

"The one near to Aunt Lucy's house?"

"That's the one. If you do talk to her, I wouldn't mention that you're my granddaughter. She and I have history."

***

I'd intended calling into the office before going to see Charlene Vallance, the widow of Mickey Vallance, AKA

Webby the clown. Those plans were scuppered when I turned the key in the ignition, and the engine made a very strange noise and refused to start. I tried several more times, but with no joy.

Jack gave me a puzzled look when I walked back into the house.

"Did you forget something?"

"No, the stupid car won't start."

"What's wrong with it?"

"How would I know?"

"Do you want me to take a look at it?"

"What good would that do? You know even less about cars than I do. I've called the AA; they said they'd be here in twenty minutes."

"Do you want a coffee while you wait?"

"Yes, please, but watch out for those floating spoons."

"Ha, ha. I didn't imagine it."

"If you say so. Where's Florence?"

"Upstairs in her bedroom."

"Playing with the dolls' house again?"

"Yeah, she's really into it at the moment."

Out in the garden, Buddy started barking like a dog possessed.

"What's up with that stupid dog?" I snapped. Jack and I both went outside to find out what he was barking at, but there was nothing to see. I walked over to him and picked him up. "That's enough of that. What were you barking at?"

"That thing."

"What *thing*?"

"I don't know what it was, but there was definitely a thing."

"Show me."

"I can't. It's gone now."

"If I put you down, do you promise not to bark anymore?"

"I promise. The thing's gone now anyway."

I put him down, and Jack and I went back into the house.

"What was that all about?" Jack said.

"I've no idea. He said he was barking at a *thing*, but he didn't know what it was. That dog is a liability."

Florence came up behind us. "I thought you'd gone to work, Mummy?"

"My car has broken down. I'm waiting for a man to come and mend it."

"Why doesn't Daddy mend it?"

"Daddy doesn't know how cars work."

"Why was Buddy barking, Mummy?"

"I don't know. He's a silly dog."

"Is it okay if I play with him?"

"Of course it is."

Twenty minutes later, there was a knock at the door.

"Good morning, love." The AA man was wearing a yellow hi-vis jacket. "Got a problem with your car?"

"It won't start."

"Come on, let's see what's wrong with it." I followed him down the path. "Can you open the bonnet for me?"

"Sure." I sat in the car and popped the bonnet.

"Okay, turn the key."

The engine made the same awful noise as it had before. He came around to the driver's side window.

"When was the last time you had this serviced, love?"

"It must be about four—"

"Months?"

"Years."

"Hmm. That explains it. It's a bit of a mess under there."

"Can you get it going?"

"I think so, but you really must take it in for a service."

"I will. I promise."

He messed around with the engine for a few minutes, and then shouted, "Try it again now."

This time it started first time. "Thanks."

"I can't promise how much longer it will keep going. You definitely need to get it seen to."

"I will. Thanks for your help."

When he'd left, Jack came out of the house.

"Is it okay now?"

"Yeah, he got it going, but he said it needs a service."

"I've been telling you that for ages. You'd better get it booked in."

"This old thing's had it. It would be throwing good money after bad. I need a new car."

"Can we afford one?"

"We'll have to. I can't do my job without one."

"We definitely can't afford to buy a new one."

"I know. I'll find something second-hand. Anyway, I'd better get going. I'm already running late. See you tonight."

After that distraction, I didn't have time to call into the office, so I drove straight to West Chipping, where Charlene Vallance lived on the top floor of an apartment block.

My day was continuing to go from bad to worse when I

spotted an 'Out of Order' notice stuck on the lift door.

Great!

By the time I reached the eighth floor, my legs had turned to jelly, and I was gasping for air. As I leaned against the wall, trying to compose myself, the lift doors opened and out stepped an elderly man carrying two shopping bags.

"Are you alright, dear? You've gone a funny colour."

"Err, yeah. I thought the lift was out of order."

"You mean the sign downstairs?" He grinned. "That's just the kids, they're always sticking that on the doors. This lift never breaks down. Would you like to come in for a cup of tea while you catch your breath?"

"No, I'm okay now, thanks."

"Are you sure?"

"Positive."

"Okay, well take care." And off he went.

This wasn't the first time I'd been caught out like this. If I got my hands on those kids, I'd turn them into frogs. Then boil them very slowly.

What? Of course I'm only joking. (Or am I?)

The woman who answered the door of flat 813 was in her sixties and had a headful of curlers.

"You must be Jill. Sorry about the curlers. I'm going to my daughter's later. It's my grandson's third birthday, so I want my hair to look its best. Are you feeling alright? You look a little out of sorts."

"I'm fine. I've just walked up the stairs."

"You should have taken the lift, dear."

"I will next time."

"Come on in. I've just made some tea—that'll sort you out. Do you take milk and sugar?"

"Just milk for me, please."

"What about biscuits? I've got some lovely bourbons."

"No, thanks. Just the tea will be fine."

We settled down in the living room, in front of a full-length window that looked out over West Chipping.

"You have a great view from up here, Mrs Vallance."

"Call me Charlene, dear. I was a little apprehensive when we first moved in because I'd always lived in bungalows and houses. When they offered us this place, we almost turned it down, but I love it now. It has a great view and because it's on the top floor, I don't have to put up with the sound of footsteps above me. When we moved here, I was worried that the lift might keep breaking down, but it's never broken down once."

"That's good to know. I take it that's your husband?" I pointed to the photograph on the sideboard: A much younger Charlene was standing arm in arm with a handsome young man who was at least a foot taller than her.

"Yeah, that's my Mickey. He was a handsome devil when he was younger. He wasn't so bad when he got older for that matter."

"How long had he been a clown?"

"He was already doing it when I first met him. If I'm honest, it put me off at first. At that age, you dream of going out with a movie star or a rich businessman, don't you? Not a clown. I used to get a lot of stick from my girlfriends, but I stood by Mickey and I'm glad I did. He was a great husband, dad and granddad. He was a brilliant clown too. I wish you could have seen his act. I have some of his videos if you'd like to watch one."

"Not right now, thanks. I'm a bit pushed for time."

"I still can't believe he's gone."

"Don Keigh mentioned that your husband had some problems with his heart."

"Yes, but as long as he took his tablets every day, he was fine."

"How was he in himself in the days before he died?"

"Happy, but then Mickey was always happy. Always laughing. That's why he made such a great clown. He loved to make people laugh, especially kids. Did you know Mickey had the longest clown shoes in the country?"

"Don did mention something about that."

"They were a devil to keep clean, I can tell you. He got me to try them on once, and I couldn't even lift my foot up. I don't know how he used to walk in them, but they made the kids howl with laughter. Are you sure you wouldn't like to see one of his videos?"

"Maybe next time. Was he okay when he left you that day?"

"He was fine. He was looking forward to the meeting at NOCA. He enjoyed the banter with the other clowns. Hang on, I tell a lie. He had got himself a bit wound up because his car wouldn't start, but he managed to get a lift, so he wasn't late for his meeting."

Chapter 10

After I left Charlene Vallance, I drove towards Washbridge where I'd arranged to meet Randy Seaburn's widow, Patricia. Randy, AKA Jolly Jelly, had been the second of the two clowns to die of a heart attack during a NOCA meeting.

Patricia Seaburn lived in an impressive house surrounded by a high wall. Clearly the clown business had paid well for Randy Seaburn. The large metal gates appeared to be locked, so I pressed the call button on the intercom.

"Hi, it's Jill Maxwell."

"Who?"

"Jill Maxwell. I phoned earlier."

"Oh yes."

"I'm parked on the road outside your house. Could you buzz me in the gate, please?"

"I'm afraid I can't. It seems to be stuck. I'm waiting for someone to repair it."

"In that case, could you come down here?"

"Sorry?"

"I said could you come down to the gate?"

"I would, but I twisted my ankle yesterday and I can barely walk on it."

"Oh dear. I suppose we could just talk through this intercom."

"Pardon?"

"CAN WE TALK THROUGH THE INTERCOM?"

"Sorry, this intercom is useless. What did you say?"

I was getting nowhere fast. If I wanted to speak to her, I was going to have to get over the gate. Normally, I would have used the 'levitate' spell, but the street was very busy, and someone might have seen me. I took a closer look at the gate; it wasn't all that tall. How difficult could it be to climb over?

As it turned out, it was very difficult, but I managed to get to the top, where I sat astride it while I caught my breath.

"Are you okay up there, missus?" a man who was walking past shouted.

"Yes, thanks."

"It'd be much easier if you just opened the gate, you know." He laughed.

"Gee, why didn't I think of that?"

I was halfway down the other side when I lost my footing and fell. Fortunately, I didn't break any bones, but I still ended up with a few scrapes on my legs. After dusting myself down, I walked up the drive to the house and knocked on the door. It was answered by a woman on crutches.

"You made it. How did you get in?"

"I had to climb over the gate. I hope you don't mind."

"Not at all." She glanced at my legs. "Have you hurt yourself?"

"It's nothing. I'm okay."

"I thought afterwards, we could have just talked on the phone."

Duh! Why hadn't I thought of that?

"Never mind. I'm here now."

"Do come in." She led the way into the lounge. "Can I get you a drink?"

"No, thanks. I've just had one at Charlene Vallance's house."

"Charlene and I have got to know one another quite well over the last few weeks. She's a lovely woman."

"She is."

"I'm still not sure why you want to talk to me. Are you a member of NOCA?"

"Err, no. I'm actually a private investigator."

"Oh? I don't understand. Randy died of natural causes."

"I realise that, but Don Keigh is keen to make sure nothing was missed. It's just a formality really. Is that okay?"

"I guess so. Did you know Randy, Jill?"

"No, I didn't."

"You haven't seen his act, then?"

"I'm afraid not."

"He was known as Jolly Jelly because his act was built around jelly. He was absolutely mad about the stuff."

"Don Keigh said as much."

"Talking of jelly, I have plenty of it in the fridge. Old habits die hard, I suppose. Would you like some?"

"No, thanks."

"Are you sure? I have all the flavours: Strawberry, orange, raspberry—"

"Not for me, thanks. Can I ask if your husband had any health issues, Patricia?"

"No, he was fit and well as far as I knew. That's why this all came as such a shock. There was no warning whatsoever."

"How was he in himself? Was he happy in the weeks and days leading up to his death?"

"Yes, but then Randy was always happy. You have to be if you're a clown. If you're not, people can tell. There's no faking it."

"How did he feel about the NOCA committee meetings? Did he enjoy them?"

"Not particularly, but he felt he should play his part."

"And on the day that he died, did anything out of the ordinary happen?"

"Not really." She hesitated. "Except—"

"Yes?"

"It was nothing really, but I do remember he was a little stressed because he'd lost his wallet. It wasn't the money that bothered him. All his credit cards and his driving licence were in there. Fortunately, Trevor found it. Randy must have left it in his car when Trevor gave him a lift the previous day."

"Would that be Trevor Hee?"

"That's right. Such a nice man. Do you know him?"

"I met him briefly at Chuckle House."

"I have a video of Randy's if you'd like to see it."

"No, thanks, Patricia. I should be making tracks. I've got everything I need for now."

"Will you be alright climbing over the gate?"

"I'll be fine, thanks."

There was no way I was going to risk climbing over that gate again. If I fell onto the pavement, I would do myself a serious injury. When I reached the wall, I checked that Patricia wasn't looking through the window, then made myself invisible and levitated over it. Once on the other side, I had to wait a few minutes until the coast was clear before reversing the 'invisible' spell.

***

The car spluttered several times before it eventually

decided to start. This situation was hopeless. How could I run a business without a reliable motor? At a push, I could have used magic to travel around, but it would have been too risky to do that all the time. I would just have to bite the bullet and buy a new car.

There was no point in going to any of the main franchises because we simply couldn't afford a brand-new car. There were several second-hand car lots around Washbridge. I'd driven past one of them on the way to Patricia Seaburn's house, so I retraced my route and pulled into Carr's Cars.

I'd always hated buying cars because, in my experience, the salesmen were all cut from the same sleazy cloth; they were all untrustworthy and very pushy.

There was row after row of cars on display, but most of them were too expensive. I'd been looking around the lot for about fifteen minutes when I spotted a man headed my way.

"Good afternoon, young lady. And welcome to Carr's Cars."

"Hi."

"Allow me to introduce myself. I'm Charlie Carr, the owner of this prestigious business. Carr by name, car by trade." He laughed.

I wondered how many times in a day he said that.

"I'm Jill."

"You won't find better cars at a better price anywhere in a hundred-mile radius, Jill. You have Charlie Carr's cast iron guarantee on that."

"Right."

"What are you looking for? A little run-around to do the shopping while hubby's at work?"

Seems I could add misogyny to the list of this guy's faults.

"Actually, I'm a private investigator."

"How fascinating. Have you seen anything that's caught your eye?"

"A couple, yeah. I quite like the blue one over there. And the green one in the row behind that."

"Would you like me to get the keys, so you can take a look inside them?"

"Yes, please."

He hurried back to the building, and returned a few minutes later, keys in hand.

"Okay, Jill, let's start with the blue one." He opened the door and invited me to sit in the driver's seat. The interior was very clean, and the mileage was relatively low. I was liking this car more and more. "Would you care to take her for a spin?"

"Can I take a look at the green one, first, please?"

"Certainly."

The interior of the green car was nowhere near as good as the blue one, and the mileage was substantially higher.

"I think I'll just test drive the blue car if that's okay."

"Absolutely."

I'm always a little nervous the first time I drive a new car. Even more so because I had Charlie Carr sitting next to me. That's probably why I managed to stall it the first time.

"Gentle on the clutch, Jill."

This man was beginning to get on my nerves.

I took her for a spin and put her through her paces. It was a smooth drive and I really liked the car. When we got back to the lot, Charlie rushed to open the door for me.

"So, Jill, what say you? Is this the car for you?"

"Maybe."

"I imagine you'll need to go home and check with hubby?"

"I don't need to check with anyone. I like the car, but what will you give me for my old one?"

"Where is it?"

"Over there."

"Is it behind that heap of scrap that someone's dumped in the car park? I do wish people wouldn't do that. They do it to save themselves the expense of getting it towed to the scrap yard."

"That heap of scrap, as you put it, *is* my car."

"Oh."

Needless to say, I was offered little more than scrap value for the old car, but to be honest, I'd expected that.

"When will I be able to pick up my new car, Charlie?"

"How about Monday? Does that suit?"

"Monday will be fine. I'll see you then."

***

The last time I was at Candlefield Bowling Club was when I'd been chasing Matilda, the enchanted lawnmower, who had gone rogue. Fortunately, I'd caught it before it could do any serious damage to the bowling green.

The last time I was there, the place had been pretty much deserted, but today most of the benches were occupied, and there were several women on the green, obviously about to play a match. I'd no sooner walked through the gate than a woman approached me.

"There you are, at last. We were beginning to think you weren't coming."

"Sorry?"

"Come on. Gwen is waiting for you."

"Oh, right, thanks."

Given that Gwen was expecting me, I had to surmise that Grandma must have been in touch with her. They had clearly managed to put aside their differences.

The woman practically dragged me onto the bowling green, and pushed me towards an elderly woman who was wearing shorts, sandals and a turquoise t-shirt with Candlefield Flyers printed on the back. Half of the women on the green were wearing identical t-shirts, the others were wearing red t-shirts with Candlefield Chipmunks printed on the back.

I would need to speak to Gwen quickly, and get out of her way before the match started, but before I could, she handed me two bowls.

"You should have been here fifteen minutes ago," she snapped.

"I didn't realise I was supposed to be here for a particular time."

"The match starts in one minute. You should have been here for the team talk."

"I think there must have been a mistake."

"I hope you're as good as they say you are. This is a crucial game. If we win, we've got every chance of taking the league."

"I'm playing then, am I?"

"Of course you're playing. Did you think you were going to be one of the substitutes?"

"Err, not exactly."

"Alright, then. We can't afford any weak links today."

Gwen was the first to play. She bowled the smaller ball, which I knew was called the jack. Her first bowl finished within a couple of feet of the jack. Next, a member of the other team bowled. Her bowl finished a foot or so behind Gwen's.

That's when everything seemed to grind to a halt, and I realised they were all looking at me.

"Rita! Come on!" Gwen said.

Rita? It was only then that I realised she was talking to me. It was too late to try and explain that I wasn't Rita, so I lined up my shot, and gave it everything I had.

Which, as it turned out, wasn't very much.

The bowl veered off-course and ended up about ten yards from the jack. It was actually closer to the jack of one of the other matches. When I turned around, Gwen was glaring at me, red-faced.

"What do you call that?" she said, in a not too hushed voice.

"I'm sorry. It slipped out of my hand."

"Make sure your next bowl is better."

"I'll try."

The second woman on the other team played an excellent shot; her bowl was nestled up against the jack. Gwen took much more time to line up her second shot, and it paid dividends because her bowl hit the jack full-on, knocking the opponent's bowl into the gutter, leaving Gwen two up.

By now, Gwen had clearly given up on me; she had realised that she would have to win the game herself. Remarkably, she did just that, and we took the game by a single point.

When it was all over, we shook hands with the opponents, then I went to shake Gwen's hand, but she grabbed me by the arm and dragged me off the green.

"Why on earth did anyone recommend you? You're hopeless."

"I'm sorry, but there seems to have been a terrible misunderstanding."

"You're telling me! It's a good job I was on top form today or we would have been hammered."

"The thing is, I'm not actually Rita."

"What do you mean, you're not Rita?"

"Just that. I didn't come here to play bowls. I didn't even know there was a match."

"So why did you agree to play, then?"

"I didn't. As soon as I walked through the gate, a woman dragged me over to you. The next thing I knew, you'd handed me the bowls."

"If you're not Rita, who are you?"

"My name is Jill Maxwell. I'm a PI. I'm investigating a murder in the human world. I was given to believe that you have the power to see events that took place in the past. I wondered if I could persuade you to come with me and take a look at the location where a child disappeared. My client was wrongly convicted of his murder."

"No."

"Why not?"

"I don't like the human world."

"Please, this is really important. There must be something I can say or do that will change your mind."

She began to study her hands. "Do you know anything about nail bars?"

"As in fingernails?" I held up my hands.

"Yes, the things on the end of your fingers."

"I know an excellent nail bar, actually. Why?"

"The place I usually go to in Candlefield has closed down and all the others are useless. If you could arrange an appointment for me at a top-notch nail bar in the human world, then maybe I could see my way clear to helping you."

"That's great. Would Monday or Tuesday next week do?"

"Either of those would work for me. I'll give you my phone number."

Chapter 11

It was Saturday morning and the three of us were at the kitchen table eating breakfast.

"You're *so* not funny, Jill," Jack said.

"Look, it's floating." I continued to move my spoon from side to side in front of his face.

"Why is Mummy doing that with the spoon, Daddy?" Florence said.

"Because Mummy thinks it's clever."

"I can do that too." Florence whipped her spoon out of her bowl of cornflakes. As she did, she splashed milk all over my face. "Sorry, Mummy."

Jack was in hysterics. "Now *that* is funny!"

"I didn't mean to do it, Mummy."

"It's alright, darling. I'm not mad at you. It was Daddy's fault."

"Mummy, are you coming to dance class today?"

"Yes, darling, I am."

"Are you sure you'll have time to take her, Jill?" Jack said. "It sounds like you have a busy day ahead."

"I want to take her. And besides, you deserve some time to yourself."

"I guess."

"Have you got anything planned?"

"Not really."

"When can I see your new car, Mummy?" Florence said.

"I'm going to get it on Monday."

The previous evening, when I'd told Jack that I'd bought a new car, he'd got all huffy with me. Not because I'd spent the money, but because he thought he should have been involved in the decision making. But as I pointed out to him, he knew nothing about cars, and I hadn't had any say when he'd bought his.

"Will I be able to go out in it on Monday, Mummy?"

"We'll have to see. It depends what time I get home."

"What colour is it?"

"Blue."

"Why didn't you get a red one? Red is my favourite colour."

"They didn't have any red ones, but the blue one is really nice. I think you'll like it."

"Is it the B-Q today, Mummy?"

"The barbecue? Yes, but you mustn't be disappointed if it's cancelled because it looks like rain."

"There's no rain forecast," Jack said, helpfully. "The barbecue will definitely go ahead, Florence. I'm looking forward to it, are you?"

"Yes. What will they have to eat?"

"I'm not sure, but I bet there'll be sausages and burgers." Jack licked his lips. "Maybe some chicken."

"Can Buddy come too?"

"No!" I got in quickly. "He'll steal all the food. He'll have to wait here until we come back."

"Can I bring some food back for him?"

"I don't see why not. I have lots to do today so I might not get back in time for the barbecue. If I don't, you and Daddy will have to go without me."

"You'd better make it back in time," Jack said. "We promised Olga that we'd all go."

"If I remember correctly, you were the one who made that particular promise. I'll do my best, but it won't be easy because I have to drop in at Deli's, and then I have to go to the book signing I told you about."

"Can't your nails wait?"

"I'm not getting my nails done. When do I ever get them done? It's all connected to one of the cases I'm working on."

"Deli's nail bar? What does that have to do with it?"

"It's a long, complicated story. I'll explain later."

"Okay. Incidentally, while you're at the dance class, don't forget to check with Donna that Wendy is still coming over here tomorrow."

"Okay."

Jack had decided to take Buddy for a walk while Florence and I were at the dance class. Given the way he had to drag the Chihuahua through the gate, I got the impression that Buddy was less than enthusiastic about the idea.

As soon as we got to the village hall, Florence went running over to Wendy. Donna beckoned me to sit next to her.

"Hey, Jill, when I drove past your place yesterday, the AA man was working on your car. Is it okay now?"

"He managed to get it going, but the thing is clapped out. I bought a new one yesterday. I collect it on Monday."

"Nice. What did you get?"

"A blue one."

She grinned. "*A blue one*? I take it you're not into cars?"

"I like sports cars, but I'll never be able to afford one of those. These days, I just need one to get me from A to B without breaking down."

"Is it still okay for Wendy to come over to your place tomorrow?"

"Yeah, Florence is looking forward to it."

"Wendy too. She's talked about nothing else. Two o'clock we said, didn't we?"

"Yeah. I thought they could play in the afternoon and then we'll give them tea."

"That'll be great. It'll give me and Ronnie some alone time because Rachel is at her friend's too." She gave me a knowing grin. "If you know what I mean."

"I know exactly what you mean, trust me."

"By the way, Jill." She suddenly began to speak in a hushed voice. "When I was on my way over here, I spotted a couple of vampires walking through the village."

"Are you sure?"

"Positive. I don't think anyone new has moved into the village, so I can only assume they're tourists. It's very rare to see sups in Middle Tweaking."

The music started, and the girls began to dance. It was impossible to hold a meaningful discussion with the music and all the activity, so we sat back and watched the girls in action. Florence was definitely improving every week. Wendy, on the other hand, was just as awkward and clumsy as ever. Still, she seemed to enjoy it and that was all that mattered.

When the class was over, the four of us walked back together to the old watermill and then said our goodbyes.

Jack was reading the newspaper.

"I take it you didn't get very far on your walk," I said.

"I should have known better than to take that dog. We managed to get about two-hundred yards up the road before he sat down and refused to budge. I ended up buying a newspaper and coming back here."

"Where is Buddy?"

"Fast asleep in the garden. Those two-hundred yards clearly exhausted him. How did the dance class go?"

"We learned a new dance, Daddy." Florence gushed. "Would you like to see it?"

"Before you show Daddy your dance, Mummy has to go to work."

"Bye, Mummy." She gave me a big hug and a kiss.

"I'll see you two later."

"What about my kiss?" Jack pretended to pout, so I gave him a kiss too. "And make sure you're back in time for the barbecue."

"I'll do my best."

"You'd better."

***

The book signing wasn't until one o'clock, so I had plenty of time to drop in at Nailed-It. The shop had expanded dramatically since it first opened. Deli had bought Grandma's beauty salon business, and she now offered the full range of treatments.

The young woman behind the counter had nails that were so long I couldn't imagine how she ever used the computer.

"Good morning, madam. Do you have an appointment?"

"No, I don't."

"I'm afraid we're fully booked for all treatments today."

"I'm actually here to see Deli. Is she in?"

"Yes. What's your name?"

"Jill Maxwell."

The young woman had only spoken a few words into the phone when Deli appeared, larger than life and twice as loud.

"Jill!" She gave me a great big hug. "It's ages since I've seen you. Where have you been hiding yourself?"

"Nowhere. I'm still working here in Washbridge."

"A little bird told me that you'd got yourself a country residence now."

"I'm not sure I'd call it a country residence, but yeah, we live in Middle Tweaking."

"Very nice. Why don't you come through to the back? I'll make us a coffee."

"Sure." I followed her into the office where the furniture was every bit as gaudy as I'd expected.

"I hope these pods are okay," she said, as she dropped one into the coffee machine. "Nails bought me this for my birthday."

"That'll be fine. Kathy has one of those."

"What brings you here to see me, Jill?"

"I have a favour to ask of you."

"Ask away. I'll help if I can. You know that."

"It's actually for a friend of mine—well, more of an acquaintance, really. By the name of Gwen Ravensbeak."

"Raven's what?"

"Beak. Ravensbeak."

"What a great name."

"Isn't it just? Anyway, Gwen has been let down by the nail bar she usually goes to, and she asked if I knew of a top-notch salon that might be able to fit her in at short notice. I immediately thought of you."

"I would hope you did. They don't come any more top

notch than Nailed-It. When was she hoping to come?"

"I know you're really busy, but ideally, Monday or Tuesday next week. If that's possible."

"Let me take a look." She passed my drink and then sat at her desk and began to tap away on the computer. "You're in luck. It's Nails' day off on Monday, but I can get him to come in for an hour to see to your lady."

"I couldn't ask him to come in on his day off."

"It's no bother. I happen to know he's coming into town for lunch with one of his friends, so I'll ask him to come in an hour early. He'll be able to fit in your friend at eleven if that's okay."

"I'm sure it will be."

"Make sure you tell your friend her appointment will be with our top nail technician. Nails has numerous awards to his name now, and he's been featured in at least three different magazines."

"I will. She'll be very impressed, I'm sure."

"Right. That's all booked for you."

"Thanks, Deli."

Deli and I chatted for a while over coffee, but then she had to attend to a customer, so I thanked her again and left.

I still had a little time to kill before the book signing, so I decided to pay a visit to Mad at her hubby's record shop, Vinyl Alley. The shop front was very small, and the window was covered in vinyl record sleeves, so I couldn't see inside. It was like stepping back in time, to a record store from the seventies. It was very basic in design, just rows and rows of tables on which were wooden boxes, crammed full of vinyl records covering every genre. If the number of customers browsing through the stock was anything to go by, vinyl had clearly made a comeback.

Mad was behind the counter. "Jill, what do you think of the place?"

"It's fantastic."

"It's a bit basic, but so was Brad's shop in Glasgow. That's what made the move so simple. All he had to do was to get the tables and stock transported down here. It took us about a week to set it all up, and then we were up and running."

"Where is this new husband of yours, anyway? I was hoping I'd meet him today."

"He's just nipped out for coffee."

"Is somebody talking about me?" A tall, skinny man with wild hair joined Mad behind the counter and put his arm around her waist.

"Brad, this is Jill. I told you all about her."

"Pleased to meet you, Jill. According to Mad, you're some kind of superstar detective."

"I'm not sure I'd go that far."

"Would you like a coffee? I can nip back out?"

"No, thanks. I've just had one. At your mum's salon, actually, Mad. How are you settling into Washbridge, Brad?"

"Okay, so far. The people all seem really friendly, and business is better than I could have hoped for, considering we've only just opened. The only downside so far is the thefts."

"From the shop?"

"Yeah. We've had quite a few records *go walkies* over the last couple of weeks. I wouldn't normally mind—the same thing happened in Glasgow—but whoever is taking them is picking out some real classics." He reeled off the names of several artists and tracks that I'd never heard of. "See what I mean, Jill? Every one a classic."

"Absolutely. What are you going to do about it?" I glanced around. "Don't you have CCTV?"

"No, but we might have to think about getting it installed if the thefts continue. Anyway, you'll have to excuse me. I have stock to sort out in the back. I'll leave you two to talk. It was nice to meet you, Jill."

"You too."

"What do you think of Brad?" Mad asked after he'd disappeared into the back.

"He's nice, but I wouldn't have thought he was your type. He strikes me as a bit too hippie-ish for you."

"I know, but we get on like a house on fire."

"It's a pity about the thefts."

"And the leaks." She pointed to a bucket in one of the aisles.

"Roof?"

"Yeah. There was no sign of a problem when we looked around the building originally, but ever since we moved in there's been one leak after another."

"Have you had someone look at it?"

"Brad's pretty handy, but as soon as he stops one leak another one springs up. If it continues, we'll have to bite the bullet and get the professionals in."

"How's the ghost hunter business doing?"

"It's really quiet and I have no idea why. Since I moved back down here, I've only had two or three cases to deal with. Not that I'm complaining. I'm pleased to be able to spend more time in the shop. What were you doing at my mother's salon? You weren't getting your nails done, I can see that."

"Asking her a favour."

"Did she come through for you?"

"Yeah, big time." I checked my watch. "Sorry, Mad, I have to get going."

"When are the four of us going to get together for dinner?"

"Soon. I'll be in touch."

Chapter 12

Washbridge's largest bookstore, where the book signing was to take place, was called Wash Books, which had always struck me as a rather naff name. It was ages since I'd been in there; the last time was when I'd bought a couple of books for Florence at Christmas.

I headed straight for the customer service desk, which was just inside the door. The eager young woman looked very bookish.

"Welcome to Wash Books. How can I help you?"

"I'm looking for Richard Watkins. I believe he's in your store today."

"He is indeed. I take it you're here for the book signing?"

"Actually, no. I just need a quick word with him on a private matter."

"I'm afraid you'll have to wait until the book signing has finished."

"Right. How long will that be?"

"He's scheduled to be here for another three hours."

"*Three hours*?"

There was no way I could wait that long because I'd miss the barbecue. If I did that, Jack would be furious (which, okay, I could live with), but Florence would be upset too, and I didn't like to let her down if I could help it. I would have to find a quicker way to get to Richard Watkins. What if I had one of his books to sign? That should get me to him quicker.

"Where can I find Richard Watkins' new book?"

"Err, they're right behind you."

I turned around to find four tables stacked high with

them.

"Right, thanks." I grabbed one and flicked open the cover to check the price. Twenty pounds! Was he having a laugh? No way was I going to spend that kind of money. I'd just hold onto the book until I'd managed to grab a few words with him.

"Where exactly is the book signing taking place?"

"At the far end of the shop, in the crime section."

"Thanks."

I'd expected to find a dozen or so people queuing. Twenty tops.

I was wrong by a factor of five. Watkins was seated at a table at the far side of the crime section. From there, a queue ran along two of the walls to where I was standing.

"Excuse me," I said to the young woman in front of me. "I take it this is the queue to get a book signed?"

"Yes, it is."

"I wasn't expecting there to be so many people here."

"Really?" She seemed surprised. "I thought there'd be more. When Richard was here to sign his last book, there were twice as many people. Have you read all of his books?"

"Not all of them."

"They're brilliant. I've read every one several times."

"Do you like Margaret Plant's books?"

"Oh yes. I love Margaret's books as well, but I've been waiting ages for her new one to come out, and I still don't know when it's going to be published."

It soon became apparent that Richard Watkins wasn't simply signing books. He was having a long chat with everyone in the queue, as well as taking selfies with most of them. At this rate, I'd still miss the barbecue.

What I needed right now was a cunning plan. Something that would allow me to get to the front of the queue much quicker. I ran through a list of spells that I might use, but there was no obvious solution. In the end, I decided on the 'rain' spell. It was far from ideal, and I would have to use much tighter control than normal.

After creating a teeny, tiny rain cloud, I manoeuvred it slowly over the full length of the queue. As it passed overhead, the people beneath began to make for the exit to avoid what they assumed was a burst pipe. In no time at all, everyone except Richard and me had deserted the crime section.

After reversing the spell, I walked over to the table where Richard Watkins was looking very confused. He was wearing glasses and had a goatee. He fitted the description of the man Mr and Mrs Comfy had seen hanging around their street on the day that Margaret Plant's manuscript had gone missing.

"Where's everyone gone?" he said.

"They probably needed the loo."

"Who shall I dedicate it to?" He reached over and tried to take the book. If he signed it, I'd be forced to pay for it, so I kept a tight hold of it. We were soon having a tug of war. "Do you want me to sign your book or not?"

"Actually, I just wanted a quick word with you."

"About what?"

"My name is Jill Maxwell. I'm a private investigator working for Margaret Plant."

"*Margaret*? Why does she need a private investigator?"

"Someone has stolen the manuscript for her next novel."

"Really?" His face lit up. "How terrible for her." I could almost see the cogs turning in his mind, and as it dawned on him why I was there, his smile faded. "Wait a minute. Why do you want to talk to me? That crazy old woman doesn't think I had anything to do with it, does she?"

"Margaret hasn't suggested anything of the kind, at least not to me. But her neighbours saw someone matching your description hanging around the street on the day it went missing."

"This is outrageous. I don't even know where Margaret lives. When is this supposed to have happened?"

"Last week."

"Do you know where I was last week?" He grinned. "I'll tell you. I was in the States doing TV interviews and book signings. All week. I'm sure it won't be difficult for you to confirm that."

Oh bum! So much for that theory.

"I see. In that case thanks for your help."

Catching me off guard, he snatched the book from my hand and signed it.

"There you go, Jill. Don't forget to pay for it on your way out."

"Thanks." For nothing.

"Oh, and by the way, when I've finished signing books, I'm going to have a word with my friends in the book press. I'm sure they'll be very interested to hear about Margaret's misfortune."

"I'm afraid I can't allow you to do that."

"And how exactly do you intend to stop me?"

After casting the 'forget' spell, I made my way out of the shop, stopping only to put the book on the pile near the door.

What? Maybe someone called Jill would buy it.

***

When I pulled up outside the old watermill, Jack was looking for me through the window. I'd no sooner got out of the car than he and Florence came walking down the drive.

"I didn't think you were going to make it." Jack tapped his watch. "I thought Florence and I would have to go to the barbecue by ourselves."

"The book signing was way busier than I expected."

"How did it go?"

"It was a complete waste of time. I thought I might be onto something because Watkins matched the description of the man seen hanging around the street where Margaret Plant lives on the day of the theft, but he was in the USA all that week."

"Where does that leave you?"

"Back at square one."

"Oh well, never mind. The barbecue will cheer you up."

"Somehow, I doubt that. Incidentally, I called in at Mad's record shop while I was waiting to go to the book signing."

"What's it like?"

"Very retro."

"Did you meet her husband?"

"Yeah, Brad seems really nice."

"Did they say how business was?"

"It sounds like it's got off to a good start. Except for the thefts."

"They haven't had a break-in already, have they?"

"No, it sounds more like shoplifters."
"They should report it to the police."
"Like that would do any good."

Olga was waiting for us at the gate. Standing beside her was a man I recognised as our postman.

"Hi, Jill," Olga said. "This is my husband, Oscar. You've probably seen him delivering the mail."

"Hi, this is Jack, and this is Florence."

"Hello, Florence. Aren't you a pretty girl? My two children, Olivia and Oliver are around the back. Shall we go and join them?"

As we made our way around to the back of the house, the smell of cooking meat greeted us.

"Kids, this is Florence. Come and say hello."

Oliver and Olivia came running over, and began to make a fuss of Florence.

"When will everyone else be here?" I said.

"It's just us and Oscar's brother who should be arriving soon, hopefully. He's travelling down from the Midlands. We thought we'd keep it a small affair today, didn't we, Oscar?"

"Yes, flower. Hey, Jack, are you interested in stamps?"

"*Stamps*?"

"It's my hobby. Would you like to take a look at my collection while we wait until the food is ready?"

"Err, sure." Jack couldn't have looked any less enthusiastic if he'd tried.

It served him right. He was the one who'd agreed to come to this shindig.

Olga seemed to be in charge of the barbecue, and judging by the expert way she was flipping the burgers, she was clearly an old hand at it.

"The two guys seem to have hit it off," she said.

"Don't they just? Jack's always had a keen interest in philately."

"Really? Oscar will be thrilled. It's his passion."

"Quite an appropriate hobby for him, considering."

"How do you mean?"

"Because of his job."

"Sorry, Jill, I still don't follow."

Oh boy!

"Postman. Letters. Stamps?"

"Oh, right. I see what you mean now. It had never occurred to me. What about you, Jill? Do you have any hobbies?"

"No. I don't really have time for them, what with work and looking after Florence."

"You really should get one. Everyone needs something to help them unwind after a busy day at work. Personally, I'm into basket-weaving."

"Really?"

Not quite as boring as stamp collecting, but very close.

"Do you see those bread baskets over there? I made those."

The baskets looked like a dog had spent the last hour chewing holes in them.

"They're—err—very nice."

"Thanks. I'd be happy to give you a few lessons. Once you've tried it, you'll soon catch the bug. It's addictive."

I very much doubted that.

"Sure. When I have some time to spare." The day after the twelfth of never.

The three children seemed to be getting along famously. The Rileys had a swing and a sandpit in their garden; Florence was making sandcastles with the help of her two new friends.

"The meat looks about ready," Olga said and then shouted to her daughter, "Olivia, go inside and get your dad and Jack, will you? Tell them food's up."

"Okay, Mum." Olivia disappeared into the house and moments later, Oscar and Jack re-emerged. The glazed expression on Jack's face told its own story.

After Olga had handed out the food, I managed to pull Jack to one side.

"Was that enjoyable?"

"He's got twenty albums full of stamps, and he's only shown me one so far. I just hope he doesn't intend to show me the rest later."

"I realised something while you were in there. These are the O-Riley's."

"I thought their surname was just Riley?"

"It is, but they're still the O-Riley's." I grinned.

"I have precisely no idea what you're talking about, Jill."

"Think about it. There's Olga, Oscar, Olivia, and Oliver. All of their names begin with an O, so that makes them the O-Riley's. Get it?" I laughed.

"Hilarious."

Just then, someone appeared from around the side of the house.

"Hi, everybody. Sorry I'm—" He stopped midsentence when he saw Jack and me.

***

After what were two of the longest hours of my life, we thanked our hosts, and made our exit. Back home, Buddy came rushing up to us as soon as we walked through the door. Normally, he paid no heed to our comings and goings, so I could only assume he'd caught scent of the barbecue.

I turned to Jack. "I didn't remember to bring Buddy anything back, did you?"

"No, I forgot all about him."

"Oh dear. Looks like we're in trouble."

"It's alright, Mummy, I brought him some food." Florence held out a burger.

"How long have you been carrying that around?"

"I asked Mrs Riley if I could have it just before we left. I promised Buddy I'd bring him something back."

By now, the Chihuahua was jumping up Florence's leg in a vain attempt to reach the burger.

"Give it to me, darling. I'll cut it into pieces for him."

"Hurry up!" Buddy screamed at me while I chopped up the burger.

"Have some patience, will you!"

"I'm starving." He was running around the kitchen in circles. It was the most energy I'd seen him expend since we'd first brought him home.

"Take this in the garden to feed him, Florence." I handed her the plate, and Buddy followed her outside.

"Well, Jack, I hope you're pleased with yourself. That was truly awful."

"How was I supposed to know that Oscar's brother was Leo Riley?"

"I'd hoped never to see that man again."

"He clearly still has a soft spot for you." Jack grinned.

"How I resisted smacking him around the face with a hotdog, I'll never know. Did you notice that he's still claiming I hindered his investigations? I solved more cases for him than he did himself."

"You look like you could do with a drink."

"That's a good idea. Why don't you pour us both a nice glass of wine?"

Thirty minutes, and a glass of wine later, I'd managed to calm down a little. "I can't believe that idiot is now heading up the murder squad in the West Midlands."

"He's done well for himself," Jack said.

"Does it make you wish you'd stayed in the force?"

"Not really. I was never cut out for the politics that were needed to rise in the ranks. And besides, I like working from home and being able to spend time with you and Florence."

As we spoke, a spoon came floating past my eyeline. "What the—?"

"What did I tell you?" Jack pointed at it. "This place is haunted. Now do you believe me?"

"I don't understand it. It's not cold in here, but there's always a chill whenever there's a ghost around."

"It must be a ghost. What else can it be? How else could the spoon move back and forth like that?"

"Hold on a minute! Florence Maxwell! Is that you?"

There was silence for a moment but then I heard a teeny giggle.

Jack looked at me with a puzzled expression. "What's going on, Jill?"

"Florence, reverse that spell, immediately!"

Moments later, Florence appeared, still holding the spoon. "That was funny, wasn't it, Mummy?"

"Who taught you the 'invisible' spell? Has Great-Grandma been around here again?"

"It wasn't Great-Grandma. I taught myself from the book. It's fun being invisible. Daddy was really scared when he saw the spoon yesterday, weren't you, Daddy?"

Chapter 13

The next morning, Jack was still trying to get his head around what had happened the previous day. He'd been gobsmacked when he'd realised that the 'floating' spoon had actually been carried across the room not by a ghost but by his invisible daughter. It turned out that, all the time we thought she'd been playing with her dolls' house, she'd actually been studying the spell book. That also explained why Buddy had become so agitated the other day. The *thing* he'd been barking at had actually been an invisible Florence.

I'd asked Jack to take Buddy out for a walk, so that I could have a quiet word with Florence.

"Why can't I go for a walk with Daddy and Buddy, Mummy?"

"Because I need to have a little talk with you about what happened yesterday."

"Do you mean about the spoon?"

"Yes, about the 'invisible' spell."

"I'm good at it, aren't I? Daddy didn't know it was me, did he?"

"No, he didn't, but that isn't—"

"You only knew it was me because I giggled."

"That's true, but do you remember when I told you that you could learn some more magic? I said that I would be the one to teach you the spells."

"But I taught it myself, Mummy. It was easy peasy."

"That's as maybe, but some of those spells in the book can be dangerous. You wouldn't want to hurt yourself or someone else, would you?"

"No."
"That's why I've put the spell book somewhere safe."
"Where is it?"
"I can't tell you that."
"Do I have to try to find it?"
"No. I've hidden it so that you can't teach yourself any more spells."
"But that's not fair."
"I'm afraid that's the way it has to be. From now on, you can only learn new spells with me. That way, everyone will be safe."
"But you only teach me one new spell a week. That's not many."
"Okay, maybe we can make it more than one."
"Ten!"
"No, definitely not ten. You can learn two, but only if you're a good girl."
"I *am* a good girl."
"Most of the time, but not when you use the 'invisible' spell to scare Daddy."
"It was funny, wasn't it?" She giggled. "He thought I was a ghost."
"No, it wasn't funny." I thought it was hilarious, but I couldn't let Florence know that. "And you mustn't do it again. Okay?"
"Okay, Mummy."
When Jack and Buddy got back, he took me to one side to ask how our little chat had gone.
"Okay. She understands that she mustn't teach herself any more spells."
"Are you sure?"
"Definitely."

Fingers firmly crossed.

***

Jack was preparing lunch.

"We're out of gravy powder," I said. "I'd better nip over to the village store."

"Good luck with that." He grinned. "I don't give much for your chances of finding any."

"I can dream. I won't be long."

As I headed towards Tweaking Stores, I spotted two vampires in the distance. I assumed it must be the same couple that Donna had mentioned at dance class. They had their backs to me, and they were walking unusually fast. A little way ahead of them was the vicar who was clearly oblivious to their presence. Were they following him? I had a horrible feeling that's exactly what they were doing, so I picked up my pace.

The vicar turned into the narrow street (little more than an alley, really) that ran between the tea room and the pharmacy; it was a well-known shortcut to the rectory. I was still clinging to the hope that the two vampires would carry on past the turning, but to my dismay, they followed him. This was getting serious, so I legged it after them.

When I reached the alley, the vicar was still unaware of the two shadowy figures who were now just a few feet behind him. Moments later, the male vampire reached out a hand, clearly intending to grab the vicar.

"Excuse me!" I yelled.

The two vampires spun around.

The vicar did too. "Jill?"

"It's alright, Vicar. I was just calling to my two friends there."

"Ah, okay. Have a wonderful day."

"You too, Vicar."

And off he went, totally oblivious to the lucky escape he'd just had.

"What on earth do you two think you're playing at?" I demanded.

"We were peckish," the female vampire said, somewhat timidly.

"*Peckish*? Are you totally insane? You do realise where you are, I assume?"

"In Middle Tweaking."

"Which, in case you hadn't noticed, is in the human world. You can't simply attack a human in broad daylight."

"But we didn't bring any synthetic blood with us because we thought we'd be able to buy it here."

"Your stupidity is hardly the vicar's fault, is it? If I hadn't stepped in, you would have drained him of blood, wouldn't you?"

"Well, err—"

"Don't try and deny it. Your fangs are still showing."

"We're sorry." The male put his hand in front of his mouth. "This is our first time in the human world. We don't really know the etiquette."

"Well, I can tell you this much: Attacking a human, and killing them by draining their blood, is definitely not the *etiquette* required."

"I guess not. Sorry. Would you happen to know where we could get some synthetic blood?"

"No, I don't. I suggest you go back to Candlefield

straight away."

"But we've only just got here."

"I don't care. You'll just have to cut short your day trip."

"We're not here on a day trip. We've booked to stay the whole week."

"Where?"

"In Hotel First Time."

"How did you hear about the hotel?"

"There's a big advertising campaign running in Candlefield."

"What type of advertising campaign?"

"The ad said that Middle Tweaking was the ideal destination for sups who have never been to the human world before."

"Unbelievable."

I was so angry it took all my willpower not to do some serious harm to these two idiots. Instead, I practically dragged them across the village back to the hotel. En route, I spotted a werewolf and two wizards. What on earth had Grandma been thinking? Why would she target her advertising at sups who had no experience of the human world?

As we got close to the hotel, the male vampire pulled away from me. "I don't care what you say. We're not cancelling our holiday. We've paid for a full week."

"I can't stop you from staying here, but you have to at least go back to Candlefield and pick up some synthetic blood."

"We will. I promise."

"You better had because if I catch you stalking anyone else, I'll contact the rogue retrievers and let them know what you've been up to. Daze happens to be a close friend of mine."

Just the mention of Daze's name put the fear of God into both of them.

"There's no need to do that. We'll go back home straight away and stock up with enough synthetic blood to see us through the week."

"Okay. Now get out of my sight." I practically pushed them through the doors of the hotel.

I considered confronting Grandma there and then, but I didn't trust myself not to do or say something I would later regret.

I was halfway to the village shop when I heard someone shout my name. Grandma was closing in on me, and she clearly wasn't happy.

That made two of us.

"What do you think you're doing to my customers? Two of them have just walked into the hotel, and they were very upset. They said a witch had been giving them a hard time. I assume that was you."

"It most certainly was."

"Would you care to explain yourself?"

"Do you know what those two idiots were doing?"

"Looking around the village, I imagine. Sightseeing."

"They were just about to attack the vicar and drain him of blood."

"Surely not. You're being melodramatic as usual."

"No, I'm not. They were this close to dragging the vicar to the floor and plunging their teeth into his neck when I stepped in."

"Oh? Alright, I'll have a word with them."

“Those stupid vampires had come to the human world for a week’s holiday and they hadn’t thought to bring any synthetic blood with them.”

“Okay, I’ve just said I’ll talk to them.”

“They told me that you’ve been running an advertising campaign in Candlefield targeting sups who’ve never been to the human world before.”

“That’s right. I saw a gap in the market and jumped in.”

“That’s all well and good, but you’ve failed to provide these newbies with even the most basic instructions on how to behave in the human world.”

“That’s hardly my responsibility. I’m not their mother.”

“It most certainly *is* your responsibility. You’re the one who invited them over here. You’re their host. I also saw a werewolf. I assume it’s his first time here as well. What happens if he suddenly turns wolf and rips Miss Drinkwater to shreds?”

“From what you’ve told me about her, he’d be doing us all a favour.”

“This is no laughing matter, Grandma. I saw a couple of wizards too. Goodness knows what they might get up to.”

“You’re making a mountain out of a molehill.”

“I don’t think so. And I warn you now that if there’s any repeat of the behaviour I’ve just witnessed, I’ll have no hesitation in calling in the rogue retrievers.”

“I’m not scared of Daze and her gang.”

“Maybe not, but your guests *will* be. And when she sends them all packing to Candlefield, you’ll have an empty hotel.”

“You wouldn’t do that.”

“Try me.”

“What exactly is it you want me to do?”

"Prepare some basic instructions for all your guests, and make sure they've read and understood them before you allow them out into the village. I suggest you start by rounding up all your current guests and giving them a good talking to."

"And if I refuse?"

"Your hotel will go bust. I guarantee it."

"You're getting too big for your boots, Jill."

"Just do as I say."

Further discussion would have been pointless, so I left Grandma standing there, still seething, and made my way to the village store.

As all I needed was gravy powder, I'd assumed I'd be in and out of the shop in no time at all.

Wrong!

I'd searched high and low in the section marked 'G', but there was no sign of it.

"Marjorie, do you have any gravy powder?"

"There should be plenty on the shelf, Jill."

"I've just looked all through 'G' section and I can't see it anywhere."

"It's under 'P'. 'P' for powder."

Of course it is. So obvious. Not.

I eventually found it in-between the washing powder and flea powder. I considered suggesting to Marjorie Stock that it might be time to revisit their shelving system before they poisoned someone, but I knew I'd be wasting my breath. I was just about to pay for the gravy powder when it occurred to me that it might be nice to buy jelly for Florence and Wendy to have after their tea. Amazingly, the jelly was in section 'J'. There was a selection of flavours to choose from; I opted for the strawberry.

On my way out of the shop, who should I bump into but Stewart, the man who had persuaded Jack to take Buddy off his hands. The man who was supposedly living with his brother in Australia.

"Hello, Stewart, fancy seeing you here."

"Hi. It's Jill, isn't it?"

"That's right. Aren't you supposed to be living in Australia?"

"Err, yeah. Unfortunately, there was a bit of a problem."

"Really? Weren't you going to live with your brother?"

"Err, that's right."

"So? What happened?"

"He—err—"

"Disappeared? Was taken away by the fairies?"

"Actually, he died."

"Oh, I'm sorry about—wait a minute—when did he die?"

"Err—" He hesitated.

"The truth, Stewart."

"Three years ago."

"And the news has only just reached you, has it?"

"I—err—"

"You never were going to move to Australia, were you?"

"Okay, no. I'm sorry I lied, but that dog and I just didn't get along. I thought he'd be happier in a family surrounding."

"Oh, I see. This was just a selfless act on your part. You were only thinking of Buddy."

"That's right."

"Do I look stupid? You and I both know that Buddy is a nightmare. You were looking for some mug to take him off your hands."

"I'm sorry, but what's done is done. I can't take him back now." He started to edge his way into the store. "I have to buy some dishwasher tablets. Give my regards to Jack, will you?"

"Are you alright, Jill?" Jack said. "I was beginning to worry about you."

"I most certainly am not alright."

"What's wrong?"

"Where do I begin? First, I've just discovered that Grandma is encouraging sups, who've never been to the human world before, to holiday at her hotel."

"Is that a problem?"

"It could be a massive problem. I just came across two vampires who were on the verge of attacking the vicar."

"Seriously?"

"Yes. If I hadn't stopped them, they'd have drained him of blood. The idiots came to the human world for a week's holiday without any supplies of synthetic blood."

"What did you do?"

"I told them to go back to Candlefield to get some, and I threatened to set Daze on them. Then I read the Riot Act to Grandma. I told her that she had to issue instructions to all of her guests on how to behave in the human world."

"Will she do that?"

"She'd better or I'll get the rogue retrievers to arrest all of her guests."

"How did your grandmother react to that?"

"She wasn't best pleased, but I don't care."

"There's no wonder you're annoyed."

"You've only heard the half of it. You'll never guess who I bumped into on my way out of the shop."

"I've no idea."

"Your friend, Stewart. You know, the guy who gave you Buddy. The guy who went to live in Australia with his brother."

"He can't have come back already, surely?"

"He never went to live with his brother, and there's a very good reason for that. His brother died three years ago."

"I don't understand."

"It's very simple. Stewart had had enough of Buddy and he was looking for some mug to take him off his hands. And guess what? He found you."

***

I was feeling a little nervous about Wendy coming to play with Florence because it was the first time she'd had a school friend over for a play date, and I wanted it to go well.

Donna dropped her daughter off at two o'clock, and we agreed she'd collect her at six-thirty, after the kids had had their tea. The girls were really giddy at first, but they soon settled down. Florence took Wendy out into the garden to play with Buddy who was being his usual obstreperous self. He refused point-blank to fetch the ball whenever Wendy threw it. That was no doubt because our agreement only covered playing ball with Florence. Fortunately, Wendy didn't seem to be too concerned; she was more than happy to just watch Florence throw the ball for Buddy to fetch.

When the girls had grown tired of that, they went up to Florence's bedroom where she proceeded to take out every one of her toys to show Wendy. When I popped my head around the door to check on them, I could barely see the bedroom floor. It would no doubt be my job to tidy them all away later. Still, I didn't mind. It was nice to see the girls having so much fun.

I wasn't sure what Wendy liked to eat, so I'd made a selection of sandwiches. We had nibbles too: crisps, biscuits, cocktail sausages, and sausage rolls. By the time the girls came downstairs again, they were ravenous, and they were soon tucking into the food. Rather than cramp their style, Jack and I put our meals on a tray, and went through to the lounge.

Twenty minutes later, Florence came through to us.

"Mummy, can we have our jelly now, please?"

"Of course you can, darling." I followed her back into the kitchen and gave the girls their jelly.

When Jack and I had finished our meals, we headed back into the kitchen. I was just about to go through the door when I stopped dead in my tracks.

Jack bumped into the back of me. "What are you doing, Jill? I almost dropped my tray."

"Look in there," I said in a hushed voice. "Look at Wendy."

He peered around the door. "What am I supposed to be looking at?"

"Her legs."

"Is that fur all over them?"

"Yes, and look, she's beginning to grow a tail."

"What's going on?"

"I think she might be starting to turn."

"Into a werewolf?"

"No, into a kangaroo. Of course into a werewolf."

"What are we going to do?"

"I don't know. It doesn't seem to be progressing any further. Let's just keep an eye on her." I led the way into the kitchen, and we pretended to be doing the washing up. After a few minutes, her tail had vanished, and the fur on her legs slowly started to recede.

"I think it's going to be okay," I whispered to Jack.

When Donna arrived, I took her through to the lounge.

"There's nothing wrong, is there, Jill? Is Wendy okay?"

"Everything's fine. The girls have had a great time."

"You had me worried there for a minute."

"Sorry. Look, something did happen that I think you should know about. While the girls were eating their tea, fur started to grow on Wendy's legs."

"What?"

"And I saw what looked like the beginnings of a tail."

"Oh, my goodness." Donna looked horrified. "She didn't turn completely, did she?"

"No, that's as far as it went, and it only lasted a minute or so. She didn't even seem to notice, and neither did Florence, but I just thought you should know."

"Right, thanks. Can I ask, what did you give them to eat?"

"Just sandwiches: ham, cheese, that sort of thing, and a few nibbles."

"What about for afters? Any dessert?"

"Strawberry jelly."

"That's it." Donna turned pale. "I'm so sorry, Jill, I

should have told you."

"Told me what?"

"There's something in jelly that can activate the change."

"I had no idea. I would never have given it to her."

"There's no reason you should know. It's entirely my fault. I should have mentioned it to you."

"Luckily, she didn't eat much of it."

"Thank goodness for that. I dread to think what might have happened."

"All's well that ends well. Shall we go through and see the girls?"

"Okay."

As Florence and Wendy said their goodbyes, I grabbed another quick word with Donna.

"I'm really sorry about what happened. I do hope this won't put you off letting Wendy come over again."

"Of course not. I think we should make this a regular thing."

Chapter 14

"Are you sure this is a good idea?" Jack said.

"Not really, but I promised Mrs V that I'd take Buddy in to see her, and she'll keep pestering me until I do, so I may as well get it over with."

"Rather you than me."

"Florence, come and give me a kiss. I'm going to work now."

"Why is Buddy going to work with you, Mummy?"

"I promised to take him to show Mrs V."

"Will he be here when I get home from school?"

"Of course he will. As soon as Mrs V has seen him, I'll bring him back home." I gave her a kiss, then picked up Buddy.

As I was walking towards the gate, he piped up, "Don't I get a say in this? I might not want to go to your office."

"I thought you'd be pleased to get out of the house."

"I'm not some sort of trophy to show off to any Tom, Dick or Harry."

"You'll like Mrs V."

"Will she have any treats for me?"

"I wouldn't have thought so."

"You should have told her to get some in."

"For goodness sake, stop moaning, will you? There's no wonder Stewart wanted rid of you."

"Don't mention that loser to me. He was even worse than you lot."

"I'll take that as a compliment."

I tried to get Buddy to walk from the car park to the office, but we'd only gone about halfway when he stopped dead in his tracks and refused to budge, so I had to pick him up. We hadn't gone much further when someone shouted from across the road.

"Is that your dog, Jill?" It was Blaze. He and Daze were once again cleaning windows.

"Yeah, this is Buddy."

"He's a lot smaller than the last time I saw him." Daze grinned.

"You're thinking of Barry. That's my other dog. Are you two still on the lookout for roof sprites?"

"Yeah, but no joy so far."

"What exactly have they been up to?"

"Thieving. Roof sprites are renowned for it. They work in gangs, as many as ten or fifteen at a time. They always gain access to a house or office via the roof—hence the name."

"And you still think they're operating in this area?"

"I'm beginning to have my doubts," Daze admitted. "We've more or less exhausted all the roofs around here, but we'll catch up with them sooner or later."

"Hey, Jill," Blaze shouted. "Why don't you ask Daze if you can see her dress."

"Shut it, Blaze!" Daze gave him her patented death stare.

"*Dress*?" I was intrigued. If Daze wasn't wearing her trademark catsuit, she was usually in jeans and a sweatshirt. "Tell me more."

"Go on, Daze, tell Jill." Blaze was clearly enjoying this, although I suspected he'd be made to pay for it later.

"I'm up for an award at the annual RR awards next weekend, so I thought I ought to make the effort."

"Do I get to see it?"

"Definitely not."
"I'll send you a photo," Blaze said.

I made my way up the stairs, and without thinking, I walked straight into the office.
"Jill!" Mrs V sighed. "I'd almost finished recording then."
"Sorry, Mrs V, I totally forgot about the knocking rule."
"Who is that little beauty?" She stood up. "What a little darling."
"Is this her?" Buddy said.
"Yes, make sure you're on your best behaviour."
"I'm always on my best behaviour around animals," Mrs V said. "Can I hold him?"
She didn't wait for an answer before she took him in her arms and started to tickle him under the chin. "I've got something for you, little doggy."
Mrs V took him around the desk, opened the drawer, and pulled out a packet of treats, which she sprinkled on the floor. As soon as she put him down, he began to vacuum them up.
"When did you buy those?" I said.
"Last week, as soon as you told me you were going to bring him in. I couldn't allow him to pay me a visit and not have a treat for him."
"You're spoiling him."
"He's worth it. He's such a lovely little thing. He must bring you lots of joy and happiness."
"Oh yeah. Tons of it. Are you alright to watch him for a minute while I nip next door?"
"Of course. Go ahead."

"I smell a dog out there," Winky said. "Have you brought that big daft thing in again?"

"No, it isn't Barry. I've brought Buddy in to meet Mrs V."

"You mean the rat?"

"He's a Chihuahua."

"I hope you don't intend to bring him through here."

"Don't worry. As soon as Mrs V's finished making a fuss of him, I'll take him back home."

"Good." He reached under the sofa. "I've got a little present for you." He handed me a Fitbit.

"*You* bought this for *me*? How come?"

"I didn't *buy it*, exactly. I got it through a friend of a friend."

"I hope it's not stolen."

"It isn't, I promise. Come on. Put it on."

"Okay." I slipped it onto my wrist.

"Right, let the challenge begin," Winky said.

"What challenge?"

"When I told you how many steps I'd done last week, you said that you'd done more."

"Of course, I did. I'm always on the go whereas you're stuck in here all day."

"We'll see, won't we? Whoever does the most steps between now and Friday is the winner."

"You're on, Winky. I can't lose."

"If you're so confident, how about a small wager?"

"Sure, how much?"

"Fifty pounds?"

"You're on."

This was going to be the easiest money I'd ever made.

I waited another ten minutes and then went to rescue Mrs V. I figured by then, she'd be ready to strangle the annoying dog.

Not so.

Buddy was standing on Mrs V's desk, and his little tail was wagging ten to the dozen. I'd never seen him so animated or so happy.

"It looks like you two are getting on well."

"He's such a little darling." Mrs V beamed. "I could play with him all day."

"I'd better take him back home now."

"I hope you'll bring him in to see me regularly."

"We'll see."

"It was lovely to meet you, young man." She gave him another fuss. "See you again soon."

"I like her," Buddy said, once we were out of the office.

"I can't believe you actually like someone."

"Why wouldn't I? She's a nice old lady. She gave me some treats and she didn't expect me to chase after a stupid ball. Can I go and live with her?"

"I wish you could."

"Why can't I?"

"Because Florence would be devastated."

"That little squirt? Who cares about her?"

"I do. She's my daughter."

"Why don't I ever have any good luck." He sighed.

"Stop moaning. Are you ready?"

"Ready for what?"

"I'm going to magic us back home."

"What do you mean, *magic us*? What's wrong with the car?"

"I don't have time to drive all the way to Middle Tweaking and back again."

"Is this going to hurt?"

"Of course not. Don't be such a wimp. Are you ready?"

"No."

I ignored him and cast the spell anyway. Moments later, we were in the kitchen at the old watermill. Jack must have heard us arrive because he came through from the lounge.

"How did it go with Mrs V?"

"Much better than I expected. This one was very taken with her. He even asked if he could go and live with her."

"That sounds like a great idea."

"I agree, but I don't think Florence would. She'd be devastated."

"You're right. Maybe when she gets fed up with him."

"Excuse me," Buddy said. "I'm standing right here."

"What did he say?" Jack asked because all he could hear was the dog barking.

"He was reminding us that he's right here. I don't think he appreciated us talking about him."

"Right. Sorry, Buddy."

I put the dog down and he went outside.

"I can't stay, Jack. I'll see you tonight." I gave him a kiss and magicked myself back to Washbridge.

When I walked into the outer office, Mrs V gave me a puzzled look.

"What have you done with Buddy?"

"Taken him home."

"But you've only been gone a few minutes."

Oh bum!

“I—err—Jack came to pick him up. He was waiting outside.”

“You’re so lucky to have that little darling.”

“I know. We count our blessings every day.”

In my office, Winky was fast asleep on the sofa. Bobby and Bertie were on the windowsill, and they seemed to be much happier than the last time I’d seen them.

“Good morning, Jill,” Bobby shouted.

“Hi, Jill.” Bertie waved a wing at me.

“Hello, you two. The last time I saw you, you were down in the dumps. What’s happened to cheer you up?”

“We have great news,” Bertie said. “Do you remember we told you we were struggling to find girlfriends? Well, there’s a new dating app available just for pigeons; it’s called Pigeon Love.” He held out his phone to show me.

“That’s great.”

“It only came out yesterday, and it’s a bit on the expensive side, but we decided to sign up, anyway. If it helps us to find girlfriends, it’ll be money well spent.”

“That’s fantastic. Any replies so far?”

“Not yet, but then we only put our profiles up this morning.”

“Fingers crossed, then. And be sure to keep me posted.”

***

My workload was crazy.

Take today for example: I had to collect Gwen Ravensbeak from Candlefield, take her to Deli’s salon to get her nails done, and then take her to the spot on the river where young Liam Roberts had disappeared.

I was also still trying to figure out whether the two clowns, who'd apparently died of heart attacks during NOCA meetings, had in fact died from natural causes, or whether there was something more sinister afoot.

Then, of course, there was Margaret Plant's missing manuscript, which I was no nearer to finding.

Busy, busy, busy.

It turned out that Gwen Ravensbeak lived on the same road as Aunt Lucy, in a small house opposite the bowling club.

"Come on, Gwen, we're going to be late," I shouted.

She'd gone upstairs to get changed fifteen minutes earlier and there was still no sign of her.

"Stop nagging. I'm ready." She appeared at the top of the stairs, dressed as though she was going to a wedding.

"Are you sure you want to wear that outfit? It's quite muddy near the river."

"That's as maybe, but I can't turn up at the beauty salon looking like a bag of rags, can I? If I'm going to be attended to by one of the human world's leading nail technicians, I want to look my best."

"Did I mention that it's a man who'll be doing your nails?"

"You did, yes. I must admit I was a little surprised at first, but as he's won so many awards and appeared in magazines, he must be a master of his craft."

"Right. Are we all set?"

"Just a second." She checked her handbag. "Yes, I think I've got everything."

"Great. Let's go." I reached out to take her hand.

"What are you doing?" She pulled away.

"I was going to magic us over there."

"I'm a witch too, you know. I'm quite capable of magicking myself over there, thank you very much."

"But you don't know where we're going."

"I'll follow you."

"Okay, if you're sure. On three: One, two, three."

I landed in a quiet alleyway across the road from Deli's salon, but there was no sign of Gwen. I knew I should have insisted that I magicked the two of us. She could be anywhere.

"Ouch!"

She'd landed right next to me and knocked me to the ground.

"Sorry, Jill. Are you okay? My bearings must have been slightly off."

"I'm alright." I got to my feet and brushed myself down. "Come on, we have to hurry."

I led the way out of the alley and across the road to the salon where the same receptionist was behind the desk.

"Hi there," I said. "I believe you have an appointment for my friend, Gwen Ravensbeak. It's with Nails at eleven."

She checked her computer. "That's right. If you'd both like to take a seat, he'll be with you shortly."

Gwen took a seat on the couch, but I remained standing.

"Gwen, I'm going to nip out because I have a few things to attend to." I turned to the receptionist. "How long is the appointment likely to last?"

She checked her computer again. "I would give it about an hour."

"I'll be back by then."

I didn't actually have any business to attend to, but I didn't want to hang around the salon in case Deli spotted me and talked me to death for the next hour. I nipped across the road to Coffee Animal where Dot was once again on duty. Mysteriously, her beauty spot was nowhere to be seen.

"You seem to be working a lot of hours, Dot. You're always here."

"A couple of people have quit recently, so I've taken on extra shifts. Me and my boyfriend, Dezzy, are saving up for a house, so the extra cash comes in handy. Your usual?"

"Yes, please."

Dot handed me the coffee and a blueberry muffin, and I was just about to look for a table when she said, "Don't forget to take your animal."

"What is it today?"

She reached under the counter and brought out a small glass cage.

"Is that a snake in there?"

"It is."

"I don't think I'll bother. I'm not a big fan of snakes."

"There's nothing to be scared of. It's perfectly harmless."

"Are you sure?"

"Absolutely. The management checked and double-checked to make sure that none of the snakes in here today are poisonous."

"Okay, if you're sure."

The snakes were clearly a big draw because the shop was the busiest I'd seen it in ages. The only free table I could find was right at the back. I'd just sat down and taken a sip of coffee when the snake hissed, "Give me some of your muffin."

"Snakes don't like muffins."

"Of course we do. We love them. What flavour is it?"

"Blueberry."

"That's my favourite. Go on, give us a bit."

"I'm not sure about putting my hand in there with you. Are you poisonous?"

"No fangs."

"*No thanks*, what?"

"I didn't say, *no thanks*. I said, *no fangs*!" He opened his mouth. "See! No fangs."

"Okay then." I broke off a small piece of muffin, opened the lid a fraction and dropped it inside.

"Thanks. Can I get out of here?"

"Definitely not."

"Why not?"

"You might slither away."

"I won't, I promise."

"Sorry, I can't take that risk."

"At least give me some more muffin, then. That wasn't a very big piece."

"Okay." I broke off another piece and dropped it into the cage.

"Do you mind if I sit here?" A young man was standing next to my table. "I've looked everywhere, and these are the only spare seats."

"Sure, help yourself."

He slid onto the seat opposite me. The cage he had with him was much larger than mine, and the snake inside it was much bigger too.

"Thanks very much," he said. "I've been trying to find a

seat for ages."

Before I knew it, he'd opened the cage and let his snake out.

"Are you sure that's safe?" I said.

"Oh yes, perfectly safe. I checked with the woman behind the counter, and she assured me that none of the snakes in here today are poisonous."

"Just make sure you keep it on your side of the table."

"Don't worry. I will."

I was watching my snake, who had just finished the muffin I'd given him, when I heard a strange noise. I looked up to find the man seated opposite me, going red in the face and waving his arms around in abject panic. He opened his mouth as if to speak, but only a gurgling sound came out, probably because his snake had wrapped itself around his neck and was slowly choking him to death. Putting my fear of snakes to one side for a moment, I grabbed it and tried to pull it off him, but it was way too strong. Another minute and the man would be dead, so I cast the 'power' spell. That did the trick—I managed to unravel the snake from the man's throat and threw it back into the glass cage.

The man gasped for air and eventually managed to splutter, "Thanks. I thought I was a goner there for sure."

Chapter 15

As I was leaving Coffee Animal, the guy I'd just rescued was remonstrating with the manager. Understandably so, because he'd come very close to being asphyxiated. From the snippet of conversation I heard, the manager was pointing out that they'd only guaranteed the snakes weren't poisonous. Not that they weren't capable of crushing someone to death. To my mind, the manager was hiding behind a technicality, but I had no intention of getting involved.

Back at Deli's salon, Gwen was sitting on the couch, talking to Nails. I could tell by her demeanour that she was pleased with the work she'd had done.

"You will allow me to come back for regular treatments, won't you, Nails?" she said.

"Of course, Gwen. I'll have the receptionist book you an appointment in four weeks if that suits."

"That would be wonderful."

Nails checked his watch. "Sorry, Gwen, but I have to go now. It's actually my day off, but I came in specially for your appointment."

"Of course. I really do appreciate you fitting me in at such short notice."

As Nails came towards the door, I pulled him to one side. "Thanks for doing this."

"No problem, Jill. Anything for an old friend."

Old?

"Gwen, judging by the look on your face, I'd say that went well."

"It certainly did, Jill." She held out her hands. "What do

you think?"

"Err—those nail extensions are very long. Is that what you asked for?"

"No, but Nails persuaded me it was the way to go, and I think he was right, don't you?"

"Err, yeah, they're very nice." Provided you never have to pick anything up. "Right then, Gwen, shall we go to the river?"

"You're the boss. How do we get there?"

"It's some distance from here, so I suggest we use magic."

"Okay."

Back in the alleyway, Gwen was about to cast a spell when I said, "Would you mind if I magicked us both over there? My knees are still sore from when you landed on me the last time."

"Fair enough. I'm sorry about that."

She gave me her hand and I magicked us to the riverbank where Liam had supposedly disappeared, and may even have been murdered.

"You weren't kidding when you said it was muddy, were you?" Gwen was trying to pull her heels out of the ground.

"I did warn you."

"Whereabouts exactly is this incident supposed to have taken place, Jill?"

"Over there. The police found the boy's blood on those rocks."

It was slow progress, but Gwen managed to make her way over there.

"Here?"

"Yeah, that's it. How does this thing work?"

"I'm going to put myself into a trance, but to do that I'll need absolute silence from you."

"Of course. Would you like me to move away?"

"That won't be necessary. Just make sure you don't make any noise."

"Okay. Got it."

She'd no sooner closed her eyes than a wasp started to buzz around my head.

"Shoo!" I tried to bat it away.

Gwen opened her eyes. "Jill, I just told you that I need absolute silence."

"Sorry, there was a wasp. It's gone now."

"Right. I'll try again."

Unbelievable! The wasp was back, but even though it was buzzing around my nose, I daren't make a noise or move in case I disturbed her again.

Fortunately, after a few minutes, it flew away.

I was watching Gwen for any indication she'd made a connection, but her expression never changed. I was just beginning to think she'd dozed off when she opened her eyes again.

"Well? What did you see, Gwen?"

"Nothing of any consequence has ever happened here."

"What do you mean, *nothing*?"

"Just what I said. No abduction or murder ever took place here."

"Are you sure?"

"Positive. My powers have never failed me."

"What about the blood?"

She shrugged.

"What does that shrug mean?"

"It means I don't know how it got there, but it wasn't

the result of a murder."

"But surely you must have seen it?"

"It doesn't work like that. Do you realise how much activity there has been here since the dawn of time? A lot. I just get the briefest glimpse as it flashes by. If there had been a murder or violent abduction, I would have spotted it, but there wasn't."

"Did you see anyone fishing here?"

"Loads of people."

"A young boy?"

"Lots of them. Look, I promised to tell you if there had been a murder or an abduction, and there was neither. Now, I need to get back to Candlefield. I've had quite enough of the human world for one day."

"Okay, thanks for trying."

Alone on the riverbank, I wasn't sure what to make of that. On the one hand, it seemed to back up Phil Black's claims that he'd had nothing to do with his stepbrother's disappearance (and possible murder). On the other, it left me with absolutely nothing to go on. It even had me questioning whether Gwen had any powers at all, or if it was all some kind of elaborate hoax. The fact that Grandma believed in her suggested she probably was legitimate because it would take something special to pull the wool over Grandma's eyes.

Before I could dwell on this any further, my phone rang.

"Jill, it's Don Keigh."

"Hi, Don. I don't have any news for you yet, I'm afraid."

"That's not why I'm calling. It's happened again. This time it was Freddie Primrose, AKA Custard Pie Face. We'd almost finished our meeting when he stood up, gripped his chest, and then collapsed."

"Have you called the police, Don?"

"They're on their way. The paramedics arrived a few minutes ago and they've already pronounced him dead. There's no way this is a coincidence, and no one is going to persuade me otherwise. I think you and I need to talk again as soon as possible."

"Do you want me to come over there now?"

"Not right now. There's too much happening here at the moment. Why don't I give you a call tomorrow, and we'll arrange something?"

"Okay, I'll speak to you then."

This day was going from bad to worse. I was getting nowhere with the Phil Black case, and now there had been another clown death.

***

I magicked myself over to Cuppy C.

"Are you alright, Jill?" Amber said. "You look really stressed out."

"That's because I am."

"Coffee?"

"No, I've not long since had one. Could I get a cup of tea, please?"

"Sure. Anything to eat with that?"

"No, just the tea."

"Why are you so stressed?"

"It's work. Every case I'm working on seems to be going nowhere."

"You'll sort it out. You always do."

"I hope so."

"Hey, Jill," Pearl said. "Were your ears burning this morning?"

"Why?"

"I overheard Grandma talking to Mum. She was furious with you."

"I don't need three guesses why. The hotel?"

"Yeah, I didn't catch everything she said, but she was livid."

"I don't care. Her hotel opened for business on Saturday, and since then there's been an influx of sups into the village. It turns out that all of them are new to the human world, and they have no clue how to behave. I caught two vampires as they were about to attack the vicar."

"Seriously?"

"If I'd been one minute later, they'd have drained him of blood. I had to drag the vampires back to the hotel, and then I let Grandma have a piece of my mind. I told her she had no right to target advertising at sups who had never been to the human world before, unless she made sure they knew how to behave."

"We have one of the brochures for her hotel in the back." Amber went to get it and handed it to me. The front cover read:

Hotel First Time.

The ideal resort for sups on their first visit to the human world.

It included several photos of the hotel and Middle Tweaking. All in all, it was a very polished brochure, which did a good job of selling the hotel. No wonder it was fully booked.

***

After magicking myself back to Washbridge, I drove to Stanley Trotter's house. I was hoping to find him in this time, and it seemed I was in luck because I could hear voices inside: A man and a woman. They were talking and laughing, but when I rang the doorbell, they fell silent. I waited but no one came to the door. I tried the bell again with the same result, so I knocked loudly on one of the door's glass panels. I was just about to give up when a man in his late sixties opened the door. He was smartly dressed and reminded me a little of Colonel Briggs.

"Yes, young lady, how can I help you?"

"Mr Trotter?"

"At your service."

"I'm very sorry to disturb you. My name is Jill Maxwell. I'm a private investigator, working for Margaret Plant, the lady who lives in the property which backs onto your garden."

"I know Margaret."

"Something was stolen from her house the week before last."

"How dreadful. How exactly can I help?"

"It appears the thief got into her house through the kitchen window. That means he must have come through the garden of one of the adjoining properties. I wondered if you'd seen anything unusual. Any strangers hanging around, that sort of thing?"

"No, I'm afraid not."

"Would it be possible to look at your garden, Mr Trotter? I realise you have company at the moment, so I can come back later if you prefer."

"You're welcome to look around now. There isn't anyone else here."

"Oh? I thought I heard you talking to someone."

"No, I live alone. You must have heard the TV."

"My mistake."

"Come in. I'll show you to the garden."

"Thanks."

He led the way through the house, which was spotlessly clean and beautifully furnished.

"You have a lovely home, Mr Trotter."

"Thank you. It's this way, through the conservatory."

The garden, which was considerably smaller than Margaret's, had high hedges on two sides. At the far end was the wall I'd seen from Margaret's property.

"Margaret told me that these two properties were originally built and owned by the same family."

"So I believe."

"Is it okay if I take a walk down the garden?"

"Help yourself, young lady."

He followed me down the path to the wall. As I got closer, I noticed that the padlock on the door wasn't locked.

"Is this door usually left unlocked?"

"Err, no. It's kept locked most of the time. I—err—took in a parcel for Margaret the other day while she was out. I used the door when I took it through to her. I must have forgotten to lock it afterwards."

"Do you go through to Margaret's garden very often?"

"Hardly ever. I've been thinking of getting the door bricked up for some time, but it's one of those things I've never got around to."

"Right, thank you very much for your time, Mr Trotter."

"My pleasure."

As I walked back to the car, I considered the possibility that Mr Trotter might have stolen the manuscript. His garden provided the easiest access, and he'd seemed a little flustered when I'd asked why the door between the gardens was unlocked. Surely, if the postman had been unable to deliver a parcel, he would have asked someone on the same street to take it in.

That wasn't the only thing that was bothering me. Mr Trotter had denied having company, but the voices I'd heard were not the TV. He had been talking to a woman. Not that there was anything wrong with that, but why had he felt the need to lie?

***

I hadn't exactly had the best of days, but at least I had one thing to look forward to—it was time to collect my new car. I just had to hope this scrapheap would keep going long enough to get me to the car lot. I crossed my fingers and turned the key. The engine made an obscene noise, but it did at least start.

Phew!

I arrived at Carr's Cars just before four o'clock. My new car was parked outside the office, and it looked even better than I remembered.

I parked my old banger out of sight, around the back of the building, and made my way into the office.

"Jill, you're very punctual," Charlie Carr greeted me. "Come inside. I have all the paperwork ready for you."

He offered me a coffee, but I declined because I wanted

to get out of there as quickly as possible. That man gave me a serious case of the creeps.

"Right, Jill, this is the agreement for the car. I just need a signature, there and there. Thank you. As I recall, we didn't get the chance to discuss the extended warranty when you were here before. I assume you'll want to buy one?"

"No, thanks."

"Are you sure? Repairs can be very expensive, and then there's the bodywork to consider."

"I'll take my chances. I definitely don't want to buy an extended warranty."

"As you wish. Where did you park your—err—*vehicle*?"

"Around the back. Here are the keys."

"Thanks. Happy motoring, Jill."

Even though it wasn't brand new, the blue car still had that new car smell that I love. When I turned the key in the ignition, the engine actually purred. I'd deliberately finished work early, so that I didn't have to rush home. I wanted to take her for a little spin.

I'd only been driving for a few minutes when I heard a knocking sound. Oh no! Don't tell me this thing was going to break down already. Maybe I should have taken the extended warranty after all.

The car was driving perfectly, but I daren't ignore the knocking sound in case it did some permanent damage. I pulled into the first lay-by I came to, and turned off the engine, but the knocking sound continued. How could that be? It took me a few seconds to work out that it was coming from the glove compartment, so I reached over and pulled it open.

I got the shock of my life when a little head appeared.
"Hi, there," the little man said.
"Who are you?"
"Henry."
"Why are you in my car?"
"I'm a car elf."
"I didn't realise there were such things."
"There aren't many of us left. You're lucky to have me."
"And you live in the glove compartment, do you?"
"Yes. It's been my home since this car came off the production line."
"Don't you scare people? Wasn't the previous owner a human?"
"Yes, but only sups can see us, and you're the first sup to own this car. What's your name, by the way?"
"I'm Jill. What exactly do you do?"
"Nothing really. Just hang around in here."
"Don't you get bored?"
"Sometimes, but I won't now I have you to talk to."
Great!

Chapter 16

The next morning, by the time I made it downstairs, Florence and Jack were already seated at the kitchen table.

"Morning, Mummy." Florence was tucking into her cornflakes.

"Good morning, my little flower." I planted a kiss on top of her head.

Before I could give Jack a kiss, he handed me an envelope.

"Happy anniversary, darling." He looked at me expectantly.

"Err, happy anniversary, sweetheart. I—err—I left my card upstairs. I'll just go and get it."

I know what you're thinking: that I'd forgotten to buy a card. Well, you're wrong. I'd bought one a couple of weeks earlier, but for the life of me, I couldn't remember where I'd put it. It would be somewhere Jack wouldn't find it, but now, neither could I.

I spent the next ten minutes going through all the drawers in our bedroom, but there was no sign of it. Defeated, I sank back on the bed, and was trying to figure out what to do when I heard little footsteps coming up the stairs.

"Mummy, why have you got all the drawers open?"

"I was looking for something."

"Shall I get Daddy's versary card for you?"

"It's anniversary, not—hang on, do you know where the versary, err anniversary card is?"

"You put it in my cupboard, Silly Billy."

"Of course I did. Let's go and get it."

I followed her through to her bedroom and retrieved

the hidden card. I was just about to take it downstairs, when she said, "You haven't written on it, Mummy."

Oh bum! All the pens were downstairs.

Unless.

"Do you have a pen in here, Florence?"

"There's one on my desk." She picked it up and handed it to me.

"Is pink the only colour you have?"

"Yes. Pink's a nice colour, isn't it?"

"It's lovely." I scribbled a message on the card and hurried back downstairs.

"Happy anniversary, darling."

Jack eyed me suspiciously. "Did you just magic yourself somewhere to buy this?"

"How could you suggest such a thing? I've had it for ages."

"I like the pink ink." He grinned. "It looks just like Florence's pen."

"Does it? Well, pink is the colour of love, isn't it?"

"You haven't forgotten we're having dinner with our parents tonight, have you?"

"I don't suppose we could cancel, could we?"

"No, we can't. They're all looking forward to it."

"I'm glad someone is. What are you planning to cook?"

"I'm not."

"You don't seriously expect me to do it, do you?"

"Of course not. I've ordered in catering."

"You have? Who?"

"A local company. They have a very good rating online."

"Hmm, I foresee a tiny problem."

"What's that?"

"How are you going to explain to the caterer that four of the guests are ghosts?"

"Oh yeah. I hadn't thought about that."

"You'll have to cancel the booking."

"It's okay. We'll be able to manage it between us."

"Stuff that for a game of soldiers. I'll talk to Aunt Lucy, to see if she knows of any caterers in Candlefield who can help."

"Do you think she will?"

"I don't know, but I don't have any other bright ideas."

"By the way, I've arranged for Florence to go to Wendy's while the six of us have dinner."

"When did you do that?"

"I had a word with Donna at school yesterday."

"Is Florence okay with that?"

"Are you kidding? She thinks it's a great idea."

After all the time I'd wasted looking for the anniversary card, I was running late. "I should be heading out, Jack."

"Have you remembered to put your Fitbit on?"

"No, I haven't. Thanks for reminding me." I hurried upstairs, retrieved it from the bedside cabinet, and rushed back down again. "I've got it."

"I still can't believe you took a bet with Winky."

"I can't lose this time. I'm on the go all day while that lazy cat just lies around the office doing nothing. I'll record twice as many steps as him easily."

"Hmm."

"What do you mean, *hmm*?"

"It's just that Winky has a habit of getting one over on you."

"Not this time."

I was just about to leave when Florence said, "Mummy, can I have a ride in your new car?"

"Yes, darling. At the weekend."

"Can't you take me to school in it today? Pleeease."

"I suppose so. Are you ready, Jack?"

"Just about."

"Come on, then. I'll drop you and Daddy at school on my way to work."

Florence insisted on sitting in the front with me, so Jack was relegated to the back seat. It was only a couple of minutes' drive across the village, so I took it really slowly. We'd only just set off, when a knocking sound came from the glove compartment.

"What's that, Mummy?" Florence said.

"It's nothing. Ignore it."

The knocking continued.

"There's something in here, Mummy." Before I could stop her, she'd pulled open the glove compartment and Henry popped his head out.

"Hi, everybody."

"Who's that little man, Mummy?"

"That's Henry. He's a car elf."

By now, Jack was totally confused because, as a human, he couldn't see the elf. "What's going on, Jill?"

"We have a car elf who lives in the glove compartment. His name is Henry."

"What's your name?" Henry asked Florence.

"Florence Maxwell." She seemed remarkably unfazed by the elf's sudden appearance.

"I'm very pleased to meet you, little witch." He turned to me. "How come the guy in the back is a human?"

"That's Jack. He's my husband."

"Is it okay for you to talk to me when he's here?"

"Yeah, it's fine, but I'd rather you kept it to yourself."

"Don't worry. My lips are sealed."

I dropped Jack and Florence near (but not too near) the school, and I was just about to set off for Washbridge when someone made me jump by knocking on the driver's side window.

It was Grandma. Great! Just what I needed to start the day.

"I'm on my way to work, Grandma."

"This won't take a minute." She pushed a folder into my hands.

"What's this?"

"Take a look."

Printed on the front was:

Hotel First Time.

Important information pack.

Inside the folder were several sheets of paper, which I flicked through quickly.

"So? What do you think, Jill?"

"You seem to have covered most things here. How did you get it done so quickly?"

"I have my contacts. I trust that you'll stop hassling my guests now."

"I wasn't *hassling your guests*. I was saving the vicar from certain death. That's hardly the same thing. And, providing your guests read and abide by these instructions, they won't have anything to fear from me."

"Good."

She was just about to leave when I said, "Grandma, how much do you know about Gwen Ravensbeak?"

"Only what I told you."

"But can she really see the past? Or is it just some kind of elaborate con?"

"It's definitely not a con. I know several people who have called upon her powers, and they all speak very highly of her. These are people I trust, so yes, I'm confident Gwen can do what she says. Why?"

"I took her to the location where a young boy was supposedly abducted, and maybe even murdered. She went into a trance, but afterwards she insisted that no such incident had taken place there."

"Maybe it hadn't."

"But the police found his blood on the rocks. That's what got my client convicted of his stepbrother's murder."

"You more than anyone should know the police don't always get it right. If Gwen Ravensbeak says nothing happened there, you can be sure she's right, and proceed with your investigation accordingly."

"I guess so. Anyway, I'd better get going."

"Before you do, I understand that you're having a dinner party at your place tonight."

"How did you hear about it?"

"I have my sources. I was just wondering what happened to my invitation?"

Oh bum! I was already dreading the dinner party. Having Grandma there too would be purgatory. But what choice did I have?

"Err, you're welcome to join us if you wish."

"Are you kidding? Wild horses wouldn't drag me there. Why would I want to share a table with that crowd? What possessed you to organise that little shindig?"

"It wasn't my idea. Jack arranged it as a surprise for our anniversary."

"That's what happens when you marry a human. It's your own fault. You reap what you sow."

It was nice to be able to listen to music while I was driving. The radio in my old car had stopped working years ago. I was singing along to a golden oldie from the nineties when the glove compartment opened and out popped Henry.

"I don't suppose you could change the music channel, could you, Jill?"

"What's wrong with this one?"

"I'm not a big fan of pop music. I'm more of a jazz person myself."

"Err, okay. I suppose so."

And, so it was that I had to endure twenty minutes of jazz on my drive to Washbridge. By the time I'd parked the car, I'd lost the will to live. It suddenly dawned on me that I was being taken for a mug. Why had I let Henry listen to the jazz channel when I hated it? Whose car was it anyway? It was time I stood up for myself. If he wanted to carry on living rent-free in the glove compartment, he would just have to put up with the music I liked.

No more Mr Nice Guy.

***

As I walked to the office building, my phone rang.

"Jill, it's Don Keigh."

"Morning, Don. How are things today?"

"Pretty rough still, as you can probably imagine. Is there any chance you could come over to Chuckle House this morning?"

"Yeah, but I need to nip into the office first. I can be there in about an hour if that's okay?"

"That's fine. We'll see you then."

As I walked up the stairs in my office building, I could hear dogs barking, which surprised me because since Bubbles had opened, I hadn't heard a peep from the canine clientele down the corridor.

I was just about to go through the door to my offices when I remembered that I needed to knock first. When I did, the barking became even louder and seemed to be coming from inside.

"You can come in, Jill!" Mrs V shouted. "It's okay."

I couldn't quite believe the sight that greeted me: sitting on Mrs V's desk was a cute little Pomeranian. On the opposite side of the room, Delilah was holding the lead of a spaniel, and Farah was trying to rein in a Rottweiler. All three dogs were barking at me.

Before I had the chance to ask what was going on, Farah said, "I'm really sorry, Jill. When I tried to unlock the door this morning, the key broke off in the lock, so we can't get in."

"Oh dear. Have you called someone?"

"I rang a locksmith ten minutes ago and he's promised to be here within the hour. As you can see, some of the dogs booked in for this morning have already arrived. Their owners dropped them off on their way to work. Mrs V saw us out in the corridor and was kind enough to invite us to come in here. I hope that's okay with you."

"Of course it is. I only popped in to check the post, then

I have to shoot straight out again, so you'll have to excuse me."

As I made my way across the room to my office, the Rottweiler was straining on its lead, so I gave it a wide berth.

Winky was sitting on the sofa, looking rather nervous. "What's going on out there? Why are all those dogs in here?"

"Don't panic. They'll be gone soon. The people at Bubbles can't get into their premises; they're waiting for the locksmith. Mrs V took pity on them and invited them to wait in here."

"I might've known the old bag lady would be behind this. She hates me."

"She didn't do it just to annoy you."

"You should charge them for being here."

"Don't be so mean. They'll be gone in a few minutes."

"Just make sure they don't come through here." He disappeared under the sofa, just in case.

Bertie and Bobby were just outside the open window.

"Hey guys, how's your love life? Have you had any joy with that new app?"

"Not yet, Jill, but we live in hope."

"I guess it'll take time for the word to get around."

"There are tons of profiles on there already. Mostly guys so far," Bertie said. "Lots of our mates have signed up."

"That's great. Hopefully, it'll only be a matter of time before the two of you are all loved up."

"Wings crossed."

When I'd finished checking the post (bills, bills and

something that looked like an award notification, but turned out to be another bill), I made my way back through the outer office, making sure to steer well clear of the Rottweiler.

***

The female clown on reception at Chuckle House showed me straight to the meeting room where Don Keigh and Trevor Hee were already seated at the conference table. Thankfully, neither of them was in clown costume.

"Jill, come and sit here." Don gestured to the seat next to him.

"Why don't you talk me through what happened yesterday," I said.

"It was terrible." Don shook his head. "We'd almost got through the meeting, and I was beginning to think that the curse had been lifted, when Freddie suddenly stood up and held his chest. The next thing I knew, he'd fallen backwards, knocked over his chair and landed with a thud on the floor. One of our committee members is trained in first aid; he applied CPR, but he wasn't able to revive Freddie. Do you have any leads yet, Jill? Anything at all?"

"I've spoken to the widows of Mickey and Randy, but nothing much came out of that. I plan on speaking to the other committee members next if you can provide me with a list."

"What about the Scrabble tiles, Jill?" Don said. "Any idea what they mean?"

"Not a clue as yet."

"It strikes me that you're clueless altogether," Trevor snapped. "What exactly are we paying you for?"

"Can I remind you that I only got involved with this case because Don insisted that I did. I'm happy to walk away from it right now if that's what you want. You won't owe me a penny."

"That isn't what we want, Jill," Don said. "Ignore Trevor, he's just upset. We all are."

"Understandably."

"You'll stay on the case, then?"

"If that's what you want, yes."

"Definitely. One way or another we need to get to the bottom of this. Trevor, get Jill a list of the members, would you?"

"This is a total waste of time." Trevor stomped out of the room.

"I do apologise for Trevor." Don was clearly embarrassed by the actions of his junior colleague.

"Don't worry about it. I'm not."

Chapter 17

By the time I got back to the office, the dogs were nowhere to be seen.

"I take it they managed to get into Bubbles, Mrs V?"

"Yes, dear, the locksmith arrived not long after you left. It's a pity because I was really taken with little Petra."

"Who's *Petra*?"

"The Pomeranian."

"Right. I didn't much care for that Rottweiler. I think he had it in for me."

"I'm sure he was only trying to be friendly."

"*Friendly*? He looked like he wanted to rip off my arm and eat it."

"Jill, I managed to find the address you wanted."

"For Phil Black's stepfather? Is he still in France?"

"Yes. He lives in Avignon."

"That's great, Mrs V. Well done."

"Are you thinking of going over there?"

"I doubt it. I'll most probably track down his phone number and give him a call."

Winky was under the sofa.

"Three hundred and forty-nine, three hundred and fifty!" He punched the air. "Get in there!"

"Winky, what are you up to?"

"Nothing." He couldn't have looked any more guilty if he'd tried.

"What were you counting?"

"I wasn't. You must be hearing things." He came out from under the sofa. "By the way, Jill, how's your step count coming along?"

"I haven't checked it for a while. You do realise you have no chance of winning, don't you? Take today, for example, I've not stopped since the moment I got out of bed, whereas you've been lying around the office doing nothing."

"We'll see." He grinned. "I wouldn't count your chickens."

"Why do people say that?"

"Say what?"

"What you just said. About counting chickens."

"It's just a saying."

"I know, but think about it. How many people actually keep chickens? Not many, I'd wager."

"Seriously?"

"And if you did keep them, would you really spend all your time counting them?"

"You've missed the point by a country mile."

My phone rang; it was Kathy.

"Jill, hi. I just called to wish you a happy anniversary."

"Thanks."

"I have a present for you and Jack."

"That's very kind of you, Kathy, but you shouldn't have. We never buy you anything for your anniversary."

"That's okay. I know you're tight-fisted."

"Gee, thanks."

"I'm only kidding. I was going to take it around to your place to give it to Jack, but our washing machine broke down this morning and I have to wait in for the repairman. Is there any chance you could pick it up on your way home?"

"Sure. In fact, I've had enough of work today, so I'll be over shortly."

"Okay. See you soon."

"I'm going to call it a day, Mrs V."

"Already? Are you feeling okay?"

"Yeah, I'm fine. It's our wedding anniversary today, so I thought I'd finish early and surprise Jack."

"You should have reminded me. I would've bought you a card."

"You don't need to do that. I'm calling at Kathy's on my way home because she's bought me a present."

"Us."

"Sorry?"

"I'm sure the present is intended for you *and Jack*."

"Right, yeah. That's what I meant."

"Are you doing anything special tonight?"

"Just having dinner."

"Out?"

"No. Florence is going to her friend's house."

"So, it'll just be the two of you, then. How romantic."

"Thanks." Some chance.

***

On my way to Kathy's, Henry stuck his head out of the glove compartment.

"Can we have the jazz channel on again, Jill?"

"Sorry, no. I'm not listening to that awful row again. I want to listen to some pop." I switched on the radio and tuned into a channel that was playing greatest hits of the eighties and nineties.

I expected Henry to go back into the glove compartment to sulk, but instead he began to sing along. That elf had the worst voice I'd ever heard.

"I didn't think you liked pop music, Henry."

"I don't really, but I do enjoy a good singalong. I'm a big karaoke fan. We should go together sometime."

"I don't really do karaoke."

"Why not? It doesn't matter if you can't sing. Not everyone can have a voice like mine."

By the time I arrived at Kathy's house, I couldn't make up my mind which was worse: listening to the jazz channel or having to endure Henry's singing.

"I'm sorry to drag you over here, Jill," Kathy said. "I'd have taken the present over to Jack, but I daren't go out in case I missed the repairman. I can't afford to be without the washing machine." She glanced over my shoulder. "You didn't tell me you were getting a new car."

"It's not new-new. Just new to me. I had to buy it because my old one had given up the ghost."

"Have you got time for a cuppa?"

"Of course."

"Go through to the orangery and I'll put the kettle on."

In the 'orangery', I took a seat next to the open French doors. As I looked out over the garden, the gnome holding a fishing rod stood up and walked across the lawn to where a gnome with a bucket was sitting. The second gnome then got up and walked over to the spot where the first gnome had come from.

When Kathy had told me she thought the gnomes were possessed, I thought she was crazy, but I'd obviously misjudged her because I'd just witnessed the gnomes swapping places. It was time I had a word with these two gentlemen.

Fortunately, the kitchen was on the side of the house, so Kathy didn't see me go out into the garden. I walked over to the gnome with the bucket, and then called to his friend.

"Hey, you with the fishing rod, come over here and join us, would you?"

"Me?"

"I don't see anyone else out here with a fishing rod."

Clearly puzzled, he walked across the garden and sat next to his friend.

"You're a witch," bucket-gnome said.

"Well spotted. Would you care to tell me what you two think you are playing at?"

"I don't know what you're talking about," fishing rod-gnome said.

"Do I look like I just came down the river on the stupid boat? You two have been swapping places, making my sister think she's crazy."

"We were only having a laugh. We didn't mean any harm by it."

"It isn't funny. What are your names?"

"I'm Len," fishing rod-gnome said.

"And I'm Ben."

"Len and Ben. Right. I'm Jill."

"If you're a witch, how can the lady in the house possibly be your sister? She's a human."

"I was adopted, but never mind about me. How come you two are living in this garden?"

"The man who lives here bought us from the garden centre. You're not going to tell the rogue retrievers, are you?" Len said. "They'll send us back to Candlefield and we really like it here."

"Yeah." Ben nodded. "This garden really catches the sun."

"I won't tell the rogue retrievers if you promise to behave, and that means not swapping places willy-nilly."

"But it gets really boring sitting in the same place all the time. If they'd just move us around occasionally, it wouldn't be so bad."

"Okay. I'll have a word with my sister and suggest that she moves you around the garden every now and then, but only if you promise to stay put the rest of the time."

Before they could respond, I heard Kathy's voice behind me.

"Jill, why are you talking to those gnomes?"

"I'm not." I laughed. "Don't be silly."

"I heard you. You said something about moving around the garden."

"I was just thinking out loud. I read an article at the weekend about garden gnomes."

"Really? In which magazine?"

"I think it was called Gnomes and Gardens. Anyway, the gist of it was that in order to get the most out of your garden gnomes, you should move them around regularly."

"What difference would that make? That sounds like nonsense to me."

"Don't be so quick to judge. The man who wrote the article was the country's leading expert in garden gnomes. He reckons moving them around makes it more likely visitors will notice and admire them. If you keep them in the same place, they just blend into the background."

"I suppose that makes sense. I'll mention it to Pete, and suggest that he moves them around every week. Come on, let's go back inside, your tea's going cold."

As Kathy started back to the house, I turned to the gnomes who both gave me the thumbs up.

"What's in it?" I shook the present she'd given me. "Can I open it?"

"No, you can't. Wait until you get home and open it with Jack."

"Won't you even give me a clue?"

"No. You were just the same when we were kids. You always tried to find your birthday presents."

"No, I didn't."

"Yes, you did. Don't you remember the year Mum and Dad bought you a CD player? You found it three days before your birthday, and you were so busy listening to the music that you didn't hear Mum come into the room. She caught you red-handed."

"I don't remember that. You're just making it up."

"If you say so. How are you and Jack celebrating tonight?"

"Nothing special. Just dinner for two."

"Where are you going?"

"We're not. We're staying in."

"That's a bit boring, isn't it? The four of us should have gone out to celebrate."

"You're right, we should have. In fact, that's given me an idea. Why don't you and Peter come over tonight?"

"Won't Jack mind? He's probably looking forward to an intimate dinner for two."

"No. He'd love it if you came over. What do you say?"

"Okay, but only if you're sure."

"Absolutely."

***

Florence hadn't needed any persuading to go around to Wendy's house for tea. In fact, she'd been asking me every five minutes whether it was time to go yet.

"Florence, are you ready? It's time now."

"I'm ready, Mummy." She came running over. "How long will I be staying at Wendy's house?"

"Just a couple of hours, then I'll come and pick you up."

Wendy and her mother, Donna, must have been looking for us because the door flew open even before we got through the gate. Wendy came running down the path and gave Florence a hug, then the two of them disappeared inside, chatting and giggling.

"Thanks for doing this, Donna," I said.

"No problem. Wendy's been looking forward to it."

"Is it okay if I pick Florence up at seven?"

"That'll be fine."

"By the way, while I think about it, you know those two vampires you saw in the village the other day?"

"Yeah?"

"There's a good chance you're going to see a lot more sups around here from now on."

"How come?"

"I told you that my grandmother had taken over the hotel in the village, didn't I? Well, it seems she's been targeting her marketing at sups who've never ventured out of the paranormal world before. The ads invite them to enjoy their first experience of the human world here in Middle Tweaking. That's why she called the hotel, Hotel

First Time."

"I take it you didn't know that's what she had planned?"

"I had no idea."

"It could be dangerous, don't you think?"

"It already is. I managed to stop those two vampires just as they were about to attack the vicar."

"No! Seriously?"

"Yeah. If I'd got there a couple of minutes later, he'd have been a goner."

"How did the vicar react?"

"Fortunately, he didn't even see them; he was oblivious to the whole thing. I dragged them back to the hotel and tore a strip off my grandmother. I told her that she had to provide all her guests with instructions on how to behave in the human world."

"How did she react to that?"

"She wasn't very happy about me sticking my nose in, but I threatened to get the rogue retrievers involved, and that was enough to persuade her to put together information packs for her guests."

"Do you think that will be enough?"

"Hopefully, but who knows? Keep your eyes peeled, would you? If you see any sups stepping out of line, let me know."

"Will do."

"I'd better get going. I'll see you at seven."

Aunt Lucy had come through for us big time—she'd managed to locate a company who not only worked in both the paranormal and human worlds, but were also able to fit us in at short notice. Candle Caterers had arrived dead on time and were busy in the kitchen.

"You're looking surprisingly happy," Jack said.

"Why wouldn't I be? It's our anniversary, after all."

"I know that, but our parents will be here soon. I expected you to have a long face all evening."

"Don't be ridiculous. I'm looking forward to it."

"Really?" He eyed me suspiciously.

Tee-hee. Little did he know.

"Where shall I put this?" Jack held up the vase Kathy had bought as an anniversary present.

"Can't you drop it on the floor, accidentally on purpose?"

"No, I can't. I don't know why you don't like it. I think it's quite handsome."

"Kathy never did have any taste. Stick it in the spare bedroom for now."

A chill fell over the room, announcing the arrival of my mother and father. Although the two of them still worked together at Cakey C, they rarely had a good word to say about one another. And, judging by the way they were looking daggers at each other, they'd already managed to fall out.

My mother threw her arms around me and gave me a hug. "I can't believe another year has gone by. Where does time go?" Then she turned to my father. "Sit down, you. You're making the place look untidy."

"Yes, dear." He rolled his eyes at me.

The temperature dipped again, and moments later, Jack's parents appeared.

"Hi, darling." Yvonne gave Jack a hug, then turned to me. "It's lovely to see you again, Jill. It's been too long."

"It's great to see you all," Jack's dad, Roy, had a smile for everyone.

We'd only just sat down, and Yvonne and my mother were already glaring at one another.

"How's Cakey C doing, Mum?" I asked, in an attempt to ease the tension in the room.

"It's going from strength to strength, thanks, darling. Sales and profits are increasing nicely."

"Did you manage to get your hygiene certificate reinstated, Darlene?" Yvonne asked.

My mother went red in the face and for a horrible moment, I thought she was going to launch herself across the table at Yvonne. "That was just a misunderstanding, as you well know."

"As I remember it, the customers deserted the shop in droves."

"That was because a lot of our clientele are witches. It stands to reason they wouldn't want to be in the same room as a witchfinder. That's why we had to let you go, Yvonne."

"Rubbish. You were just annoyed because I refused to serve food until you got the hygiene certificate renewed."

"Maybe we should change the subject, ladies." Jack tried to defuse the situation, but to no avail because my mother had the bit between her teeth now.

"My friend, Rita Rawhide, was killed by one of your kind." She pointed an accusing finger at Yvonne.

"What do you mean, *my kind*?"

Just then, there was a knock at the door.

"I'll get it." I hurried out into the hallway.

"Happy anniversary!" Kathy was holding a bunch of

flowers. Peter was by her side, with a bottle of wine in his hand.

"Kathy? Peter? What a lovely surprise."

Kathy gave me a knowing wink.

By the time we walked into the dining room, Jack was all alone at the table. Our parents had obviously heard Kathy and Peter and made themselves scarce.

"Happy anniversary, Jack," Kathy said. "I hope you don't mind us gatecrashing like this."

"We don't mind at all," I said. "Do we, Jack?"

"Err, no." Jack gave me an icy look. "Of course not."

One of the caterers popped his head around the door. "Are you ready to eat now?"

"Yes, please," I said. "It'll be the four of us."

"Four?" He looked puzzled. "I understood it was six."

"No, just four, thanks."

It was Kathy's turn to look confused. "Why did he think there were going to be six, Jill?"

I shrugged. "Miscommunication, I guess."

"What shall I do with these?" Kathy held out the flowers.

"Why don't you put them in the vase Kathy bought us, Jill?" Jack said. "It's lovely."

"Do you think so, Jack?" Kathy beamed. "I wasn't sure if Jill would like it."

"Are you kidding? She said it was the nicest vase she's ever seen, didn't you, Jill?"

"Err, yeah, it's lovely. I'll just go and get it."

Chapter 18

"You can keep saying it until the cows come home, Jill, but I'm never going to believe you."

It was the next morning and Jack was putting out food for Buddy. He categorically refused to believe that I'd had no idea Kathy and Peter were going to call around the previous evening.

"How could I possibly have known they were going to come over?" I said, all innocent-like. "I was just as surprised to see them as you were."

"Rubbish. I should have realised you were up to something when you were so upbeat earlier in the evening. I couldn't work out why you weren't in a foul mood because our parents were coming over. It was because you knew Kathy and Peter were going to turn up."

"That's not true, but you have to admit it worked out for the best. You saw how your mother and mine were going at it, and we'd only been at the table for five minutes. Can you imagine what it would have been like if we'd had to endure another two hours of that?"

"I'll give you that much. I felt sure those two would have put aside their differences by now."

"You clearly don't know my mother. No one can hold a grudge quite like her. All things considered, it turned out to be an enjoyable evening, don't you think?"

"Yeah, it was," Jack admitted. "I particularly liked the part where you had to scramble around in the spare room to get the vase Kathy gave us."

"Why did you tell her I loved it? We'll have to keep it out on display now."

"Serves you right."

"Mummy!" Florence came rushing into the kitchen. "When can I go to Candlefield again?"

"I'm not sure, darling, we'll have to see."

"Wendy says she goes to Candlefield when it's a full moon. What's a full moon, Mummy?"

"It's when the moon is a circle."

"Why does Wendy go to Candlefield when the moon is a circle?"

"Do you remember she told you that she can turn into a wolf?"

"Yes. It's scary, isn't it? I'm glad I don't turn into a wolf. I'd like to turn into a cute lamb, though."

"Wendy has to go to Candlefield when there's a full moon because that's when she turns into a wolf."

"Could I go and watch her do it?"

"No, because it would be dangerous."

"Wendy's my friend. She wouldn't hurt me."

"She won't while she's a little girl, but she might when she's a wolf. You wouldn't like it if she ate you for her dinner, would you?"

"No, I wouldn't. That would be horrible."

***

I'd got into the habit of knocking on the door before I walked into the office.

"Come in," Mrs V shouted.

"Aren't you making a video today, Mrs V?"

"I'm just about to record one, and I was going to ask you to help."

"Help how?"

"I've just completed a cardigan and I thought you could model it."

"On camera?"

"Yes. It's one thing to see it laid out on a table, but it would be much better to see it on a model."

"Sorry, Mrs V, I'd really rather not."

"Why not? You're an attractive young lady and very photogenic."

"Although that's undoubtedly true, the answer is still no. You'll have to find yourself another model."

Winky was on the window ledge, and there was a clicking sound coming from his direction. My curiosity was piqued, so I made my way across the office to get a closer look. It turned out that he was snapping photos with a small digital camera.

"What are you up to, Winky?"

"Do you have to creep up on me like that? I almost fell off the ledge."

"Sorry. What are you photographing?"

"Just the cityscape."

"Why?"

"I—err—I may hold an exhibition."

"Pull the other one."

"It's true. I'll call it a cat's eye view of the city."

Before I could question him further, Mrs V came through to my office.

"Jill, I have a policeman to see you. A Detective McDonald."

"Are you sure he isn't a farmer?"

Mrs V rolled her eyes, and rightly so. That quip was terrible even by my standards.

What do you mean, *what standards*?

McDonald was a giant of a man with a red moustache and beard. His Scottish accent was so thick, I struggled to make out what he was saying, but it quickly became clear that he was a member of the 'policemen who hate PIs' club.

"I expect you to drop your investigation immediately," he bellowed. "This is an extremely serious matter, involving three murders, potentially."

"It's a pity you lot didn't think that after the first or second murders."

"I wouldn't know about that. I only transferred to Washbridge a few days ago. All of that is irrelevant. All you need to know is that I don't want you anywhere near this case."

"Duly noted."

"I understand from Don Keigh that you have the Scrabble tiles that were sent to NOCA."

"Would they be the same Scrabble tiles that your people dismissed as no more than a practical joke?"

"Do you have them or not?"

"I do, but they aren't here."

"Where are they?"

"At my house."

"I'm going to need you to bring them to the station."

"Aye, aye, Captain."

"A-S-A-P."

"Absolutely. Message received and understood."

***

I'd been unable to find a phone number for Phil Black's

stepfather, so if I wanted to speak to him, I would have to go to France and do it face to face. I couldn't even be sure the address that Mrs V had found was still his current place of residence, but in the absence of any other information, I would have to check it out.

There simply wasn't time to take a plane, so I would have to resort to magic again. After using the map on my phone to locate the town, I prepared to cast the spell. This journey would be the furthest I'd ever magicked myself and I was a little nervous; I'd have to make sure I gave it my full focus.

I'd just closed my eyes when Winky piped up, "What are you doing?"

"Magicking myself to France."

"*France*? Ooh la la. Can I come with you, s'il vous plaît?"

"No, you can't."

"Go on. I've never been to France."

"You've always said that you don't like being magicked to places because it makes you nauseous."

"Yeah, but for a trip to France, it would be worth it."

"Sorry, Winky, but this is strictly business. I can't have you tagging along. You'd be a distraction."

"Go on. You won't even know I'm there."

"No, sorry."

"You're so mean."

I tuned out his whinging, closed my eyes and cast the spell.

The temperature in Avignon was at least five degrees warmer than in Washbridge. From what little I could see of it, Avignon looked like a beautiful place. I would have loved to look around, maybe even had a dance on the bridge, but I had work to do.

The address Mrs V had found was a house in the ancient town centre. The woman who answered the door said something in French that I didn't understand. Fortunately, I was able to call upon the 'translate' spell, which allowed me to speak English, and have the person I was talking to hear my words in their own language. Likewise, whatever they said would be translated into English for me.

What do you mean, I just make this stuff up as I go along? Of course the 'translate' spell is a real spell. You don't have to take my word for it—take a look in the official spell book.

Anyway, I digress. Once I'd cast the 'translate' spell, I asked her to repeat what she'd said.

She was clearly annoyed at having to repeat herself. "I said, I'm busy and I don't want whatever it is you're selling."

"I'm not selling anything, I promise."

"That's what they all say."

"It's true. I'm looking for a man by the name of Andrew or Andy Roberts. I was told he lived at this address."

"Oh?" Her expression softened a little. "He did live here a while ago."

"By himself?"

"No, with his wife and a boy."

"How old was the boy?"

"Fifteen, probably."

"It's very important that I speak to Mr Roberts. Do you happen to have his new address?"

"Yes, I do. Just wait there." She disappeared into the

house and came back minutes later with a scrap of paper.

"He moved back to England? Are you sure?"

"That's the address he gave to me."

I'd no sooner stepped away from the door than my phone rang.

"Hi, Kathy. Is everything okay?"

"Why are you speaking in French, Jill?"

Oh, bum!

I quickly reversed the 'translate' spell. "Sorry about that. I've been taking French classes."

"Why?"

"Jack and I have been talking about taking a holiday in France, so I thought it would be nice to learn the language."

"You'll soon get bored like you always do."

"Rubbish. Once I start something, I always see it through."

"Like the piano lessons?"

"My fingers aren't cut out for the piano."

"Or the horse riding lessons?"

"Did you actually want something, Kathy?"

"I just called to say that we had a terrific time last night."

"Yeah, us too."

"Really? I thought Jack looked a bit put out when we first arrived."

"No, he was pleased to see you both. Look, I'm sorry but I really do have to go. I'm run off my feet at the moment. I'll catch up with you later."

***

I magicked myself back to the car park in Washbridge from where I rang Mrs V.

"It's Jill. I'm just calling to let you know I'm going to Margaret Plant's house and that I probably won't be back in the office today."

"I don't understand."

Her response rather threw me. What was there to understand?

"I said I won't be—"

"No, I mean, why are you ringing me from your office. Couldn't you have just told me on your way out?"

Oh bum!

Mrs V had seen me go into my office, but I'd magicked myself from there to France. As far as she was aware, I was still in the room next door to her.

"I'm actually in the car park, Mrs V."

"But how did you get there? I didn't see you leave."

"Please don't think I'm criticising because I'm not, but when I came through the outer office, you'd actually nodded off."

"I was asleep? Are you sure?"

"Positive, but don't worry about it. Making those videos must take it out of you."

"I'm really sorry, Jill."

"Forget it. It's fine."

***

I was gagging for a drink, but I didn't want to risk going to Coffee Animal again. The last time I'd been there, the guy opposite me had almost been crushed to death by a snake. What animal would they have on offer today? Poisonous spiders? Scorpions? Alligators? No, thank you.

Instead, I decided to pay a visit to Aunt Lucy. I could always rely on getting a nice cup of tea there, and it wouldn't cost me a penny. Plus, the only animals I'd have to contend with were Barry, who might try to lick me to death, and Rhymes, who I suppose could try to bore me to death with his poetry.

When I arrived at her house, Aunt Lucy was just coming out of the door.

"Jill? I wasn't expecting you, was I?"

"No, I just called on the off chance."

"I'm on my way into town. There's a couple of things I need to buy, but you're welcome to come with me. We can get a drink while we're there."

"That sounds great."

It was a lovely day for a walk, and just what I needed to shrug off the stress of the cases I was working on. Aunt Lucy told me that her neighbour, Charlie, had now put his house up for sale.

"Good riddance if you ask me, after the way he treated you."

"I still can't believe he did those awful things to my garden. By the way, Barry was quite taken with the new dog groomer."

"That's a shame. I was hoping he'd hate it and that he'd refuse to go back there again."

"You're out of luck, I'm afraid. He said he wants to go there every time."

"That's great. Just great!"

When we arrived at the market, Aunt Lucy suggested

we split up so she could get the things she needed while I browsed. We agreed to meet back at the Market Cafe in thirty minutes.

It was ages since I'd had a good look around Candlefield Market. There were all manner of stalls: Some selling conventional goods that you'd find in most markets in the human world. Others were selling goods aimed at sups: spell books, magical potions and even synthetic blood for vampires.

I wasn't looking for anything in particular, but one stall did catch my eye. Until then, I hadn't realised that the vinyl record revival had reached Candlefield. The man running the stall was a wizard.

"Are you looking for a particular record, young lady?"

"No, I'm just browsing, thanks."

"Okay. If you need any help, give me a shout."

"Will do."

His stock was quite limited, just half a dozen boxes of records. As I looked through them, alarm bells started to ring inside my head.

"You have some very rare titles here," I said.

"Yes, that's our speciality."

"Could I ask how you manage to source them?"

"I can't tell you that." He laughed. "That's a trade secret."

"My husband collects rare vinyls. I'm going to make a note of some of these titles to see if he's interested in them."

"Okay. I'm here most days. Tell him to drop by anytime."

When I'd finished taking notes, I went over to the cafe to join Aunt Lucy, who insisted on buying the drinks.

"You'd better not tell the twins we've been in here," she said. "They get upset if I give my custom to any of their competitors."

"Don't worry. They won't hear it from me."

"Did you buy anything, Jill?"

"No. Nothing caught my eye."

"I saw you looking at the record stall. You have one of those old-fashioned record players, don't you?"

"Not anymore. I used to have one when I lived by myself, but when Jack and I got together, there simply wasn't enough room for all of our stuff. I think it must have got thrown away. It's a pity really, because vinyl is definitely making a comeback."

Chapter 19

According to the woman I'd spoken to in France, Phil Black's stepfather, Andy, had been living there with a woman, assumed to be his wife, and a teenage boy. His new address was supposedly in Bristol. Driving there and back would have taken too long, so once again, I elected to use magic.

The terraced house was located a few miles from the Clifton Suspension Bridge. The teenage boy who answered the door barely made eye-contact with me; he was much too busy fiddling around on his phone.

"Hi, is your father or mother in?"

"No." Clearly a man of few words.

"Do you know when either of them will be back?"

"My mother doesn't live here anymore. My parents split up."

"Right, sorry. Did you used to live in France, by any chance?"

"Yeah." He slid his phone into the pocket of his jeans. "Until about a year ago. Who are you anyway?"

"My name's Jill. I'm an old friend of your father's. I was hoping to have a word with him."

"He's gone into town to do some shopping. He won't be long."

"Can I come inside and wait?"

He shrugged. "I guess." He led the way to the kitchen where the laptop on the table had a game paused onscreen.

"I'm sorry if I interrupted your game."

"Don't matter. It was rubbish, anyway."

"I don't know your name, sorry."

"Mila."

"How do you spell that?"

"M-I-L-A." It was clear from the way he responded that he must get asked that all the time.

"How long did you live in France, Mila?"

"Not sure. Since I was little."

"So you must speak French."

"Course. I used to go to a French school."

"Which do you like best, living in France or here in England?"

"Don't care, really. Food's better over there, but I've got more friends here."

"Do you think I could get a drink of water, please?"

"We've got Coke if you want that."

"That would be great, thanks."

He took the bottle of Coke from the fridge and poured us both a glass.

"Did your mother live with you and your father in France?"

"Yeah. Until she decided to take off, then me and my Dad came here."

"What's that game you were playing?"

"Countdown to Death."

"It sounds a bit scary."

"Not really. It's pretty tame." He took a sip of his drink.

The original reason for my visit had been to talk to Andrew Roberts, but after speaking to Mila, I was now worried that if he saw me, it might spook him, and he could do a runner. I needed to get out of the house before Andrew Roberts came back, and I had to make sure that Mila didn't mention my visit.

After casting the 'forget' spell, and while Mila was still a little dazed, I emptied his glass, and dropped it into my bag. As I left the house, I spotted a man, with a number of carrier bags, walking towards the house. I had no way of knowing if it was Andrew Roberts, but I didn't want to take any chances, so I set off in the opposite direction. Once I was a couple of streets away, I called Phil Black. If my hunch was correct, that would change everything.

"Phil, we need to talk. Where are you?"

"In a coffee shop in Washbridge."

"Can you spare me a few minutes?"

"Sure. Shall I come to your office?"

"No need. I'll come to you. Which coffee shop are you in?"

"It's called Coffee Animal. Do you know it?"

"I certainly do. I'll be with you in a few minutes."

***

When I walked into the coffee shop, the volume of chatter was unbelievable. As I made my way to the counter, I realised it wasn't the customers who were making all the noise; it was the parrots in cages on every table.

The much-travelled beauty spot was now back on Dot's left cheek.

"Hi, Jill. Your usual?"

"Just a coffee today, please, Dot. It's very noisy in here, isn't it?"

"Tell me about it. It's driving me crackers. I think the management seriously underestimated how much noise these birds would make." She reached under the counter and produced a cage with a small green parrot in it.

"There you go, Jill. I'll just get your coffee."

"Who's a pretty boy?" the parrot said.

"Not you. That's for sure."

"How very rude. They aren't paying me enough to put up with your insults."

"Sheesh! I was only joking. I didn't mean it."

"Do you think I enjoy having to repeat the same stupid line over and over again? I'm an intelligent bird. I can hold a meaningful conversation with anyone, but instead I have to say all this gibberish."

"There's no need to have a go at me. It isn't my fault."

Once I had my coffee, I picked up the cage and went in search of Phil Black. He was seated at a table in a corner of the room. Phil's parrot was twice the size of mine and very colourful: yellow, blue, green, and red. As I joined him at the table, his parrot said, "Pieces of eight, pieces of eight."

"It's the first time I've been in here," Phil said. "It's quite a novel idea, isn't it? The animal theme, I mean."

"Hmm. *Novel* is one way to describe it."

"I take it you've been in here before?"

"Many times."

"Do you have some news for me, Jill?"

"Not really. I hope I didn't get your hopes up too much. I just thought it was time to update you on my investigation so far."

"Okay."

"Up until now, I've mainly focused my efforts on the riverbank where Liam's blood was found. I called in one of the country's leading experts on crime scenes. She's adamant that Liam couldn't have been murdered there."

"Really?" Phil's face lit up. "That's good news, isn't it?"

"It might be if she's right, and I believe she is. It certainly casts serious doubt on the evidence the police used to convict you."

"That's brilliant."

"Unfortunately, that's not going to be enough to clear your name. We're going to need much more. Ideally, we need to find out what really happened to Liam. That isn't going to be easy."

"But you still think there's hope?"

"There's always hope, but I thought it only fair to warn you that the longer I spend on the case, the more expensive it's going to be."

"I understand that, Jill, and I don't care. If I have to spend all the money my grandmother saved for me, I'll happily do that. What's your next move?"

"I've got one or two leads that I need to follow up, but there's nothing concrete to report today. Obviously, I'll keep you posted."

"I have faith in you, Jill. I know you'll come through for me." He checked his phone. "Look, I'm really sorry, but after you phoned, I got a call about a job interview. It's the first one I've had since I was released, so I'm going to have to shoot off."

"That's fine. You go, and good luck."

"Thanks. Jill, would you do me a favour, and take my parrot back to the counter when you take yours?"

"Sure, I'll see to it."

He left, leaving me the proud keeper of two parrots.

"Why didn't you buy us something to eat?" Phil's parrot asked me. "I'm starving."

"Me too," my parrot chirped in. "What's the point of us being in this cafe if you don't buy us a treat?"

"I'm sorry guys, but I wasn't hungry."

"Isn't that just typical of a human? You only think of yourself."

I didn't have the time or inclination to argue with two parrots, so I ignored them. I hadn't mentioned my hunch to Phil because I didn't want to raise his hopes until I was sure of my ground. To confirm my suspicions, I was going to need the cup he'd been drinking from. Unfortunately, I chose to put it into my bag just as the manager was walking past the table.

"Excuse me," he growled. "What do you think you're doing?"

"Sorry?"

"You just put one of our cups in your bag."

"No, I didn't."

"Yes, you did. I can still see it."

"Oh yeah, so I did. Sorry."

"Will you put it back on the table, please."

"I really need a new coffee cup. Surely, you can spare one."

"If you need a coffee cup, there are plenty of shops on the high street that will sell you one."

"But I really like this one."

"It's not for sale."

"Go on. I'll give you a fiver for it."

"I've just told you, it's not for sale."

"Please. Name your price."

"Twenty-five pounds."

"Are you kidding? Twenty-five pounds for one coffee cup?"

"Take it or leave it."

"Okay." Somewhat begrudgingly, I handed over the

money. "This is daylight robbery."

"Thank you, madam." He grinned. "It's been a real pleasure doing business with you. If you'd like any more of those cups at the same price, do let me know."

The two parrots were still moaning and groaning when I took them back to the counter, but despite having to put up with those annoying birds, the meeting had been very useful and might yet prove to be the key to solving this case.

***

After leaving Coffee Animal, I made my way to Vinyl Alley where Mad was by herself behind the counter. The shop was much quieter than on my last visit with only a few customers looking through the boxes of records.

"Am I glad to see you, Jill," Mad said. "It's been really quiet so far today; I could do with a good chinwag."

"I'm sorry to disappoint you, Mad, but I can't stay long. I'm up to my neck in work. Is Brad in?"

"Yeah, he's in the back. Do you want me to go and get him?"

"No, not yet. I need a quiet word with you first."

"Is something up?"

"I think I might know who's stealing your records."

"I should get Brad, then."

"Hang on. If my hunch is correct, the thefts are being carried out by sups."

"Are you sure?"

"No, that's why I wanted to check if the records that have been stolen are the ones on this list."

"I don't understand."

"I went to Candlefield Market with Aunt Lucy earlier today, and I came across a stall selling vinyl records. The guy running it was a wizard. He didn't have a lot of stock, just a few boxes full of records. As I was browsing through them, I spotted several of the titles that Brad mentioned when he told me about the thefts. I've made a note of several others which I want to check with you."

"Let me get Brad."

"You can't tell him about—"

"It's okay. He knows all about the paranormal world."

"How?"

"I told him of course."

"Mad! Are you insane?"

"It's okay. I figured I'd already told him about ghosts, so I might as well go the whole hog and tell him about you lot."

"*Us lot*?"

"Sorry, no offence. I meant sups."

"Does that mean he knows I'm a witch?"

"Yeah. I hope you don't mind."

"Not as long as he doesn't tell anyone else."

"He won't. He's the soul of discretion. Wait there." She disappeared into the back and moments later, the two of them returned. "Show Brad the list, Jill."

He glanced through it. "Yeah, yeah, yeah, yeah. These have all been stolen from us in the last two weeks. Who did it, Jill?"

"Roof sprites."

"I've never heard of them," Mad said.

"Neither had I until a few days ago when I bumped into Daze and Blaze. They told me they were looking for a gang of roof sprites whose MO is to get into buildings through the roof, hence their name."

Mad glanced over at the bucket. "Do you think they caused the leaks in the roof?"

"I'd bet my life on it."

"What do these sprites look like?" Brad said.

"Your guess is as good as mine."

"What about the guy running the stall?" Mad said.

"I asked him where he sourced his records, but he wouldn't tell me. He was being very cagey. My guess is that the sprites are fencing the stolen records through him."

"Do you think he knows they're stolen?"

"Almost certainly."

"What can we do about it?" Brad said. "How can we catch them?"

"I assume they're getting into the shop at night after you've closed. Why don't I see if I can disrupt their plans?"

"We couldn't expect you to do that, Jill," Mad said.

"I don't mind, and besides, it's definitely going to take magic to catch these little blighters. What time do you normally close?"

"Five-thirty."

"Okay. I can't do it today, but I can come around tomorrow night."

"That would be great, Jill, thanks. We really do appreciate this."

"I'll be here just after seven."

***

After dinner, Florence went out into the garden to play

with a very unenthusiastic Buddy.

"Jack, my darling," I said in my sweetest voice.

"What do you want, Jill?"

"What makes you think I want something?"

"Because the only time you talk to me like that is when you do."

"That's really unfair. You've hurt my feelings."

"Yeah, right. So, what is it you want?"

I picked up my bag and took out the glass I'd taken from Mila, and the coffee cup that Phil Black had been drinking from.

"Why does that cup have Coffee Animal on it, Jill? Did you steal it?"

"Of course I didn't. What do you think I am? I paid twenty-five pounds for that."

"If you're going to lie, at least try and make it credible. Nobody in their right mind would pay twenty-five pounds for a cup like that."

"I had no choice. It was the only way the manager of the shop would let me take it."

"So, what's with the glass and the cup?"

"Do you still have any contacts at the police labs?"

"So, you *do* want a favour, after all?"

"Only a teeny tiny one."

"What do you mean by *labs*? What exactly are you after?"

"I need someone to check the DNA on these."

"I assume this is related to one of the cases you're working on?"

"Yeah, it's the one I told you about, where my client was convicted of murdering his kid brother."

"You want to know if the same person's DNA is on both

of these?"

"Not exactly."

"What then?"

"I need to know if there's a family connection between the two DNAs. Do you know anyone who can do it?"

He thought about it for a minute. "There's Walt, I suppose. Walter Wheelie."

"Is that *Wheelie* his name?" I grinned.

"Jill, here's a tip. If you want someone to help you, don't make fun of their name."

"Sorry. Force of habit. Do you think this Wheelie guy will be able to help?"

"Maybe. I still see him occasionally at the bowling alley."

"So you'll ask him?"

"I suppose so, but I can't promise anything."

"Thanks, Jack, you're the best." I gave him a hug and a big kiss.

"And you're a manipulative creep."

"I've been called worse things. When can you get in touch with him?"

"I'll give him a call now."

"Great. Oh, and while I think about it, I have to go out tomorrow after dinner, and I might be gone most of the night."

"Why?"

"You remember I told you there had been a spate of thefts from Vinyl Alley. I think I know who's behind them."

"Who?"

"Roof sprites."

"What are they?"

"I'm not entirely sure, but I hope to find out tomorrow night."

Chapter 20

Florence clearly had something on her mind as she ate her breakfast of boiled egg and soldiers. "Mummy, you haven't taught me a new spell this week."

"I know, darling, and I'm very sorry, but Mummy has been really busy."

"You promised you would."

"I know I did, and I will."

"Can you teach me one tonight?"

"Not tonight because Mummy has to go out to work. We can do it on Saturday."

"But I go to dance class on Saturday."

"I know, but there'll be plenty of time in the afternoon."

"Okay. Which spell are you going to teach me?"

"I think it would be a good idea if you learned the 'propel' spell."

"What's that?"

"Do you remember when we went to the seaside last year and Daddy tried to win you a cuddly toy?"

"I wanted the cuddly spider."

"Yes, I remember."

"I was going to call him Spider, but Daddy didn't win him."

"That's right. That's because Daddy's rubbish at darts."

"I'm standing right here," Jack said. "And I still say someone had tampered with those darts."

"What is it they say about a bad workman?" I turned back to Florence. "Anyway, the 'propel' spell lets you throw things with great force."

"Cool."

"Did you just say *cool*? When did you start to say that?"

"Theo in my class says it. He says it's cool to say cool."
"Does he now?"
"What can I throw?
"I've not decided yet."
"Can I throw a dart?"
"Probably best not to throw anything with a point on it."
"What can I throw, then?"
"I'm not sure. I'll give it some thought, and we'll do it on Saturday."

After she'd finished her breakfast, Florence went out to play with Buddy.
"Jack, did your Mr Wheelie Bin say how long the DNA test would take?"
"*Mr Wheelie Bin*? You just can't help yourself, can you, Jill?"
"I'm only having a bit of fun. So, did Walter Wheelie say how long it would take?"
"I've arranged to take the glass and cup over there after I've taken Florence to school. I'll ask him then, but I got the impression that he'd be able to turn it around pretty quickly."
"Thank you, darling. You're such a sweetheart."
"So you keep telling me. I thought you might have had a lie-in this morning, seeing as you're going to be working tonight."
"That would have been nice, but I'm rushed off my feet. I can't spare the time."
"At least you'll be able to relax this weekend. We don't have anything on, do we? Apart from Florence's dance class, obviously."

"The way things are lining up, there's a good chance I may have to work." I took the envelope containing the Scrabble tiles out of my bag and tipped them onto the kitchen table.

"I thought you said you were busy," Jack said.

"I am."

"But you have time for a game of Scrabble?" He grinned.

"These were sent to the chairman of NOCA after the second committee member dropped dead during a meeting."

"Why are some of them coloured red?"

I rearranged the tiles. "The red ones spell the word *revenge*. See?"

"What about the rest of the tiles?"

"I don't think they're relevant."

"Why send them, then?"

"I don't know, Jack, but I'd get on a lot better without you looking over my shoulder."

***

Although Mrs V had given me the all-clear to enter the office, it was obvious that she had plans to make a video because the tripod and camera were set up on her desk. Standing next to Mrs V, was a very attractive young woman who, if I wasn't mistaken, was wearing the cardigan I'd been asked to model.

"Good morning, Jill," Mrs V said. "This is Ramona."

"Hi." Ramona gave me a little wave.

"Ramona is going to model my cardigan."

"Great. Are you two—err—friends?"

"No," Mrs V said. "I only met Ramona a few minutes ago."

Ramona elaborated, "Annabel stopped me in the street and asked if I'd ever done any modelling."

"O—kay?"

"I told her I hadn't, but that it was something I'd always dreamed of doing. She said this could be my opportunity to get into the business."

"Did she now?"

"I understand her channel has a large following."

"Hmm. So, this will be your first time modelling?"

"Yes, I'm a little bit nervous."

"You'll be fine, I'm sure. You strike me as someone who has a natural ability for it."

"Do you really think so?" She giggled. "Thank you for saying that."

"I'd better leave you two to get on. I have lots of work to do."

I couldn't believe the nerve of Mrs V, picking a random stranger off the street, and getting her to model the cardigan. Poor Ramona clearly thought this was her first step into the big time. Little did she know she'd probably be seen by no more than a few hundred yarnies. If she was lucky.

Winky was nowhere to be seen, but Bobby and Bertie were sitting on the ledge outside the window, so I went over to chat with them.

"Good morning, guys. How are things?"

"Okay, I guess." Bertie sighed.

"I thought you two were okay now you have the pigeon dating app."

"We're starting to have our doubts about that."

"How come?"

"We're beginning to wonder if it's just a scam."

"What makes you say that?"

"Look at this." He took out his phone, brought up the app, and began to flick through the profiles. "What do you see, Jill?"

"Err, some very handsome male pigeons."

"Now, look at these." He flicked through another selection of photos.

"What's going on with those?"

"That's what we'd like to know. The profile photos of male pigeons are selfies with the guy looking straight at the camera. Those weird looking photos are supposedly profiles of lady pigeons."

"None of the lady pigeons are looking at the camera."

"Exactly."

"Let me take another look at them."

He handed me the camera and I flicked through a selection of the female profiles. Very few of the photos actually showed the pigeon's face.

"Do you see what I mean, Jill?" Bobby said.

"Yeah. These don't look like selfies at all."

"We're beginning to think this whole thing is a con."

"Have you actually tried contacting any of the females?"

"Yes. Bertie and I have tried to connect with a number of them, but we haven't had a single response."

"To be fair, that's not so unusual with dating apps. At least, so I'm told."

"Yeah, but the same thing has happened to all our male friends. None of them has had any kind of response."

"That is odd." I handed back his phone.

It was more than odd; it was downright suspicious, and although I didn't say anything to Bobby and Bertie, I had a feeling I knew exactly what was going on. If I was right, someone had a lot to answer for.

***

Mrs Flattery answered the door at Margaret Plant's house, with a feather duster in her hand.

"Hello again, Jill. Is Margaret expecting you?"

"Actually, no, but I was hoping to grab a quick word with her."

"I'm not sure that's going to be possible. She's been hard at work in her office all day. I don't really like to disturb her."

"It is rather important."

"I daren't just burst in, it's more than my job's worth. I can knock on the door and see what response we get if you like."

"Yes, please."

As we approached the office, I could hear the sound of typewriter keys. Mrs Flattery knocked on the door but there was no response, and the typing carried on unabated.

"Will you try again, please?" I said.

She did as I asked, but there was still no response, and the typing continued.

"I don't think it would be wise for us to venture inside," Mrs Flattery said. "Maybe you could call back another time."

"Err, okay." I was all for going into the study, but I

didn't want to get Mrs Flattery into trouble, so I allowed her to show me out.

I hadn't given up yet, though.

Once outside, I checked there was no-one around, and then levitated over the gate at the side of the house. I'd intended to knock on the window to attract Margaret's attention, but the door into the study was open, so I popped my head inside. There was no sign of Margaret, which was weird. But not half as weird as the fact that I could still hear the typewriter keys, even though the typewriter was standing idle on the desk.

I went inside and followed the sound of typing, which seemed to be coming from one of the drawers in Margaret's desk. I pulled it open to reveal a tape recorder. Why would Margaret have made a recording of herself typing? And, more importantly, where was she?

I had a hunch that I knew the answers to those questions, and if I was right, that would explain what had happened to the manuscript. But first, I needed a closer look at Daisy.

***

It was ages since I'd been to Washbridge Library. In fact, the last time was when Mad was supposedly working there. I say *supposedly* because if memory serves me right, she spent most of her time hiding in a storeroom, practising her crossbow skills. Still, it had provided a good cover for her ghost hunting activities.

The library had undergone a complete revamp since my last visit—and not before time. There were lots of people browsing the bookshelves, and a similar number were seated at tables. And yet there was total silence: No one was talking, and I couldn't even hear anyone unwrapping sweets. I headed straight for the customer service desk behind which sat a young woman, wearing horn-rimmed glasses on a chain around her neck.

"Excuse me," I said.

"Shush!" She put a finger to her lips.

"Sorry, it's just that I—"

"Shush!" Her icy stare almost cut me in two.

"I—err—"

"Shush!" She pushed a notepad and pen across the desk.

"You want me to—?"

"Shush!" She nodded and made a scribbling motion with her hand.

I wrote my enquiry onto the notepad:

I am looking for books by Margaret Plant. Which section would I find them in, please?

I pushed the notepad and pen back to her. She read my note, turned to a blank page and wrote her reply:

On the mezzanine level in the general fiction section under P.

She pushed the notepad and pen back to me.

This time I wrote:

I'm looking for her latest book. Do you happen to know what it's called?

She studied my message, and then turned to her computer. Remarkably, she seemed to have developed the ability to use the keyboard and mouse without making a sound. After studying the screen for a few minutes, she wrote another message:

Margaret Plant's latest book is called Call for Murder. Our records show we have three copies in stock.

In response, I wrote:

Thank you.

After passing the notepad and pen back to her, I made my way to the stairs that led to the mezzanine level. Every other step creaked, and I could feel the woman's eyes burning a hole in the back of my head, but what was I supposed to do? It's not like I could levitate myself to the upper level.

Okay, if you want to be really pedantic, I *could* have levitated, but I doubt it would have gone unnoticed.

I grabbed a copy of Margaret Plant's latest book and flicked to the final pages of the story.

Eureka! Just as I thought.

I was about to take the book downstairs when it occurred to me that I wasn't a member of the library, so I wouldn't be able to check it out. As a resident of Washbridge, I was entitled to join, but that would have taken forever, particularly having to do it by passing notes back and forth. I didn't have time for that nonsense, so I made sure no one was watching, then used the 'hide' spell to make the book invisible. After creaking my way back down the stairs, I walked casually towards the door.

My silent friend had other ideas, though, and she signalled me to go over to the desk.

Oh bum! Were there security cameras upstairs? Had she seen me take the book from the shelf?

She wrote on the notepad and passed it across the desk to me:

***Couldn't you find the book you were looking for*?**

I wrote in reply:

I did find it thanks, but I realised that I've already read it. Thank you for your help, anyway.

Before she could write any more messages, I hurried out of the library.

***

When I got back to the office, Ramona had left.

"How did the video shoot go, Mrs V?"

"Excellent, Jill. Ramona is a natural. You should have seen her walking up and down the office in my cardigan. It was like she was on the catwalk in Milan."

"I must admit I thought it was a little cheeky of you to approach someone in the street like that and ask them to model for you."

"Ramona was delighted to have the opportunity to take her first step on the ladder to a modelling career."

"Err, right."

"In fact, she asked if she could do some more modelling for me. She even suggested that her boyfriend might be interested too."

"That's great. Have you uploaded the video yet?"

"No, but I was just about to. The Yarnies won't know what's hit them."

Winky was sitting on the sofa, talking on his phone.

"It's like I told you, Ricky," he said. "That guy doesn't know what he's talking about. Who are you going to trust, me or some chancer?"

Winky didn't notice me creep up behind him until I'd snatched the phone from his hand.

"What do you think you're doing? Give that back!"

"I just need to check something."

"I was talking to someone."

"Ricky? I'm sorry, but Winky has been called away. He says he'll call you back later. Okay, bye."

"How dare you!" Winky was spitting feathers. "That was an important business call."

He followed me to my desk and tried to grab the phone back, but I held him at bay while I flicked through the photo gallery until I found what I was looking for.

"Just as I thought. You, sir, are beyond despicable."

"What are you talking about?"

"I'm talking about these photos." I turned the phone around to show him.

"What about them? They're my cityscape photos for my exhibition."

"Rubbish. There is no exhibition, cityscape or otherwise. You were taking photos of pigeons."

"I have no idea what you're talking about. Why would I want a photo of a pigeon?"

"The game's up, Winky. I know you're the one behind the Pigeon Love app. That's what you were doing the other day when I caught you whooping it up under the sofa. You were counting the number of sign-ups you'd had."

"I—err—don't—err—"

"There's no point in denying it. I have all the evidence I need."

"So what if I run Pigeon Love? I'm providing a valuable service to lonely heart pigeons."

"Fleecing them, more like. They're never going to get a date through your app. You totally overestimated how many female pigeons would sign up, didn't you? When you realised how few there were, the right thing to do would have been to give refunds to those males who had already signed up, but instead, you added a load of false female profiles, and then tried desperately to get some photos to accompany them. When I saw you out on the ledge the other day, you were trying to snap photos of lady pigeons, weren't you?"

"No comment."

"Just wait until I tell Bobby and Bertie, and they tell their friends. I'm sure they'll all want to pay you a visit."

"You wouldn't do that."

"Wanna bet? I owe it to Bobby and Bertie."

"There must be another way. How about I share the profits with you? I'll give you twenty percent."

"No, thank you. I don't want any of your ill-gotten gains."

"Forty per cent."

"No. You have to refund all the payments and close down the app."

"I can't do that. It'll cost me a fortune."

"I'd better have a word with Bobby and Bertie, then."

"Okay, okay, I'll do it. I'll refund everybody's money."

"And close down the app?"

"Yes. Motherhood has turned you into a hard woman, Jill."

Chapter 21

It was probably fair to say that I wasn't Winky's favourite person. He'd just spent the last half hour giving me dirty looks, and mumbling under his breath about how terrible his life was. Needless to say, none of this had any effect on me. He deserved everything he got. I thought I'd grown immune to his underhanded schemes, but this latest one was particularly despicable. How could he take money under false pretences from his own friends? It really was beyond the pale.

My phone rang.

"Jill, it's Mrs Flattery, Margaret Plant's housekeeper."

"Hi."

"Margaret has just finished work for the day. She asked me to give you a call and said I should apologise on her behalf that she wasn't able to see you when you came around earlier."

"That's okay. I understand."

"She's feeling rather tired now and is going to have a lie down, but she wondered if you could pop over to see her in the morning? She suggested ten o'clock."

"That'll be fine. Tell Margaret I'll see her then, and thanks for calling."

When I'd left the house that morning, I'd totally forgotten about my plans to go to Freddie Primrose's funeral in the afternoon. Consequently, the white top and green skirt I was wearing weren't exactly appropriate attire. I could have magicked myself back to the house and got changed, but that would have involved too much faffing around. Instead, I used magic to change the colour of my top and skirt to black.

Winky looked up from his moaning and did a double take.

"What just happened to your clothes?"

"Aren't you supposed to be colour blind?"

"Don't be ridiculous. I may only have one eye, but I can tell the difference between green and white, and black. You look like you're going to a funeral."

"That's exactly where I am going."

"Before you leave, are you sure you won't reconsider my offer to share profits on the pigeon app? I'm prepared to make it a fifty-fifty split."

"Definitely not, and you'd better start issuing those refunds otherwise I'll tell Bobby and Bertie everything."

When I went through to the outer office, Mrs V did a similar double take.

"You weren't wearing those clothes earlier, were you, Jill?"

"Err, no. I'm going to a funeral."

"Oh dear. A relative? Friend?"

"No, it's no one I know. It's related to the clown case I'm working on."

"Right. I had no idea you kept a change of clothes in your office."

"Oh yes. Just for occasions such as this."

"I've never seen them. Where do you keep them?"

I glanced at my watch. "Is that the time? Sorry, Mrs V, I really do have to go, or I'll be late.

***

I'd changed the colour of my clothes so that I wouldn't look conspicuous at the funeral.

Epic fail.

How could I be expected to know that all those attending would be dressed in clown costume? Every single one of them! Even the pallbearers, who included both Don Keigh and Trevor Hee. And, instead of a conventional hearse, the coffin arrived in a clown's car, complete with wobbly wheels and an exhaust pipe that blew bubbles. I could have magicked myself a clown's outfit, but just the thought of that gave me the creeps. Instead, I waited outside the church and then kept my distance from the graveside. I wasn't even sure what I was hoping to see, but I had no other leads to pursue.

Freddie Primrose had clearly been popular because there were dozens of people in attendance. I was leaning against a tree, trying to stay out of sight, when someone came up behind me and tapped me on the shoulder, making me jump.

"Sorry, I didn't mean to scare you," she said. In keeping with the other attendees, the woman was dressed as a clown: she had bright pink hair, an orange nose, and she was wearing a red and green checked baggy jacket and trousers. "Didn't you get the note?"

"What note?"

"That Freddie had requested everyone dress in clown costume for his funeral."

"I'm afraid not."

"I must admit I feel a little silly dressed like this. I'm Freddie's friend, Matilda."

"I'm Jill."

"Are you family, Jill?"

“No. Actually, I’m a private investigator.”
“Oh? Why are you here?”
“I’ve been hired by Don Keigh, the head of NOCA, to investigate the spate of deaths that have occurred during committee meetings. Including Freddie’s.”
“But my understanding was that he died of natural causes.”
“More than likely, but Don just wants to be absolutely sure there was no foul play. It’s just a formality for insurance purposes really.”
“I see.”
“There’s a lot of people here today, Matilda.”
“I’m not surprised. Freddie was a very popular person, inside the clown community and beyond. Did you know he was a member of the Washbridge Dance Club?”
“I didn’t, no.”
“That’s where we met. In fact, he and I won the cup for the waltz last year. I still can’t believe he’s gone. Did you ever catch his clown act, Jill?”
“I’m afraid I didn’t.”
“It was hilarious. The things he could do with a dickie bow boggled the mind.” She glanced over to the graveside where the service had now finished, and people were beginning to drift away. “I’m going to go and offer my condolences to Petunia.”
“Freddie’s widow?”
“That’s right. Do you want to join me, Jill?”
“I don’t think it would be appropriate. I wonder, though, if you might do me a favour.”
“What’s that?”
“Would you mind asking Petunia if she’d be willing to speak to me.”

"I doubt she'll be up to that."

"I don't mean today. Maybe in a few days' time." I took out one of my business cards and handed it to her. "Would you give her this?"

"Okay, but I don't know if it will do any good."

"I understand. Thanks very much. I really appreciate it."

I was just about to walk through the cemetery gates when someone called my name. I turned around to see a sight that was enough to send a shiver down my spine: A clown running towards me. The only reason I didn't turn and run was because I recognised Don Keigh.

"Jill, I thought it was you. Why didn't you come and join the service?"

"I thought it best to keep my distance, and besides, I'm not really dressed for the occasion."

"Have the police been to see you?"

"Yeah, Archie McDonald paid me a visit, and told me to butt out of the investigation."

"How come you're here today, then? Aren't you scared you'll get in trouble?"

"Annoying the police is an occupational hazard. I'll stay on the case until you tell me otherwise."

"That's good to hear because I have no faith in them. They weren't interested until Freddie died. Did they ask you about the Scrabble tiles?"

"Yeah, I promised to let him have them. It's a good job you reminded me because I'd forgotten all about that. What are your plans for NOCA now, Don?"

"I'm not sure. Trevor has insisted we hold an emergency meeting this Sunday."

"Isn't that tempting fate?"

"It's not going to be the full committee, just Trevor and me. We're going to hammer out where we go from here."

***

As I was driving into Middle Tweaking, I noticed two figures walking along the side of the road, arm in arm. As I drove past them, I realised that it was the vicar and Marjorie Stock. It appeared that Barbara Babble, the village gossip, had been correct. Or at least fifty percent correct because according to her the Stock sisters were both romantically involved with the vicar.

When I walked into the house, Jack gave me a puzzled look.

"What's wrong?" I said.

"That's not the outfit you were wearing when you left this morning."

Before I could respond, Florence came running downstairs. "Mummy, you're home!" She stopped dead in her tracks and looked me up and down. "Why are you wearing black?"

"I had to use magic to change the colour of my outfit." I quickly reversed the spell. "Is that better?"

"Yes, I like the green and white." Florence gave me a hug and a kiss. "Can I learn that spell, Mummy? I want to change the colour of my clothes."

"I don't think so."

"Please! Can I learn it instead of the 'propel' spell?"

"No, darling. I'll show you how to change the colour of your clothes another week."

"Okay, and then can I change the colour of my clothes

while I'm at school?"

"No, you can't. You know the rules. You mustn't use magic when there are humans around."

"Apart from Daddy."

"That's right. Apart from Daddy."

"Why aren't there more sups in my school, Mummy?"

"Because we live in the human world. If we lived in Candlefield, everyone there would be a sup."

"Why don't we go and live in Candlefield, then?"

"What about Daddy? He couldn't come with us."

"Oh yes. I'd forgotten about Daddy. Let's stay here, then. I'm going to go and play in my bedroom." She dashed upstairs.

"Phew!" Jack pretended to mop his brow. "I thought for a minute she was going to say that she'd leave me behind."

"She'd never do that. She loves you too much. Hey, you'll never guess who I saw when I was driving into the village just now."

"Not more vampires, attacking people, I hope."

"No. I saw Marjorie Stock, arm in arm with the vicar."

"The gossip was true, then?"

"Could be. You haven't forgotten that I'm going out after dinner tonight, have you?"

"No. What time are you going?"

"I told Mad and Brad that I'd get to the shop about seven."

"How long are you likely to be gone?"

"I've no idea. It all depends what happens. I'm not even sure that the roof sprites are responsible for the thefts, so this could turn out to be a complete waste of time. Even if it is them, there's no guarantee they'll turn up tonight."

"You should take a book with you."

"If I do that, I'm guaranteed to fall asleep."

"Will you be able to have a lie-in tomorrow?"

"No chance, I'm afraid. All the cases I'm working on seem to be coming to a head at the same time." I glanced around. "Where did you put those Scrabble tiles? I have to let Big Mac have them before he locks me up."

"They're on the coffee table. I managed to come up with two more words."

"Oh?" I walked through to the lounge. "*Green* and *Yellow*? Is that it?"

"They use all the letters except the 'V'. Are you impressed?"

"Not really."

"It could be a clue."

"Right. I'll be sure to keep my eyes open for a green and yellow man." I picked up the tiles and put them back into the envelope.

***

I arrived at Vinyl Alley just before seven o'clock. Mad had obviously been watching for me because by the time I got to the door, she was already unlocking it.

"Come in, Jill. Are you sure you don't mind doing this?"

"Of course not."

"It doesn't seem right. Won't you at least let me stay with you?"

"No, I'd rather handle this myself."

"Fair enough. I've put some stuff out for you behind the counter. Come and see."

"A sleeping bag?"

"It's Brad's."

"I'd better not climb inside that or I'll fall asleep."

"We thought it would be more comfortable to sit on than the floor. There are biscuits, crisps and a can of pop too. Is there anything else you need?"

"No, that's great."

"You'll call me if anything happens, won't you?"

"Yeah, but don't stay up because there's no guarantee they'll even show up."

"Okay, thanks, Jill. We owe you one for this, big time."

"You certainly do."

After Mad had left, I settled down behind the counter on the sleeping bag. I'd not long since eaten dinner, so I wasn't hungry, but I did have a drink. Then I waited.

And waited some more.

Every minute seemed to last a lifetime. The only sounds I heard, were the occasional passer-by on the street outside, and the plop, plop, plop of water as it dripped into the bucket.

At some point, I must have nodded off because I woke up with a start. I glanced at my watch; it was one-fifteen. Had I heard something, or had it just been part of my dream? I wasn't sure, but then I definitely heard a noise. Something or someone was in the shop with me.

I crept slowly out from behind the counter to get a better view. Hanging from the ceiling, directly above the bucket, was a small creature. Dressed in blue dungarees and wearing bright red shoes, it was remarkably cute. His long hair was as white as snow. This must be a roof sprite.

His little hands gripped onto the edge of the hole in the

ceiling, through which the water was still dripping. Moments later, an identical creature appeared and began to climb down his colleague. This second sprite was also wearing dungarees, but his were lime green. The second sprite clung onto the feet of the first one, before whistling to the next one to join them. This continued for some time until there was a chain of sprites long enough to reach the tables. The next sprite to appear climbed down the chain, and then jumped onto the table. He took a list from his pocket and began to check each box; he was obviously looking for specific records. When he found the one he was looking for, he hurried back to the sprite chain, climbed it, and handed the record to a sprite who was in the gap between the ceiling and the roof. I watched him repeat this several times before making my move.

"You lot are busted!" I stood up and started towards them.

The sprite at the top of the chain was so shocked by my appearance that he lost his grip and fell, causing the others to plunge to the floor. They all began to run around in a blind panic, but before they could escape, I cast the 'freeze' spell on them all. The one who had been rifling through the boxes, still had a vinyl record in his hand.

I grabbed my phone and called Daze.

"Yes?" She sounded half-asleep.

"Daze, it's Jill."

"Jill? Jill who?"

"Jill Maxwell."

"Oh? Sorry, Jill, I was asleep. What time is it?"

"About half past one."

"Why are you calling me at this hour?"

"I've caught your roof sprites."

"*The roof sprites*?" She suddenly sounded much more awake. "Are you sure?"

"I'm positive. They were stealing records from Mad's store. I caught them red-handed."

"Where is the store?"

"Just off the marketplace. It's called Vinyl Alley."

"Okay, we'll be there in ten minutes."

"There's no rush. These guys aren't going anywhere."

It took her closer to twenty minutes to get there. Blaze looked half asleep.

"How did you know they'd be here, Jill?" Daze said.

"When I visited the shop the first time, Mad's husband mentioned they'd had several records stolen. Yesterday, I was in Candlefield Market with Aunt Lucy, and I saw a wizard selling vinyl records. I took a look through them, and a lot of the titles sounded familiar, so I checked with Brad, that's Mad's husband. He confirmed they were the records that had been stolen. They'd also been having trouble with a leaking roof which had obviously been caused by the sprites. I camped out here tonight on the off-chance the sprites would turn up, and lo and behold, they did."

Daze looked around at the sprites who were still frozen in place. "Blaze, round these guys up, will you?"

"It'll be my pleasure." He walked around the shop, picking up the frozen sprites and putting them in a pile on the table. Once he had them all, he threw his net over them and took them back to Candlefield.

"Thanks again," Daze said. "We really owe you one. Is there anything I can do in return?"

"There is, actually. How about you send me a photo of you in that dress?"

Chapter 22

The next morning, I took the opposite route out of the village because I needed to call at the petrol station on my way to work. I'd just paid for the fuel when another car pulled onto the forecourt. In the driver's seat was the vicar; sitting next to him was one of the Stock sisters, but this time it was Cynthia. This was proof positive that what Barbara Babble had said was correct: The vicar appeared to be romantically involved with both Stock sisters. What a scandal! Not that I would ever lower myself to tittle-tattle about such things.

Just wait until I got home and told Jack about it.

***

My first port of call was Washbridge police station where I intended to drop off the envelope containing the Scrabble tiles.

"These are for Detective McDonald." I handed them to the desk sergeant.

"And you are?"

"Jill Maxwell."

"Jack's wife?"

"That's right. I didn't think there was anyone still working here who knew him."

"They haven't got around to putting me out to pasture yet. I'm Tommy Gray." He offered his hand. "Jack and I used to go bowling regularly. Is he still a bad loser?" He grinned.

"The worst. You should give him a call sometime. He's always looking for someone to lose to."

"I might just do that."

The previous day, Mrs V and I had had a discussion vis-à-vis the video recording situation. I'd made it clear I wasn't happy about having to knock on the door every time I arrived at the office. Between the two of us, we'd come up with the idea of her tying one of her silk scarves to the door handle whenever she was recording a video. That way, if there was no scarf, I knew it was safe to go inside, as was the case that morning.

Mrs V had company: Ramona was there again, and with her was a very handsome young man.

"Good morning, Jill," Mrs V said.

"Morning, Mrs V. Hello again, Ramona."

"Hi, Jill. Did you see the video I did for Mrs V?"

"I haven't had the chance to look at it yet, but Mrs V tells me you're a natural."

"I'm so excited," she gushed. "Sorry, Jill, I should have introduced you to my boyfriend. This is Piers."

"Hi, Piers." I offered my hand.

Instead of shaking it, he gave me a little salute. This guy clearly thought he was too cool for school.

"Are you here to do some modelling, too, Piers?" I asked.

"Yes, but this isn't my first rodeo. I have quite a lot of experience, don't I, Ramona?"

"Yes, Piers is a foot model."

"Is he? How—err—interesting."

Piers lifted one foot. "You can't tell at the moment because I'm wearing boots, but my feet have perfect proportions, which is why they're in such demand."

"Fascinating."

"My normal fees are quite high, but I've agreed to waive them as a favour to Ramona."

"That's very generous of you. I assume you'll be modelling Mrs V's socks?"

"They both will," Mrs V chimed in. "I'm just trying to find matching pairs."

"Right, well I'll leave the three of you to get on."

There was no sign of Winky in my office, but Bertie and Bobby were once again on the window ledge.

"Jill," Bertie beckoned me over. "We have some news."

"Have you found yourselves girlfriends on the Pigeon Love app?"

"No, that thing was a total waste of time, but at least we've got our money back. That's what we wanted to tell you."

"You have?" I said, acting suitably surprised.

"Yeah, this morning, totally out of the blue, the money was refunded."

"Any idea why?"

"Not a clue," Bobby said. "But around the same time, the app disappeared altogether. It looks like it's been closed down."

"That is strange, isn't it? Still, it's good news for you two."

"Yes and no." Bertie sighed. "We're no longer out of pocket, but we're back to square one on the girlfriend front."

"Two handsome pigeons, such as yourselves, will find girlfriends eventually. You just need to have patience."

"I hope you're right. Anyway, we can't stay and chat. It's breakfast time and there are good peckings to be had down there." And with that, off they flew.

I'd no sooner sat at my desk than Winky came in through the window.

"Bobby and Bertie tell me they've had their money refunded." I grinned. "That was very kind of you."

"Like I had a choice."

"Trust me, in the long run, you'll feel much better about yourself for having done it."

"I very much doubt that." He jumped onto my desk. "So, are you ready?"

"Am I ready for what?"

"To compare our step counts. You haven't forgotten, have you?"

"Of course not. The question is are you ready to hand over fifty pounds?"

"In your dreams." He laughed. "Let's see how many steps you've clocked up."

I clicked the button on my Fitbit and brought up my step count since Monday. "I've done fifty-eight thousand, seven hundred and sixty-five steps." I held out my wrist so he could see the display. "Read'em and weep. That'll be fifty pounds, please."

"Not so fast." He pressed the button on his FitCat. "Three-hundred and twenty-one thousand, seven-hundred and thirty-two."

"What?" I gasped. "That's not possible. That's over five times as many as I did."

"That's what I've been telling you all along. Just because you only see me in the office, doesn't mean I stay here all day. I'm out and about as much as you are, wandering the city far and wide."

"But I—err, but—"

"That's fifty pounds you owe me. Thank you very much."

How had that cat managed to record so many steps? Did he really spend hours wandering around the city when I wasn't there? Jack was right: I should never have taken a bet from Winky because I always ended up losing.

When I went through to the outer office, Ramona and Piers were both sitting, barefoot, on the desk. Mrs V was busy going through her box of socks, which she kept in the cupboard, presumably picking out the ones she wanted her models to wear for the video shoot.

I had to admit that Piers did indeed have perfectly proportioned feet, even if his toenails were a little on the long side.

"Mrs V." I waited until she looked up from the cupboard. "I'm going to Margaret Plant's house. I should be back later, but if I get delayed, I'll give you a call."

"Alright, dear. When you come back, keep a lookout for the scarf on the door."

"Don't worry, I will. Good luck with the video shoot."

***

Mrs Flattery greeted me at the door and took me through to the office where Margaret Plant was seated at her desk.

"I'm sorry I wasn't able to see you yesterday, Jill, but I've had writer's block for so long that when the inspiration does strike, I have to make the most of it."

"No problem."

"Take a seat." She gestured to the sofa. "Mrs Flattery tells me you have something important you want to discuss with me. Do you have any leads on the manuscript?"

"No, I don't, but that's hardly surprising seeing as the manuscript doesn't exist and never has."

"What?" She sat back in her chair. "Of course it exists. It was stolen. That's why I hired you to find it."

"That's obviously what you'd like your publisher and agent to believe, but you and I know it's not true, don't we?"

She was clearly becoming agitated. "Jill, if this case is beyond you, just say so."

"It's time to stop the pretence, Margaret." I walked over to her desk, pulled open the drawer, and pressed the play button on the tape recorder. The sound of typewriter keys began to echo around the room. "This is what I heard when I called yesterday, isn't it?"

"No, I was working in here when you came," she insisted. "Although, I do sometimes play that recording when I don't want Mrs Flattery to disturb me."

"You're lying, Margaret. You weren't even in the house when I called yesterday."

"How dare you!"

"I came in through that door, and the office was empty." I switched off the tape recorder.

She hesitated for the longest moment. "Okay, you're right. I wasn't here when you called."

"It's time you came clean with me, Margaret. How long have you been in a relationship with Mr Trotter?"

"Stanley? I don't know what you're talking about. That's an outrageous thing to suggest."

"I heard the two of you talking when I called at his house the other day. That's why the door between your gardens was open."

"You've got it all wrong."

"I don't think so. What I don't understand is why you feel the need to hide your relationship."

"I—err—we—err—" Her words drifted away.

"My guess is that the two of you have been seeing each other for some time now, and that your relationship has encroached upon your writing. So much so that you haven't even started on your new book."

"Nonsense. It's almost finished."

I reached into my bag and brought out her latest book, which I'd 'borrowed' from the library. "I assume you recognise this, Margaret."

"Of course I do. It's the last book I published."

"It is indeed." I flicked to the final page. "A rather dramatic final line: ***And so, he took his final breath.***"

"I know what it says. I wrote it."

"You did indeed, and if I'm not mistaken, you did so on this very typewriter."

"I've written all my books on Daisy."

"Excuse me." I opened the front of the typewriter, removed the ribbon, and held it up to the light from the window. "Look at the last few words on the ribbon. ***And so, he took his final breath.*** That was the last time you did any work on this typewriter. You haven't started your new book."

She said nothing for several minutes.

Then. "You're right, Jill. I'm sorry I tried to deceive you. Stanley and his wife, Marsha, lived on the other side of the wall for over twenty years. I was friends with both of them. When Marsha became ill, Stanley nursed her for six years. It wasn't easy for him, and he'd sometimes come over here for a chat and a cup of tea—just to get away from the constant stress. During that time, we developed feelings for one another, but nothing happened, I swear. Not while Marsha was still alive. After she died, we continued to see one another and grew even closer."

"But why hide it? Neither of you has anything to be ashamed of."

"I know that, but Stanley feels it's too early. He believes people will think badly of him."

"That's nonsense. He has every right to get on with his life."

"I agree, but I felt I had to respect his wishes. The more time we spent together, the longer I put off working on the new book, which as you correctly deduced, I still haven't started. The publisher was piling pressure on Georgie who in turn was pushing me. I kept breaking one promise after another until, in the end, I knew I had to do something radical. That's when I came up with the idea of faking the break-in. I thought that would solve the problem, but of course I didn't take you into account. I suppose you'll have to tell Georgie."

"Not necessarily."

"Oh?"

"As far as I'm concerned, you're my client. If you don't want me to tell her the truth, I won't."

"What will you tell her?"

"That I've exhausted my investigations and I've drawn a blank."

"You'd be prepared to do that?"

"Sure, but it won't help you unless you're going to start

work on the new book. If you don't, you'll just end up back in the same situation."

"I will. I promise. If you can convince Georgie that the manuscript is lost, that will give me some breathing space."

"What about Stanley? If you carry on seeing him as often as you have been doing, nothing's going to change."

"We've already discussed this, and he's agreed that I should spend more time on my writing." She stood up from her desk. "Why don't you come and meet him?"

"He and I have already spoken."

"I know, but I'd like to introduce you properly." She led the way out of the door, across the garden and through the door in the wall. When she reached Stanley Trotter's back door, she let herself in.

"Stanley, darling, it's Margaret." He came hurrying out of the kitchen, but stopped dead in his tracks when he saw me. "It's alright, Stanley, Jill knows everything."

"She does?"

"Yes, she's one smart young lady. She managed to see through our little ploy."

"Oh dear."

"It's okay. She's promised to tell Georgie that the manuscript can't be found."

"It's very nice to meet you formally, Stanley," I said.

"You too." He offered his hand. "I'm sorry I lied to you the other day, but I'm sure Margaret has explained the circumstances."

"She has, and although it's none of my business, I really think it's time you brought your relationship into the open. I've just told Margaret the same thing. Neither of you has done anything wrong."

"It isn't that easy."

"Wouldn't Marsha want you to find happiness in your remaining years?"

He nodded. "Yes, she would."

"There you are, then. No more subterfuge."

Chapter 23

I was feeling pretty good about the 'stolen' manuscript case, even though I would have to pretend that I'd failed miserably when I spoke to Margaret's agent, Georgie Walpole. Margaret and Stanley had decided to 'come out' and make their relationship public. When I left them, they'd both seemed pleased and relieved at their decision.

I was on my way back to the car when my phone rang.

"Is that Jill Maxwell?"

"Speaking. Who's this?"

"Petunia Primrose. You had someone pass your card to me at the funeral."

"Hi, I wasn't sure if I'd hear from you, especially not so soon."

"I believe you're investigating the recent deaths at NOCA. Is that correct?"

"Yes, it is. It's more than likely just a tragic coincidence, but—"

"I don't think it is. There's something not right about Freddie's death. He was as fit as a fiddle. Would you like to come and talk to me?"

"Definitely, but only if you're sure you're up to it. When would be a good time?"

"Why don't you come over right now?"

"Now? Okay. Give me your address, and I'll be straight over."

Petunia Primrose's house was a fifteen-minute drive away. I'd only just set off when the glove compartment opened, and Henry stuck his head out.

"Are you planning on cleaning this car at the weekend,

Jill?"

"I don't think so. I've only had it a few days."

"You really should clean it every week if you want to maintain its resale value. Did you look after your previous car?"

"Err, yeah. Sometimes."

"People make the mistake of focussing on the exterior, but it's just as important to look after the interior."

"Absolutely. My sentiments exactly, but I do have a lot on this weekend."

"I could valet the interior for you if you wish."

"You'd be willing to do that?"

"Yes, for a small fee."

"How small?"

"Only five pounds. That's a bargain, I'm sure you'll agree."

"Hmm, I'm not sure."

"If it's my qualifications you're concerned about, I do have references. Would you like to see them?"

"No, that's not necessary. Go on, then, you can do it."

***

I wasn't sure if the woman who answered the door was Petunia Primrose or not because all the people at the funeral had been dressed in clown costume.

"Petunia?"

"No, I'm Hyacinth, Petunia's sister. Petunia is in the lounge. Would you like to come through?"

The curtains in the lounge were closed; the only light came from a standard lamp in the corner of the room. Petunia was swaying back and forth in a rocking chair.

"Would you like me to stay with you, Petunia?" Hyacinth asked.

"No, thanks. I'd rather speak to Jill alone."

"Okay. I'll be in the kitchen if you need me."

"Have a seat." Petunia pointed to the armchair opposite her. "Thanks for coming over so quickly."

"Not at all."

"Have you spoken to the widows of the other two men who died at NOCA meetings?"

"Patricia and Charlene? Yes, I have."

"Do you really think there's a possibility of foul play?"

"I honestly don't know, but I think it's important that we at least rule it out."

"I totally agree. I'm finding it hard to accept what happened to Freddie."

"Why don't you tell me about your husband?"

"We were together for twelve years, married for ten of those. It was a second marriage for both of us. Freddie was very different to my first husband, Bernard, God rest his soul. Bernard was a civil servant; he was a kind, generous man, but he wasn't exactly known for his sense of humour. Two years after Bernard died in a car crash, Freddie and I got together."

"How did you meet?"

"It was fate." She smiled at the memory. "It was my niece's birthday, and Freddie had been hired to provide the entertainment. We got talking and just seemed to hit it off; we've been together ever since. Most of that time we've spent laughing. Freddie made his living from being a clown, but the truth is he never switched off. He just loved to make people laugh; he would have done it even if he hadn't been paid. Did you ever catch his act, Jill?"

"No, I'm sorry to say I didn't."

"It's okay. I won't ask you to watch his videos. I know you're afraid of clowns."

"What makes you think that?"

"Why else would you have dressed in your normal clothes and stayed back from the service yesterday? It's okay, we all have our phobias."

"Err, right. You mentioned on the phone that your husband had been in good health?"

"That's right. Freddie was very health conscious. He exercised regularly and ate healthily. He was in great condition for a man of his age."

"What about his mental health? Was he under any kind of stress?"

"Stress? Freddie?" She laughed. "He didn't know the meaning of the word. He was always happy, always joking. He always looked on the bright side of life. For example, on the day he died, he went out to the car and found he had a flat tyre. I'd have been totally stressed out about something like that, but Freddie just took it in his stride. He said that he'd call a taxi, and he'd get it fixed when he came home. But then Trevor called, and said he'd swing by to give Freddie a lift."

"Trevor Hee?"

"Yes. Such a nice young man. That was the last time I saw Freddie alive." She began to cry. "I'm sorry, Jill. I don't think I can do this anymore today."

"I understand. Thanks for talking to me."

When I left Petunia's house, Hyacinth was trying to console her sister. I felt bad at having intruded at such a difficult time, but the conversation had certainly given me food for thought.

Before I got into the car, I called Charlene Vallance.

"Charlene, it's Jill Maxwell. I came to see you the other day."

"Hi."

"Just a quick question, please. You mentioned that Mickey's car had broken down on the day of the NOCA meeting, but that he'd managed to get a lift with someone."

"That's right. I wish he hadn't made it to the meeting. He might still be alive."

"Who gave him a lift?"

"Trevor Hee. Why?"

"Err, no reason. I just wondered. Thanks, Charlene." I ended the call before she could ask any more questions.

It was now clear there was one common denominator that linked the three men's deaths, and that was Trevor Hee. Freddie Primrose and Mickey Vallance had both had car trouble on the day they died, and it had been the gallant Trevor Hee who'd given them a lift to the NOCA meeting. When Randy Seaburn had lost his wallet, it had once again been Trevor Hee who had come to the rescue. This was way too much of a coincidence for my liking. I would need to take a closer look at Mr Hee, but that would have to wait because while I'd been on the phone to Charlene, I'd received a text from Georgie Walpole. She'd just spoken to Margaret Plant who'd told her that I wanted to speak to her. The text said she would be calling into my office that afternoon and that she was hoping to hear good news.

She was in for a big disappointment.

***

As I approached the office building, I spotted something out of the corner of my eye: Coming out of the window of my office was a cat.

But it wasn't Winky.

I watched the tabby as he made his way down the fire escape. When he got closer to the ground, I could see that he had something tucked into his collar: A twenty-pound note.

"Hey, you! What are you up to?"

He jumped. "You shouldn't go around shouting at people like that. I could have had a heart attack. You witches have no consideration."

"What's that money tucked into your collar?"

"What's it got to do with you? Mind your own business."

"Actually, it is *my* business because that's my office you just came out of."

"Oh, right. I didn't realise."

"Did you take that money from my desk?"

"No, I didn't. I'm not a thief and I don't appreciate you insinuating that I am."

"Where did the money come from, then?"

"If you must know, it's the proceeds of a business transaction."

"With Winky, I assume?"

"That's right. He and I go way back."

"What kind of business transaction?"

"I don't suppose it can do any harm to tell you because it's all done and dusted now. As you can probably tell from my athletic physique, I'm into sports, mainly marathon running. Winky gave me a call at the beginning of the week and offered me some cash if I'd test drive his FitCat."

"What do you mean, *test drive*?"

"He wanted me to wear it while I was doing my training."

"Did he now? And how long did you do that for?"

"I started wearing it on Monday, and I gave it back to him first thing this morning. He didn't have the cash for me then, so I had to pop back for it just now."

"Sorry, I didn't catch your name."

"Marti. Everyone knows me as Marti the Marathon."

"Right, Marti, thanks for your time."

There wasn't a scarf tied around the door handle, so I let myself into the office.

"Sorry, Jill. I can't talk." Mrs V was busy on the computer. "I'm in the middle of editing the socks video."

"No problem. I'll catch up with you later."

Winky was lying on the sofa, looking like butter wouldn't melt.

"Tell me, Winky, how is it that whenever I come into the office, you're always lounging around. And yet, somehow, you managed to clock up more steps than I did?"

"It's like I said before, I spend most of the day out and about in the city. I get plenty of exercise."

"It's just a coincidence that you're almost always here when I come in, is it?"

"Yep."

"Interesting. On my way in just now, I got talking to a friend of yours."

"Oh?"

"Now, what was his name? Oh yes, I remember; it was Marti."

Winky's face fell. "I don't think I know any Martis."

"Think harder. Apparently, most people know him as Marti the Marathon."

"I—err—sorry, it still doesn't ring any bells."

"That's rather strange because Marti certainly knows you. In fact, he was just telling me about your little business arrangement. The one where he wore your FitCat during the week and you paid him twenty pounds."

"I—err—"

"It's no good denying it. The game's up." I held out my hand.

"What's that for?"

"The hundred pounds you owe me. That's the fifty you cheated me out of, and the fifty you owe me for beating your step count."

"But I've just given Marti twenty pounds."

"I thought you didn't know him. You are a liar and a cheat."

"I—err—okay, I do know him, but the whole thing was only a joke."

"And very funny it was too. Look, I'm laughing. Ha, ha, ha. Now give me my money."

It would be fair to say that Winky wasn't having the best of weeks. First, he'd had to refund all the payments he'd received through his pigeon dating app. Then, he'd had to pay out on our bet, as well as paying Marti the Marathon his twenty pounds.

He was now sulking under the sofa. Not that he would

get any sympathy from me because he'd brought it all on himself.

Mrs V popped her head around the door.

"Jill, Georgina Walpole is here to see you."

Oh bum! I really wasn't looking forward to this meeting.

"Send her in, Mrs V, would you?"

"What's going on, Jill?" Georgie demanded. "I asked Margaret what the situation was with the manuscript, but she said I had to ask you. I hope you have good news for me."

"I'm afraid not."

"You must have some leads, though?"

"None. I've hit a brick wall which is why I have to drop the case."

"Drop it?"

"I wouldn't want to continue to take your money when I know there's no hope of a positive outcome."

"What do you mean, *continue to take it*? You can't possibly intend to bill us at all. You've done nothing."

"I can assure you, Georgie, that—"

"It's Ms Walpole to you." She snapped.

"Right. I can assure you, *Ms Walpole,* that I've carried out a thorough investigation."

"There's no way we'll be paying you a single penny. Not only have you produced no results, but because of you, we've wasted another two weeks during which time Margaret could have begun her rewrite. It's going to be at least another year before the book can be published now. This is going to cost us a small fortune. I don't know how you have the nerve to call yourself a private investigator.

You're just an amateur." And with that she turned on her heels and stormed out of the room.

Fortunately, Margaret Plant had told me to submit my invoice directly to her, and had promised that she would pay it herself. She'd even said that she intended to add a small bonus.

Georgie had no sooner left, than Winky came out from under the sofa.

"Another satisfied client." He smirked.

"Shut it, you. You're on very thin ice. If you're not careful, you'll be looking for a new home."

"You'd never throw me out. You couldn't live without me. By the way, how's that recruitment drive of yours going? Have you found yourself another private investigator yet? It sounds like you could do with someone who knows what they're doing."

I hadn't checked my job ad for a few days, so I pulled up the website and logged into my account. So far, there had been only three applications. The first one was a complete no-hoper: The woman had apparently worked for several years as a hygiene inspector, and she somehow thought that qualified her to work as a private investigator. The second applicant was no better: This guy had spent most of his life behind bars; his pitch was that he could be poacher turned gamekeeper. He too went onto the rejection pile. The third applicant looked much more promising. The guy was called Felix Perkins and had, apparently, spent several years in the private investigator arena, during which time he'd had experience of cases of all kinds. He described himself as a self-starter who could make an immediate impact. This guy was definitely worth adding to my shortlist (of one). I would give it a few more days for more applications to come in, and then think about arranging interviews.

Chapter 24

It was Saturday morning and I was taking Florence to dance class. Jack had had a phone call the previous night from Tommy Gray, the desk sergeant I'd spoken to when I handed the Scrabble tiles in. Being the kind-hearted and selfless wife that I am, I'd told Jack that he could go bowling with his old friend.

What? I know he didn't need my permission, but I granted it anyway.

Young children have a habit of speaking their minds. That isn't necessarily a bad thing, but it can be a little embarrassing sometimes.

"Mummy, look!" Florence tugged at my arm. "Why is that man wobbling around?"

I could feel the colour rising in my cheeks as I turned to see who she was pointing at. I was desperately hoping that whoever it was hadn't heard what she'd said. I assumed it would be an old man, unsteady on his feet, or maybe someone the worse for drink.

It was neither of those.

Unless I was very much mistaken, the 'man' wasn't actually a man at all. At least, not a *human* man. The 'man' was a number of pixies, standing on each other's shoulders, under an overcoat. I'd seen exactly the same thing some years ago when a pixie called Colin Wragg had visited my office. Because pixies are so small, it's impossible for them to move around the human world unnoticed unless they have some kind of disguise. This group were definitely going to have to work on their balancing skills.

I didn't see any point in lying to Florence.

"That's not a man, darling. It's pixies. Under that coat, there are probably nine or ten of them, standing on each other's shoulders. That's why they're wobbling around so much."

"I hope they don't fall over, Mummy."

"Me too."

Donna and I were sitting next to one another in the village hall, watching Florence, Wendy and the rest of their group going through their latest dance routine (which looked remarkably like their previous two routines).

"This is definitely the business to be in," I said. "The woman who runs these classes must be coining it."

"Can you dance, Jill?"

"Me? Yeah, I'm a natural."

"Really?"

"No, I've got two left feet. My sister, Kathy, was the dancer in our family. You could barely move in our house for all the medals she brought home."

"That reminds me. Did Florence give you the leaflet about the dance exams?"

"No, I haven't seen one. Maybe she gave it to Jack. What exams?"

"They're in a couple of weeks. They try to get all the girls to take them." She leaned closer and said in a hushed voice, "It's just an excuse to charge more money. From what the other parents have told me, no one ever fails them."

"That sounds exactly the same as Kathy's dance class. She got a medal just for showing up."

"By the way, Jill, I've seen a few sups around the village. I assume they're staying at your grandmother's hotel."

"Almost certainly. She must be making bank too."

"I saw a vampire, standing in the street, drinking a bottle of synthetic blood just now. At least, I hope it was synthetic."

"Why couldn't he have done that in the hotel? I'll have to have another word with Grandma. On our way here, Florence and I saw a group of pixies."

"*Pixies*? How can they possibly go unnoticed? They're tiny."

"I've seen it done before. A bunch of them stand on each other's shoulders, and then put on an overcoat so it looks like a human man."

"That's clever."

"Only if their balancing skills are up to it. The ones I saw this morning were struggling to stay upright."

"Oh dear." She smiled. "Ronnie and I are taking Wendy to my mother's this afternoon. I can't say I'm looking forward to it. My mother and I don't get on particularly well, but Wendy loves her Grandma. What about you, Jill? Have you got anything planned for later?"

"I promised to teach Florence a new spell."

"How are her magic lessons coming along?"

"Okay, although she gave us a bit of a shock in the week."

"What happened?"

"Unbeknown to me, the little madam had taught herself the 'invisible' spell and used it to scare Jack. He saw a spoon floating across the kitchen, and thought we had a ghost in the house."

Donna laughed. "Poor Jack."

"I thought it was hilarious, but I couldn't let Florence know that. I had to pretend to be annoyed and tell her off. Hey, Donna, would it be okay if I nipped out to the store? We're out of spaghetti rings, Florence's favourite."

"Sure, it'll be another half hour until they finish. You shoot off."

I hurried out of the hall and across the village. As I was approaching the store, I spotted the vicar going inside. Which of the Stock sisters was he visiting, I wondered? I soon had my answer because he was standing at the counter, chatting to Marjorie.

I headed to the 'S' section, but after five minutes, I'd been unable to locate the spaghetti rings. I was about to go to the counter to ask for assistance when Cynthia walked into the shop. Oh boy! The sparks were going to fly now. I held back, waiting for the shouting to begin, but instead I heard the three of them chatting and laughing. Curiosity got the better of me, so I headed to the counter.

"Hi, Jill," Marjorie said. "Did you find what you were looking for?"

"Actually, no. I'm after some spaghetti rings, but I couldn't see them in the 'S' section."

"You need the 'R' section. R for rings."

"Right. I should have realised."

"You know our cousin, the vicar, don't you, Jill?"

The vicar turned around. "Jill and I have spoken a few times, haven't we?"

"Err, yeah. I didn't realise Marjorie and Cynthia were your cousins. I thought—err—that's to say, Barbara said—err—" I stopped before I dug myself any deeper into the hole.

"*Barbara*?" The vicar gave me a puzzled look. "What did she say?"

"Not *Barbara*. The *barber*. He said—err—I should get some—err—cheese while I was here. I almost forgot."

"The barber told you to buy cheese?" It was Marjorie's turn to look confused.

"Yeah, he insists he cuts hair much better with a bit of cheddar to nibble on."

Now all three of them looked bewildered, but I ignored their puzzled expressions, grabbed a lump of cheddar cheese, paid for my purchase and hightailed it out of there.

"Did you get them?" Donna asked when I got back to the village hall.

"Sorry?"

"The spaghetti rings, did you manage to get any?"

"I—err—no, I bought some cheese instead."

***

Thankfully, dance class was over. After Florence and I had said our goodbyes to Donna and Wendy, we went home and had a light lunch.

"Mummy, is it time to learn the 'propel' spell?" Florence gobbled down the last of her sandwich.

"Yes, I'll just go and get the spell book."

"Where have you hidden it, Mummy?"

"That would be telling, wouldn't it? You wait down here while I go and get it. And no sneaking up after me. If you do, I won't teach you any more magic."

"I'll wait here, I promise."

When I got to our bedroom, I quickly checked Florence

hadn't followed me, then took the spell book from its hiding place, under a pile of boxes in the bottom of the wardrobe. When I got back downstairs, Buddy was standing in front of his bowl, looking very sorry for himself.

"Florence, you'd better give Buddy some food before we start."

"Can't you give it to him, Mummy? His food smells."

"No, I can't. He's your dog, so you have to feed him sometimes. I've opened the pouch for you."

She gave a huge sigh, but then grabbed the pouch and a spoon, and put the food into his bowl.

Buddy clearly didn't mind the smell because he began to wolf it down.

"Okay, darling, let's get started." We sat at the kitchen table, and I'd just found the page for the 'propel' spell when there was a knock at the door. "Wait there while I go and see who that is." I went through to the hall and opened the door to find Grandma standing there.

"Grandma? What are you doing here?"

"That's a nice greeting, I must say. How about: *how lovely to see you Grandma?* Or *would you like a cup of tea, Grandma?*"

"I'm really busy at the moment."

"Teaching your beautiful daughter the 'propel' spell. Yes, I know."

"How?"

"You should know by now, Jill, I am all seeing."

Before I could stop her, she'd pushed past me into the kitchen.

"Great-Grandma!" Florence jumped off her chair and threw herself into Grandma's arms.

"Hello, poppet, I haven't seen you in ages. I've been so busy with my new hotel. How are you?"

"Okay. Mummy is going to teach me the 'propel' spell."

"Is she really? In that case, I think I'll stay and watch."

"Grandma, could I have a quick word?" I gestured to the hallway.

"I'm just going to have a little talk with Mummy," she said, and then followed me into the hall. "Yes, Jill, what is it?"

"You can't be here. I promised Jack that you'd have nothing to do with teaching Florence magic."

"And I won't. I'm just here to observe and have a cup of tea. You won't even know I'm here."

Before I could object, she went back into the kitchen and put some water into the kettle. I walked up behind her and whispered, "Okay, but you can't get involved."

"Don't worry. I'll just watch. Would you like a cup of tea while I'm making one?"

"Yes, please."

While Grandma made the tea, I re-joined Florence at the table.

"Okay, darling. You need to learn all the images for the spell."

"I did that while you were talking to Great-Grandma. I think I know them all."

"Take one more look, just to be sure. Then you can give it a try."

Grandma handed me the tea, then took a seat at the opposite side of the table from us.

"Right, Mummy," Florence said. "I know them now."

"Okay, I'll just get a spoon for you to try the spell on." I went over to the cutlery drawer, took out a spoon, and placed it in front of her. "Right, hold out your hand, close your eyes and then cast the spell."

"A-hem." Grandma interrupted. "Haven't you forgotten something?"

"Like what?" I was fuming.

"You didn't tell her to focus."

"She already knows that, don't you, Florence?"

"Yes. Mummy says that's the most important part."

"Good." Grandma smiled approvingly. "Off you go, then."

Florence held out her hand and closed her eyes—her face was a picture of concentration. A few moments later, the spoon shuddered but it didn't move.

She opened her eyes. "Why didn't it work, Mummy?"

"You didn't focus hard enough." Grandma got in before I had the chance to respond. "Try again, but this time maximum focus."

"Okay, Great-Grandma, I'll try."

This time, the spoon flew across the table and hit the wall.

"Yay! I did it!" Florence yelled, triumphantly.

"That's very good, darling." I gave her a kiss on the top of her head.

"Well done, young lady." Grandma clapped. "You're much better than your Mummy was when she was learning."

"Am I really, Great-Grandma?"

"Oh yes. Your Mummy was hopeless at first."

"I wouldn't say I was *hopeless*," I said, defensively. "It's just that I didn't get to learn magic when I was young like you, Florence."

"Why not?"

“I’ve already told you that story. Mummy didn’t know she was a witch until she was grown up.”

“Can I cast the spell again?”

“Okay, darling.”

“Just a minute.” Grandma stood up, walked over to the drawer, and took out a handful of spoons, which she placed on the table in front of Florence. “Okay, Florence, try again and see if you can do it with all of these.”

I glared at Grandma, but she didn’t even notice.

Florence repeated the spell, and all of the spoons flew across the table and hit the wall.

“You’re a superstar witch.” Grandma clapped again. “You’re going to grow up to be even more powerful than your Mummy.”

“Isn’t it time you were getting back to the hotel, Grandma?” I started for the door.

“There’s no hurry and besides, there’s something I wanted to talk to you about related to the hotel.”

Florence jumped off the chair. “Mummy, can I go outside and play with Buddy now?”

“Yes, darling. Off you pop.”

“Wait, Florence,” Grandma called. “Come and give Great-Grandma a kiss first.”

Florence had always been a little wary of the wart on the end of Grandma’s nose, so as usual, she made a point of kissing her on the cheek.

“Bye, Great-Grandma.”

“Bye, and well done on the ‘propel’ spell.”

Once Florence was out of earshot in the garden, I turned on Grandma. “You were supposed to be just observing.”

“That’s all I did.”

“Rubbish. You stuck your oar in, as usual. I don’t need

your help to teach my daughter magic."

"Keep your wig on."

"You said you wanted to talk about the hotel. I hope it's to tell me that you've changed your mind about targeting your advertising at sups who've never been to the human world before."

"Why would I change my mind?"

"Because they're a liability. My friend, Donna, saw a vampire in the village, drinking synthetic blood."

"I assume your friend is a sup?"

"Yes, so what?"

"If it had been a human who'd seen them, they'd have just assumed it was a raspberry smoothie. You're overreacting."

"And I saw some pixies pretending to be a man. They were walking down the street wearing an overcoat, and they were wobbling all over the place."

"That's a bit harsh, isn't it? Have you ever tried balancing nine people on your shoulders while walking around? It can't be easy. How about you cut them some slack?"

"What was it you wanted to talk to me about?"

"I'm here to offer your human a job."

"His name is Jack and he already has a job."

"Why does he stay at home all day, then?"

"Because he works from home."

"Doing what, exactly?"

"I've told you this before. He runs a website for ten-pin bowling enthusiasts."

"Seriously?" She laughed. "He's never going to make any money doing that. He should come and work for me."

"Doing what?"

"I need a bellboy."

"*A bellboy*?" I laughed. "Jack's not going to be your bellboy."

"I pay minimum wage plus the tips will be very good. He looks healthy enough. He could carry a few suitcases around, couldn't he?"

"Of course he could, but there's no way Jack is going to work for you. Ever."

"I'll leave the position open for a few days. Get him to contact me if he's interested."

***

Jack arrived home just as I was beginning to prepare dinner.

"Did you have a nice day?" I asked.

"Superb. We played three matches and guess how many I won."

"Judging by the stupid grin on your face, I'd say all three of them."

"Correctamundo—a clean sweep. We had a nice lunch too."

"I hope you've left plenty of room for dinner."

"Of course. Where's Florence?"

"In her bedroom."

"How was dancing?"

"As thrilling as ever. Apparently, they're going to be doing an exam soon. Did you get a note about it?"

"No, I would have told you. What kind of exam?"

"I don't know, but according to Donna, it's just an excuse for the dance school to make extra money."

"How did your magic lesson go?"

"Okay, until Grandma showed up."

"I thought we'd agreed that you were going to be the one to teach Florence magic."

"It's okay. Grandma didn't take part in the lesson. She just watched. Oh, and she wanted to offer you a job."

"Me? What kind of job?"

"She thinks you'd make a good bellboy."

"That's a joke, right?"

"Nope. Apparently, it's minimum wage plus tips."

"I trust you told her what she could do with her job?"

"Actually, I said I thought you'd be ideal for it. I reckon you'd look sexy in a bellboy's uniform."

Chapter 25

It was Sunday morning and Jack had somehow managed to persuade Florence to try muesli for the first time. He was getting milk out of the fridge when for some reason he seemed to freeze (no pun intended).

"Are you alright, Jack?" I said.

"I'm trying to work out why we've got so much cheese in here."

"Oh, yeah, right. That was the barber's fault."

"Sorry? The *barber*?"

"Yeah. He told me to buy it."

"I think you've been overworking, Jill. Maybe you ought to take a few days off?" He closed the fridge door, came over to the table and poured milk into his and Florence's bowls.

I figured an explanation was called for, so I told him how I'd bumped into the vicar and the Stock sisters, and I'd discovered they were cousins.

"I still don't see where the barber comes into it?"

"I almost let it slip that Barbara Babble had been gossiping about the three of them, and that she'd suggested they were romantically involved. But, with a bit of quick thinking on my part, I managed to cover my tracks by telling them that your barber had asked me to buy some cheese. Clever, eh?"

He shook his head. "That is without a shadow of a doubt the worst lie I've ever heard in my life. You can't seriously believe they bought that nonsense, can you?"

"Why not?"

"Think about it. Why would anyone believe that my barber told you to buy some cheese? In what universe would that happen?"

"Now you put it like that, it does sound a little implausible, but I couldn't let them know I'd been gossiping with Barbara Babble about them, could I?"

"It wouldn't have been any worse than telling them my barber told you to buy cheese. They'll think you're a nutjob. Me too, probably."

"Mummy," Florence said. "I like moosy."

"It's muesli, darling, and you don't have to say that just to please Daddy. If you don't like it, you don't have to eat it."

"I do like it." She put another spoonful into her mouth. "It's yummy."

"And very healthy for you too." Jack smirked. "Not like that horrible cereal Mummy is eating."

"There's nothing wrong with Chococandy Pops."

I didn't believe Florence really liked muesli. Jack must have bribed her to say that. Perhaps he'd promised to buy her a toy.

"Mummy, can I show Daddy what I can do with the 'propel' spell?"

"Yes, but not until we've all finished breakfast."

While I was loading the dishwasher, Florence said to Jack, "Watch me, Daddy."

"I'm watching, pumpkin."

She closed her eyes, and moments later, her spoon flew across the table.

Unfortunately, so too did her knife, which missed Jack's head by only a couple of inches.

"Florence!" I yelled.

"Sorry. I only meant the spoon to move."

"That's why you have to be really careful every time you cast a spell."

"Sorry, Daddy," Florence said.

"It's okay, pumpkin. No harm done."

"Can I go into the garden to play?"

"Of course you can."

"Are you okay, Jack? You gone a little pale."

"I thought I was a goner there for a minute."

"Thank goodness it didn't hit you. I haven't renewed the life insurance yet."

"You're so funny."

"I know. It comes naturally. By the way, have you thought any more about Grandma's job offer?"

"I have, actually, and I think I might take her up on it."

"What? You can't do that."

"I'm joking, Jill."

"Right. Good."

"Or am I?"

***

I knew very little about Trevor Hee. An online search had revealed next to nothing about him; the only articles I'd been able to find were all within the last couple of years, and they were all related to NOCA. Curiously, he appeared to have no social media presence whatsoever, so if I wanted to find out more about him, I was going to have to look elsewhere.

Although I could have thought of a million and one things I'd rather be doing on a Sunday, this was the ideal opportunity to search Trevor Hee's apartment because he and Don had agreed to meet that very morning at Chuckle

House to discuss the future of NOCA.

I magicked myself over to Trevor's apartment, and rang the doorbell, just in case the meeting had been cancelled or someone else lived there with him. Fortunately, there was no response, so I checked to make sure no one was around, then I magicked myself inside.

I had no idea what I was looking for or where I might find it, so I started in the nearest room, which turned out to be the lounge. Trevor obviously favoured the minimalist approach: there was very little furniture, and no photographs or ornaments on display. Next, I checked the kitchen. Half of the cupboards and drawers were empty, and the others contained only food, pots and pans and cutlery.

There were two bedrooms: A small one, which was obviously being used for storage, and the master bedroom, which was dominated by a king-size bed. The built-in wardrobe was divided into two halves. The right-hand side contained Trevor's everyday clothes: suits, jackets, trousers, that kind of thing. The left-hand side was reserved for his clown outfits, of which he had many. The drawers were full of jumpers, socks and underwear. The bottom of the wardrobe was full of shoe boxes, all of which contained only shoes.

The spare bedroom was going to be the biggest challenge. It was full of boxes of all shapes and sizes. I had no idea how long Trevor's meeting was likely to last, but I was certain I wouldn't have time to check every box. I would need to be selective, so I picked out those boxes which weren't sealed, on the assumption that he might have accessed their contents recently.

I drew a blank with the first four boxes. Why did people

insist on holding onto so much rubbish? When I opened the next box, there was a clown's outfit on top. Initially, I assumed it must be one of Trevor's old costumes, but when I took it out and held it up, I could see the green and yellow checked garment had been made for someone much taller. As I dug deeper into the box, I uncovered all manner of clown paraphernalia: wigs, noses, bow ties etc. They had all obviously had plenty of wear. Underneath those, was another clown outfit—a different design, but the same two colours: green and yellow. After putting everything back, I started on the box next to it. This one was full of old photo albums. The first one I looked at was full of images of a young couple with a baby. The first few pages showed the proud parents with their newborn, and then, over the course of the album, the baby in the photos grew into a toddler. The next album was more of the same, but these photos had clearly been taken some years later because the child now looked to be about four or five years old. In one of those photos, the young boy was standing next to a clown, who was wearing the yellow and green checked costume that I'd seen in the other box. I continued to flick through the albums, witnessing the boy growing older in each one. After the boy reached eight or nine years of age, his mother no longer appeared in the photos—it was just him and his father.

But it was only when the boy turned into a teenager and his father grew older that it dawned on me. I knew both of them.

***

Much as I hated to admit it, Jack had been right about

the Scrabble tiles. I'd been too focussed on the tiles that spelled the word *revenge*. As my brilliant husband had pointed out, if you used the rest of the tiles, you could spell out the words *yellow* and *green*.

The yellow and green clown outfits in the spare bedroom had not belonged to Trevor Hee, but to his father, Andrew Clowne. The young boy in the photo standing next to the clown was Trevor; the clown was his father.

There was now little doubt that Trevor was behind the deaths at NOCA, but how had he done it? I couldn't afford to dwell on that now because Trevor and Don were at Chuckle House, and I had a horrible feeling that Trevor had a similar fate planned for Don. There was no time to lose, so I magicked myself over there.

The female clown behind the reception desk stared at me, clearly puzzled. "Where did you come from?"

"Through the door."

"No, you didn't. I would have seen you."

"How else do you think I got here? Do you think I magicked myself here out of thin air?"

"I—err—what do you want, anyway?"

"Where are Don Keigh and Trevor Hee?"

"They gave strict instructions that they weren't to be disturbed."

"Are they upstairs in the meeting room?"

"I can't tell you that."

"Never mind." I didn't bother with the Chucklevator. Instead, I rushed up the stairs, down the corridor and charged into the meeting room, to find Don Keigh lying on the floor; Trevor was kneeling over him with a syringe in his hand.

“Help me, Jill!” Don yelled. “He’s gone crazy!”

“Get back, Jill!” Trevor shouted.

“Sorry, Trevor, but I can’t do that.” I cast the ‘power’ spell, took hold of him and threw him across the room. Don took his opportunity to scramble away towards the door.

Trevor hadn’t finished yet. He got to his feet and started towards me, the syringe still in his hand. He had a manic look on his face.

“Put the syringe down, Trevor,” I said.

“They killed him, Jill. All of them.”

“I assume you’re talking about your father, Andrew Clowne?”

“You’re Andrew’s son?” Don said, incredulously.

Ignoring Don, Trevor directed his words to me. “My father was the best clown this country has ever known. He had more talent in his little finger than the rest of the NOCA committee members put together, but look at the way they treated him.”

“He stole money from NOCA,” I said.

“It was only ever intended as a loan. He would have paid it back.”

“He had no intention of paying it back. Have you forgotten that he killed Mr Bobo to try and cover his tracks?”

“I don’t believe that for a minute.” Trevor shook his head. “My father would never do anything like that.” As he spoke, he was getting closer and closer to me. “I’m sorry you had to be here, Jill. I didn’t want to hurt you.”

“I wouldn’t worry about it, Trevor, because that’s not going to happen.” I grabbed his arm and shook the syringe out of his hand, threw him to the floor, and shouted to Don, "Get out of here. Call the police!"

Don didn't move; he seemed paralysed with fear.

"Don! Now! Move!"

This time, he snapped out of it, and rushed out of the door. As soon as he'd gone, I used magic to produce a couple of lengths of rope with which I tied Trevor's hands and feet.

Lying on the floor, all the fight had gone out of him. "You should have let me kill him, Jill, just like he killed my father."

"No one killed your father, Trevor. He died of natural causes."

"He would never have had a heart attack if he hadn't been sent to prison. He couldn't handle it in there. I went to see him a few days before he died, and it was clear that the stress was too much for him. It was the NOCA committee that killed him, just as surely as if they'd put a knife through his heart."

"I assume that's when you decided to take your revenge."

"I was at medical school, training to be a doctor when my father was sent to prison. I wanted to give it up there and then, but he pleaded with me to stay the course. I did as he asked, but when he died, I couldn't see the point anymore. I left university, came back home, and began to hone my clown act. I'd watched my father for years, so I soon got up to speed. After a year on the circuit, I applied to NOCA. They were only too keen to bring in some young blood."

"Didn't they realise you were Andrew's son?"

"Of course not. They didn't care about him or his family. They only ever saw the clown, not the man."

Chapter 26

It was Monday morning and Florence was upstairs getting ready for school.

"I imagine you'll be in the new guy's good books now," Jack said.

"Are you kidding? Detective Archie McDonald is just like every other policeman I've ever had to deal with, and I include *you* in that list."

"Me? You can't be serious."

"I'm deadly serious. When you first moved to Washbridge you were a real pain in the backside."

"But you fancied me, anyway." He grinned.

"I barely noticed you. If I remember rightly, you were the one who chased after me."

"Funny you should say that because Kathy told me you had the hots for me from day one."

"You shouldn't believe anything my sister says. Anyway, like I was saying, Big Mac is just as bad as you, Leo Riley and Sushi. Why do you think I was late for dinner last night? Because that idiot kept me at the station for two hours even though Trevor Hee had confessed. If I hadn't turned up at Chuckle House when I did, Don Keigh would have been his fourth victim. But did I get any thanks from Big Mac? Did I heck. He was too busy having a go at me because I hadn't kept my nose out like he'd told me to."

"If you'd just listened to me, Jill, you'd have solved the case even sooner."

"Just because you came up with two words from the Scrabble tiles doesn't mean you solved the case. Those two words didn't mean a thing until I saw Andrew

Clowne's old costumes and photos. Until then I had no idea that green and yellow were his trademark colours."

"And now his son is going to follow him to prison."

"I can't help but feel sorry for Trevor. His mother died when he was just a kid; after that it was his father who brought him up. Trevor clearly adored his father, so when he was sent to prison, his world collapsed. He simply couldn't bring himself to accept that his father was actually guilty of the crimes he'd been convicted of. And later when his father died in prison, Trevor totally lost the plot."

"Do you know how he killed his victims?"

"I have no idea, but I think it's safe to assume that his training as a doctor helped in that regard. He'd manipulated events so that he got to spend time with all three of his victims before the fateful NOCA committee meetings. My guess is that he slipped them a drug of some kind. I've no doubt the police will want to exhume the bodies of the three clowns to verify that."

Jack's phone beeped with a message. "It's from Walter. He's sent the initial results from the DNA testing."

"Go on, then, don't keep me in suspense."

"Here." He handed me his phone. "This will probably make more sense to you than it does to me."

I quickly read through the message. Most of it was gobbledygook, but it did tell me the main thing I needed to know.

I gave Phil Black a call. "Phil, it's Jill. I'm sorry to ring you so early."

"That's okay. Do you have news for me?"

"Yes, but I'd prefer not to discuss it over the phone. Can you call into my office this morning? Say, ten o'clock?"

"Sure. I'll be there."

"Good news?" Jack said.

"I think so, but I'll have to update you tonight because I'm running late."

"Don't forget I'm at the dentist later, but I'll be done in time to pick Florence up."

"Oh yeah, it's your filling today, isn't it?" I did my impression of a dentist's drill. "Have fun."

***

I'd just got into the car and was about to drive off when I spotted two vampires on the opposite side of the road: a man and a young boy. The two of them were walking into the village, and the young boy was drinking from a bottle of synthetic blood.

Just how blatant could you be? Fortunately, there were no other villagers around.

I got out of the car, slammed the door closed, and stormed across the road. "Hey, you!" I shouted.

"Yes?" The man seemed surprised to see me.

"What do you think you're playing at?"

"We've just been for a walk, and we're on our way back to the hotel. Why?"

"*Why*? Are you serious?" I grabbed the bottle from the boy's hand. "Why would you let him drink this in public?" I turned the bottle upside down and poured the contents onto the ground.

"Dad, she threw my pop away." The boy looked on the verge of tears.

"Why did you do that?" the man shouted.

"Take a wild guess. Why would you let him drink

synthetic blood in the village?"

"That wasn't synthetic blood. That was cherry cola. I bought it from the village shop before we went for our walk."

"Don't lie to me. Do you think I'm stupid?"

"Check the label for yourself."

I turned the bottle around, and sure enough, the label read cherry cola.

"Yes, but—err—you could have used an empty cherry cola bottle and put synthetic blood in it."

"We could have, but we didn't. Taste it if you don't believe me."

I rubbed my finger around the rim of the bottle, put it to my tongue, and sure enough it was cherry cola.

"Err, right. Sorry." I handed the empty bottle back to the man.

"What about my cherry cola?" the kid said.

"Yeah, what about his cherry cola?" his father demanded.

"I—err—" I reached into my pocket and pulled out a five-pound note. "Sorry, this is all I have. I haven't got any change."

"That'll do." He snatched it from me. "Come on, son, let's get away from this crazy witch."

And with that, the two of them disappeared in the direction of Tweaking Stores.

This was all Grandma's fault.

***

When I arrived at work, the outer office was bustling with young women, one of whom was Ramona. Mrs V was behind the desk chatting to them, and she clearly hadn't noticed my arrival.

"Good morning, Mrs V. You have an office full today."

"These are all friends of Ramona. They've been kind enough to agree to model my giant scarf. You remember the one, don't you, Jill? The one I knitted for charity?"

"Err—I think so, but then you knit so many."

"Ladies!" Mrs V called them to attention. "Please put on the scarf."

They picked up the huge scarf, and one by one wrapped it around their necks. It was to be hoped that one of them didn't trip because if that happened, they would all end up on the floor.

"Oh, yes, I remember it now. I'd better leave you to make your video."

Next door, Bobby and Bertie were on the window ledge, cooing away merrily to each other.

"Good morning, Jill," Bobby shouted.

"Morning, Jill." Bertie waved a wing.

"You two are looking very chipper."

"We've done it," Bertie said. "We've found girlfriends."

"That's great. I couldn't be happier for the two of you."

"We were in the park yesterday, under the bench, the one near the fountain. Do you know it?"

"Err, yeah, I think I know the one you mean."

"We were nibbling on a burger bun when we bumped into two lovely ladies—sisters, actually. We got chatting to them and they've agreed to go out with us on a double date tomorrow. Their names are Bianca and Briana."

"Wow, what a lot of 'B's."

"Where?" Bobby flinched.

"I hate bees," Bertie said.

"No, I don't mean bumblebees. I meant 'B', as in your names: Bobby, Bertie, Bianca and Briana. All the 'B's."

"Oh yes, of course." Bobby laughed. "It hadn't occurred to me."

"Well, good luck with your double date, boys. I hope it goes well."

"Thanks, Jill."

And off they flew.

***

Phil Black was as pale as a sheet when he walked into my office.

"I've been on tenterhooks ever since you called, Jill. What have you found out? Is it good news or bad?"

"What I'm about to tell you is going to come as a shock, so I think you should sit down first."

"Okay." He practically flung himself into the chair. "Tell me, please."

"Liam isn't dead."

It took a moment or two for my words to register.

"What do you mean, he isn't dead? Are you sure?"

"I'm positive. I've spoken to him."

"Where is he?"

"Living in Bristol. He goes by the name of Mila now."

"*Bristol*? Are you sure it's him?"

"Pretty much. I managed to get hold of a glass that he'd drunk from. And when you and I met in Coffee Animal, I took the liberty of taking the coffee cup that you'd used. I had them both analysed for DNA."

"You knew about Liam when I met you in the coffee shop? Why didn't you say anything then?"

"Because I needed to be sure it was him first. I got the report back this morning, and there's now no doubt that the two of you share the same mother."

"If he's in Bristol, who is he living with?"

"Your stepfather."

"I'm sorry, Jill, I don't understand any of this. How can he be with my stepfather?"

"I don't have all the answers, but I do have a theory about what happened if you want to hear it."

"I do."

"I'm pretty sure your stepfather was seeing someone else while he was still living with your mother, you and Liam."

"Having an affair, you mean?"

"Yeah, I think so. I believe he'd decided to make a new life with his new woman, but he didn't want to leave Liam behind. My guess is that he didn't trust the courts to award him custody, so he came up with a plan to make sure he wouldn't lose him."

"A plan to snatch Liam? Is that what you're saying?"

"More or less, although I don't think he was the one who physically took Liam. I think his lady friend probably did that."

"How?"

"Tell me again what your parents claim happened on the morning that Liam went missing."

"They were both in bed, having a lie-in. My stepfather got up to go to the loo, and he saw Liam who told him that I was taking him fishing."

"So, your mother never actually saw Liam?"

"No. Just my stepfather."

"That's what I thought."

"Are you saying he was lying? Don't you think my stepfather saw Liam?"

"I'm sure he saw him, but it was to hand him over to his lady friend."

"But Liam knew not to talk to strangers."

"He wouldn't have seen the woman in that light. Not if his own father had told him it was okay. Your stepfather probably told Liam he'd be following them shortly."

"Where did she take him?"

"I don't know, but I do know the three of them eventually settled in France."

"*France*? Are you sure?"

"Positive. I visited the house where they used to live. Liam is bilingual now."

"Really? My little brother, bilingual? Wow. How is he?"

"He seemed fine, but I got the impression he doesn't remember much, if anything, of his—err—previous life."

"Not even me?"

"Probably not."

"What happened to the woman who snatched him?"

"She's gone. She and your stepfather lived in France for some years, but then they went their separate ways. That's when your stepfather brought Liam back to this country."

"If what you're suggesting is true, why did my stepfather stay with my mother for so long after Liam disappeared?"

"He had to stay long enough to play the part of the grieving parent. Only when things had died down, did he make his next move. He left your mother and joined his new family in France. No one questioned his walking out—they put it down to a marriage that had crumbled under incredible pressure."

"You're telling me that he stood back and allowed me to be sent to prison for a murder he knew I hadn't committed."

"I'm afraid so. The only thing I'm not sure about is whether that was an unforeseen consequence or all part of the plan."

"Do you think he put Liam's blood on my fishing rod?"

"I honestly don't know. There's only one person who can answer that question."

"I can't believe it. I knew he didn't like me, but I didn't think he'd do something like that. Where does all this leave me, Jill?"

"I don't know. You have some difficult decisions to make. The DNA evidence should be enough to identify Liam and clear your name, but that would just be the beginning."

"If I did that, and they arrested my stepfather, what would happen to Liam?"

"Presumably, he would go back to your mother who, by the way, owes you a big apology. Will you ever be able to forgive her?"

"I'm not sure. I guess so if it means I'll be able to see Liam."

"I suggest you go away and think this through. Talk it over with your grandmother before you do anything rash. Then, when you've decided what to do, you're going to need a good solicitor, and he'll want this." I passed him a copy of the DNA report.

"Thanks, Jill. For everything."

"My pleasure. Let me know how things turn out, will you?"

"Of course."

***

"I hope you saw that, Winky," I said. "Another satisfied customer."

"First one this year." He grinned.

"Cheek."

"I have some exciting news."

"What's that?"

"I'm going to offer you the opportunity of a lifetime."

"No thanks."

"What do you mean, *no thanks*? You don't even know what it is yet."

"Whatever it is, the answer's no."

"Are you sure about that? Are you really going to turn down the chance to take part in the feline lottery?"

"I don't believe there is such a thing."

"There hasn't been until now. The first ever draw takes place in two weeks. The prize pot is going to be huge, and out of the goodness of my heart, I'm prepared to let you go fifty/fifty with me, even though, strictly speaking, it's not open to two-leggeds."

"How very kind of you."

"I know, right. I've decided to invest twenty pounds, so if you put in the same, I'll buy the tickets, and we'll split any winnings."

"You must think I'm stupid."

"That goes without saying, but what does that have to do with anything?"

"This is another one of your scams, just like the pigeon dating app."

"No, it isn't. I promise. It's absolutely genuine. I can

show you the flyers if you like."

"Anyone can print a few leaflets. I'm not interested."

"Is that your final word? Because if I win, you're going to feel really bad about this."

"I'm positive. I'll take that risk."

My phone rang, and it took me a moment or two to realise it was Jack because he sounded really weird.

"Jack, are you alright?"

"Yeah, I'm in the dentist's chair; they're halfway through filling my tooth."

"In that case, why are you ringing me?"

"I've just had a phone call from the school."

"Is Florence okay?"

"Yes, she's fine."

"Why did they call you, then?"

"Miss Hope rang to ask if one of us could go over there as soon as possible."

"Are you sure Florence is alright?"

"Positive. Miss Hope promised me she was fine. Apparently, there's been some kind of incident, and Miss Hope said she needed a quick word with one of us. I won't be finished here for at least half an hour. Is there any chance you could nip over there?"

"Of course I will. I'm on my way now."

I said goodbye to Mrs V, hurried to the car and drove straight to the school. The school secretary took me through to Florence's classroom; the only two people in there were Florence and Miss Soap. To my relief, Florence looked fine, but her desk was covered with paper clips, screws, hair clips, and even a couple of pairs of scissors.

Miss Soap spotted me and came over to the door.

"Is Florence okay, Miss Soap?"

"It's Hope."

"Sorry, that's what I meant."

"Yes, she's fine. I'm sorry to call you in, but there was an unusual incident this afternoon. We were halfway through a lesson about colours when—" Miss Hope gestured to Florence's desk. "All that stuff flew across the room and landed on there. It was quite scary to tell you the truth. Luckily, no one was hurt. The headmistress says she thinks it must have been some sort of electrical surge. I was worried it might have upset Florence, but she seems perfectly fine."

"She does, doesn't she? Is it okay if I take her home now?"

"Of course. The other children were sent home earlier."

I took Florence's hand and led her out of the school.

"Right, little lady, is there anything you'd like to tell me?"

ALSO BY ADELE ABBOTT

The Witch P.I. Mysteries
(A Candlefield/Washbridge Series)

Witch Is When... (Season #1)

Witch Is When It All Began
Witch Is When Life Got Complicated
Witch Is When Everything Went Crazy
Witch Is When Things Fell Apart
Witch Is When The Bubble Burst
Witch Is When The Penny Dropped
Witch Is When The Floodgates Opened
Witch Is When The Hammer Fell
Witch Is When My Heart Broke
Witch Is When I Said Goodbye
Witch Is When Stuff Got Serious
Witch Is When All Was Revealed

Witch Is Why... (Season #2)

Witch Is Why Time Stood Still
Witch is Why The Laughter Stopped
Witch is Why Another Door Opened
Witch is Why Two Became One
Witch is Why The Moon Disappeared
Witch is Why The Wolf Howled
Witch is Why The Music Stopped
Witch is Why A Pin Dropped
Witch is Why The Owl Returned
Witch is Why The Search Began
Witch is Why Promises Were Broken
Witch is Why It Was Over

Witch Is How... (Season #3)
Witch is How Things Had Changed
Witch is How Berries Tasted Good
Witch is How The Mirror Lied
Witch is How The Tables Turned
Witch is How The Drought Ended
Witch is How The Dice Fell
Witch is How The Biscuits Disappeared
Witch is How Dreams Became Reality
Witch is How Bells Were Saved
Witch is How To Fool Cats
Witch is How To Lose Big
Witch is How Life Changed Forever

Witch Is Where... (Season #4)
Witch is Where Magic Lives Now
Witch Is Where Clowns Go To Die
Witch Is Where Squirrels Go Nuts

Susan Hall Investigates
(A Candlefield/Washbridge Series)
Whoops! Our New Flatmate Is A Human.
Whoops! All The Money Went Missing.
Whoops! Someone Is On Our Case.
Whoops! We're In Big Trouble Now.

Murder On Account (A Kay Royle Novel)

Web site: AdeleAbbott.com
Facebook: facebook.com/AdeleAbbottAuthor

Manufactured by Amazon.ca
Bolton, ON

18755281R00169